SCHOOL'S...OUT...FOR...EVER

ANTHONY ASPREY

TODAY...

The corners of Billy Crabtree's mouth sagged and his pupils slid up under his eyelids; he was fighting to keep unconsciousness at bay. Each time he blinked, his eyes stayed closed a little longer. The dozen or so of his Mothers' sleeping pills swilled down with almost a half bottle of whiskey that he had taken twenty minutes earlier were beginning to take effect. He emitted a long drawn out yawn. Soon, all of his failings and humiliations would end. After fifty-eight years of beige mediocrity, he was pondering on the last, insane twenty-eight days of his life.

In just shy of four weeks, Billy had experienced such a range of emotions: extreme fear, intense sexual satisfaction, the deepest of sadness, and shockingly violent anger. He struggled to comprehend the events that had brought him to where he was now. Just a few weeks ago he was floating in a world of boredom and solitude and now everything was different.

As his consciousness gradually faded, disjointed images began to float through his mind. Images of what he could have - *should have* - done with his life before being diagnosed with a terminal illness. Memories swirled around him. All that loneliness, sadness, bitterness, all that regret and heart-rending pain, and if he could just have had one more chance... how many opportunities had he missed?

Too late now.

Billy clasped his hands across his chest as if he were lying in an open coffin at the undertakers. Peace and tranquillity had replaced the turmoil that had been haunting him for so long.

A diminutive sigh escaped from his lips. His eyelids drooped again, and he forced them open; his Mothers' medication was kicking in a little sooner than he had expected. Billy had been walking a knife-edge of emotion for so long, but now serenity had settled over him like a warm, snug duvet.

Just before succumbing to the welcome fog of heavy sedation, he pulled back his sleeve with a hooked finger to reveal his watch. He went, "Mmm," and summoned up the last reserves of his energy to turn through ninety degrees'.

Billy had arranged company; they were to share their last few minutes in this world together. "There's only one thing I regret about this situation, Mister Dean," he slurred, "and that is the fact that I will be unable to piss on your grave. Now then, we have eight minutes left, how about we go out with a rousing song, mmm?" He cackled freakishly.

Mister Dean – 'Deano' - would have replied with a string of foul, abusive expletives if his mouth, hands and feet were not bound with gaffer tape. Pearls of sweat dotted his forehead; he was waiting anxiously for the rescue that would never come.

28 DAYS AGO...

1

"Are you going to eat that or just play with it?"

Billy Crabtree's creased face remained passive, but it was not the passage of time that had ravaged his features. Bitterness and a weary air of defeat had prematurely lined his visage. His eyes and expression were dull with some unreadable emotion.

Billy sat motionless with his elbows resting on the kitchen table; his chin perched on top of tightly clenched fists. He glanced down unblinkingly at his cold and clotted boiled egg and sighed heavily. His mind was a whirl as he picked up a toasted soldier and absent-mindedly began turning it between the thumb and forefinger of each hand. The muscles below his ears twitched as he clenched and unclenched his teeth; a dull headache was forming just above and behind his left eye.

"Well, are you going to eat that or just glare at it all morning?"

The pain in the pit of Billy's stomach was intense; beads of sweat began to pop out of his forehead. Lifting his mug of luke warm tea, he sipped it, screwed up his face, and replaced it back on the table, but not before sweeping an arm across the surface in an attempt to remove sticky
overlapping tea and coffee rings. Leaning back in his chair he combed what little grey hair he had remaining with splayed fingers and then knitted them together behind his head.

Billy's sad eyes roamed. He stared at apple-green walls, the paint cracking and peeling. A small, light brown bulge in the ceiling – in the shape of Italy of all things – water leaking from behind the toilet in the bathroom. A cupboard door beneath the sink was hanging precariously on one hinge. Just a few of a dozen or so jobs that he had been promising to put right. Just a couple of the dozen or so jobs that would never be put right. A tap was leaking incessantly, making a rhythmic and irritating plonking noise. Directly in front of him, on the wall, a kitchen clock whose tick seemed amplified beyond all endurance. The big finger shaped like a knife, the little finger a fork. Each five-minute time slot took the form of a miniature ceramic fruit or veg. Billy hated it. In fact, he hated the kitchen, he hated the house, and above all else, he hated existing. A sharp twinge. He ran both palms down his face. *Shit, it's only been an hour since I took the last painkillers.* An energy sapping melancholy was his constant companion.

"I said are you going to eat..."

Billy bought down a clenched fist onto the table. "Mum, I heard you the first time, give it a rest, will you?" He sighed quite audibly; his eyebrows had come together in an angry 'V'. "I, I don't feel too good, Mum, I'm not going to school today," he said, without averting his gaze from the clock.

If Billy were to be honest, he had come down for breakfast looking for any excuse for an argument and not for the first time lately.

He had had a terrible night. Awful dreams when he had managed to drop

off, awful thoughts when he woke again a few moments later.

Mrs. Crabtree billowed her cheeks and let out a slow breath. "Not again, Billy we've had all this before, just pull yourself togeth..."

"I can't go, Mum...I'm being bullied," Billy blurted out. He picked up his mug, cupped it between his hands and stared into it.

"Bullied!" Mrs. Crabtree hooked her fingers under the back of a chair and dragged it out. The squealing metal feet irritated Billy and he pulled an exaggerated face to let her know the fact. She flopped herself down at the table, laying her hands down flat. "What do you mean, son, bullied?"

Billy slowly raised his head. "My God, listen to me, bullied! I'm talking like a ten-year-old kid." He rubbed his face vigorously with both palms. After yet another long sigh he continued: "You know the Shorevale Council estate?"

His Mums brow slowly collapsed. "Mmm, what about it, love?"

Billy sucked in a deep breath. "Well, there are three year-eleven's who live there, and they've got it in for me in a big way, they're making my life hell. I just can't go to school today."

A cold wet snout slid across the back of Billy's hand. He instinctively snatched his hand away and pointed toward the corner of the kitchen, "Get in your basket, I ain't in the mood."

Sophie got the message and slouched away with her tail firmly lodged between her legs. She didn't head for the basket but instead crawled under a low kitchen unit that was supported on four legs – her favourite hidey-hole. She curled her body into a tight ball with just her twitching nose poking out. Sophie then gave Billy a reproachful look, as if to say, *am I getting any toast this morning?* Billy folded a toasted soldier in half and popped it into his mouth. It took almost more energy than he had available to chew and swallow. He placed his palms together in front of his face as if in prayer. Shortly, Mrs Crabtree reached out and stroked the back of his head with a hand that was shaky, veiny and dotted with liver spots.

"There's no need to take it out on the dog, Billy. Look at her poor little face she doesn't know what she did wrong. Billy, love, you're the caretaker, you must go. Who's going to open up the school?"

Billy shrugged in place of an answer. He rubbed a hand across his face in a gesture of weariness.

She bought her gnarled fingers together in a pyramid beneath her chin and continued, "Billy you're a man of fifty-eight how on earth can you be being bullied by kids, haven't you told anyone?"

Billy blew air from his nose in an audible rush. He stood up, scraping his chair back loudly. The chair toppled and clattered across the worn and pitted vinyl covered floor. He walked over to the sink and leant on it with both palms flat, his head bowed. *You daft old cow.* He gazed out at the once verdant garden that his father had tended so lovingly; it was overrun with weeds and tangles of ivy.

"How the hell can I tell anyone?" He asked through clamped teeth, "Like you say I'm a grown man. You don't understand Mum, these aren't kids they're sixteen, seventeen-year olds, I'd been at work two years at their age. The youth of today are untouchable; they say and do as they please. Oh, the management would have them in for an ear bashing, but they just stand there smirking and then go out and do the same thing again, only ten times worse."

Mrs. Crabtree rose unsteadily, her bones creaking and groaning. She moved in a weary, round-shouldered way as if she were carrying a bag of cement on her back. Placing a friendly hand on Billy's shoulder she said, "Well at least tell me about it, how long has this been going on for? What have these three yobs been doing to you?"

Billy snorted a short sharp laugh. "Oh, they're very sly, very street wise, there are never any witnesses. Nasty pieces of work they are. Evil. The odd snide remark as they pass in the corridor, or they'll spit on your back, they nick my tools and write obscene graffiti on the bog walls about me."

"Mmm," his Mum went, "but, son you need to rise above it, sticks and stones and all that? Just ignore them. In a few weeks' time when the exams are over they'll be out of your hair and you'll never see them again."

Billy shrugged away his Mother's hand and paced the kitchen. Sophie leapt from beneath the kitchen unit and trotted behind him thinking she was about to go out for her morning walk. Billy then faced his Mother, gripping the back of a chair. "You don't understand, Mum, things have changed since our day. They don't crack you on the back of the hand with a ruler any more and then everything's tickety-boo. You upset these people and they fuckin' kill you, don't you understand? The gang they're members of, The Subway Rats, they killed a man last year and got away with it, don't you remember? People fear them, and they're scared of them because they don't make empty threats. They go where they want, and they do what they want, and nobody dares to try and stop them, even the police." He sucked in a breath trying to compose himself.

"It gets to you Mum. Twenty-three years I've been there and every term it gets worse. These kids come in at year seven with no social skills whatsoever and they leave five years later exactly the same. We had the cane in our day, Mum, that always put you on the right track, nowadays there's nothing, whatever the parents and teachers are doing it just ain't working...you know what the kids call me?"

Mrs. Crabtree shook her head.

"Crabby, crabby Crabtree."

Billy's Mum held out her hands palm side up. "But, love it's just name calling. Billy, hating people that much – inwardly – can make you ill, it'll drain you, Billy and make it difficult to think about anything else...look, sit down and I'll make us a nice cup of fresh tea."

Patience was never one of Billy's strong points and he dismissed the offer with a despondent, intolerant wave. He had been gripping the back of the chair tightly enough to turn his knuckles noticeably white. "You think a cup of tea cures everything don't you? Let's just drop it, Mum, leave me alone will you?" He snatched his newspaper up from the table. "I'm going for a crap."

As Billy made for the door, he rested his hand on the handle and half-turned. Sophie had followed him slavishly and stood directly behind him, tail wagging. He shook his head slowly and the wag rate increased. Billy inflated his cheeks and let out a slow breath; he really *did* love that dog. Her needs were simple, she loved being loved, she loved being fed, and she loved her morning walk. The more people he had met over the years, the more he loved his dog.

Billy returned to the kitchen table, picked up a couple of toasted soldiers, and knelt to embrace the dog. He ruffled her head reassuringly, scratched behind her ears and then fought off an avalanche of licks. Sophie nuzzled his neck and then Billy fed her the morsels, which she swallowed completely.

Then Billy, the veins at his temples throbbing, his face flushed, flounced from the room.

Sophie slumped down with a sigh of contentment and, licking traces of butter from the fur around her mouth, she sighed, rested her head on her paws and closed her eyes.

2

Billy wore the face of a man carrying a multitude of burdens, bitter and growing old in isolation. His whole life was characterised by a sense of desolation that was impossible to shake off. He was tired. Things that were easy became suddenly very difficult. The vitality that had once seemed endless was now something to use in a miserly fashion. Billy was losing his grasp of the minute details that kept him alive as he slowly flaked away to nothing but dust. His bouts of depression could no longer be controlled by willpower alone. His aged Mum hanging like a large stone around his neck made things much much worse; it was if the umbilical cord had never been severed. He unintentionally tended to take out his frustrations on her. And now, life was about to stick a knife into his guts and twist it very slowly. A man who had sunk so low that he now found no point to the banality of his existence. All he wanted was an end to anguish, pain, long nights of nightmares, and a release from the need to care about anything and anybody. He was more afraid now than he had ever been in his life, because Billy Crabtree had known for a while that he was a dying man. Each and every symptom that he suffered was getting gradually worse and was a constant reminder that 'God' was going to see him out with this thing slowly and agonisingly eating him away. The maximum strength painkillers had done their job initially, but now he was taking more and more, and closer and closer together. Billy had endured enough pain and loneliness and now he had turned a corner; it seemed his only escape was to put his house in order, and then put an end to it all.

Billy shook away the negative thoughts in his head and found he was still in the hallway with a hand clamped on the banister. With a sinking feeling, he began hauling himself up the stairs. It took quite a while. *Moving like a seventy-year-old.* Before reaching the bathroom, Billy slipped into his bedroom and picked up yet more painkillers, the strongest that you can purchase over the counter. He swallowed them quickly with a glass of water that he kept by the side of the bed. He shuffled across the landing and into the bathroom. Lately, he would try to avoid the mirror, but he took a sideways glance; he would have loved to have seen a Brad Pitt look-a-like staring back at him. The truth of the matter was that he looked like pure shit. Grey and dejected. There was anger, desperation, and pain reflected in his eyes, which were red-rimmed and droopy with fatigue, his face hollow and creased.

The pain struck with no warning at all. It felt like a mini Mike Tyson was inside of him trying to punch his way through his abdomen. It was accompanied by a wave of nausea and gripping cramps. He grasped at the radiator with both hands and slowly lowered himself down onto the toilet seat. The next half-hour turned out to be one of the longest half-hours he'd ever lived through. Cold rivulets of sweat snaked down his forehead and dripped from his nose. Pain creased across his stomach sending tendrils of shock along his arms and legs. This was part of Billy's daily routine now. *Oh, Christ the pain, unbearable, unbearable pain, for Christ's sake help me.* Christ didn't lift a finger. *Why does it have to be like this? Why can't someone just switch me off like a light bulb? This must stop. This will stop. Death would now be a welcome release.*

The back of the bathroom door blurred in and out of focus before his weary eyes and it appeared grey at the fringes. He buried his face in his hands for what seemed like long minutes as even the slightest movement sent searing pain through his entire body. The pain was now so acute he couldn't even moan.

After a while, the painkillers finally kicked in and he welcomed a gradual easing in the severity of his discomfort.

Now feeling a little more at ease, he rose slowly to his feet. His leg muscles trembled, and he was huffing for breath. He hobbled over to the mirror, his trousers still shackling his ankles. Looking into the mirror again it could have been his father staring back at him; it seemed as if his father was taking him over - a man of fifty-eight going on seventy. There were scraps of hair, blond once, now silver and thinning at an alarming rate. Normally neatly brushed, now it was greasy and wet and lay in strands across his forehead. Not that that was uppermost on his mind. His shirt and jumper felt glued to his skin, he had lost weight, and he looked exhausted. His cheeks were chalky white, his lips thin and bloodless; dark rings bruised the skin under his eyes. He had gazed at his reflection over the last year and watched himself shrink and wither. He could hear rain spattering against the bathroom window. *Can loneliness get any worse than this?*

The memory of his father's death came vividly into his mind. A powerful memory. *Dad was about my age when he went.* Billy inspected his tongue in the mirror. *He was too sick to do anything in the end. We watched him shrivel up into a walnut and die an agonisingly slow death. Although our father-son relationship was far from perfect, it had still made me physically sick to watch. Now this awful malignant evil has me, the bastard. What did the doctor say? 'Ah! Sounds to me like a bit of the old Irritable Bowel Syndrome, Mister Crabtree. We'll soon sort you out with a change of diet.' What a twat. These so-called experts are crap. This dark disease is taking the same path as Dad's illness and it's too late to do anything about it.*

By the time the correct diagnosis was established, Billy had been informed that it was inoperable. The consultant had spoken to Billy about chemotherapy and the opportunity it provides to prolong life. As long as 2 years with, or maybe 6 months without. Seeing what it had done to his father, and also having read up about his advanced condition, Billy didn't see the point. The end result was always going to be the same. If they had offered to shorten his life then he would have jumped at the chance, and anyway he had seen what it had done to his Dad and he certainly did not want to go through what he had. In between his chemotherapy sessions he was always exhausted and went through waves of pain and nausea. Billy slumped back down onto the toilet seat.

Billy was sinking down into impenetrable blackness, clinging on by his fingertips, becoming more and more isolated and withdrawn. His downward spiral into lassitude had led him to a point where he wanted everything to stop; he wanted to cease to exist. He had already decided that he wasn't going out like his father. He wanted to go swiftly and in a painless manner. After all, who'd miss him? The house was paid for and when he was gone, it would be sold off. His Mother would see out the rest of her days in some nice warm care home with people around her and be fed three meals a day. He visualised himself in a few months' time. Just skin on bone, tubes protruding from every orifice, intra-venous drips, oxygen mask, nausea, slipping in and out of consciousness, and then his graveside with his Mother there and perhaps a representative from the school and that would be about it. No one else. Oh, no, no one would ever miss Billy Crabtree.

Billy reached for some loo paper, but the roll was empty; he tutted and blew out his cheeks. He twisted and felt for the spare roll, which was perched on top of the toilet brush holder down behind the toilet bowl. His hand fell onto a bottle of bleach, which he took instead. He unscrewed the top and took a sniff. He wrinkled his nose and recoiled slightly, *I've smelt worse.* He glared at it for long seconds. *Why not now? Here and now, why not? My life no longer has any meaning and there is nothing left for me here.* Billy stared at the bottle for a few moments longer and then took a gingerly sip; he immediately felt a burning sensation attack his lips and tongue. He turned to his left, spat several times into the sink, and then, turning on the cold tap, splashed water into and around his mouth. *Shit, if ever there were proof that I'm a total failure! I can't even kill myself properly, that was a fucking stupid idea. I ain't got the courage to live and I ain't got the courage to end it. I'm desperate to seek some form of escape and determined to die but I must make sure it's quick and painless; I'll have to give this some serious thought.*

Billy wiped himself down. He stood up, flushed the toilet, and watched in despair as the crimson-brown goo swirled away. *Christ, I know life is supposed to be sacred but this definitely ain't life. Why me? What have I done to deserve this? I've never done anyone any harm, why couldn't it have happened to someone else like the Robinson's across the road. Fat, idle dole-scrounging bastards, why not them? People who should get it never do.*

He turned to face the mirror again; he pulled down his eyelids and stuck out his throbbing red tongue. He looked so frail now, so pathetic and useless. His illness was gradually diminishing him, reducing the flesh, bringing the bones nearer to the surface; he was irretrievably doomed as he descended a vortex of emptiness and agony. *I don't want to be here, I'm supposed to be dead.* Strength left him. He dropped to his knees and, planting his hands on the bathroom floor, muffled convulsive sobs into the shag pile bath mat. Unfortunately, the blackness didn't allow him any time off. Red and yellow flashing stars appeared at the periphery of his vision as another wave of nausea gripped him. He crawled quickly across the stained tiled floor and, coughing violently, he hovered over the toilet. His eyes burned, and tears flowed down his face with the effort he used trying to control his vomiting.

When he was finished purging what little there was left in his stomach, Billy leant his back against the bath, rested his head on the rim and shut his eyes tightly. Tears of frustration, anger, and heartache escaped from behind the lids. He found that if he kept perfectly still the pain eased somewhat to a dull ache, so he didn't move a muscle. Even to the point of trying not to swallow, not wanting to upset the delicate balance that was keeping the dry heaves at bay.

Things faded into black.

3

Up until the 1960's Boreley Hill had been a small, sleepy market town in rural Staffordshire. Since then the town and surrounding countryside had been slowly stifled and imprisoned by the M6, M6 TOLL and the A5 triangle. Apart from the 24/7 background hum of heavy traffic, little had changed in the old part of town. There were well-maintained parks along the river and some of the narrow streets were lined with a blanket of trees. The surrounds though had changed drastically. The locals decried the loss of village atmosphere and quality of life that they'd long enjoyed. Did they want change? No! Did they get it? Of course.

A committee of sober town planners had decided change was necessary. They had agreed (without even visiting the area) that certain farms, commons, woods and green open spaces needed to be raised and converted into industrial estates, business parks and sprawling urban carbuncles of concrete that needed feeding by service-station mini-markets. Huge warehouse sized supermarkets that took a day to walk round, a multiplex cinema, and huge football pitch-sized car parks, which you actually had to pay for! 'Come shopping, and we'll charge you for the privilege!' An ugly, concrete tumour now surrounded this once quite beautiful little town, or as the town planners would have you believe 'a rural success story'. The faceless authorities had assumed that it would be too much of an effort for the locals to travel the two miles or so into the nearest town for their Sainsbury's, Asda, or Primark etc., etc. Therefore, they had decided that what this little town desperately needed was their very own mixture of urban and industrial sprawl. Boreley Hill could also boast that if you were to stand on the roof of their new McDonald's you could also see the McDonald's on the outskirts of the next town.

Another one of their gems was to build the Shorevale council estate - 'a tribute to modern architecture' - where other councils could dump their problem families and wash their hands of them. The new residents got to work as soon as they had moved in and, with some vigour had turned the place into the dump it now was. Therefore, after such a 'Resounding Success Story', similar types of neighbourhoods had sprung up around the town until each bordered the other.

Crime was rife on the Shorevale estate and most people tended to ignore it. Keeping yourself to yourself was the only way to get by without being engulfed by the fear and mind-numbing despair. On the edge of this 'Village' had been constructed Boreley Hill Sport and Community High School, a 1970's dull but functional three-storey block of concrete and glass rectangles. Originally, with views over open farmland, it now boasted a panoramic view of the M6 toll motorway. It was classed as a 'Moderate' school regarding its position in the nation-wide league table drawn up by the governing education authority. It accommodated just over 1,200 pupils and the majority came to school on a regular basis and did what was asked of them. There were certainly naughty kids and cheeky ones, but for the last few terms, the menace of gang culture had become an increasing threat. Each term a handful of kids - certainly single figures - were considered alarmingly violent and on occasions, knives had been discovered when there had been random searches of the kids' lockers. After protests from parents, though, this practice had now stopped as it violated their 'Human rights'.

This term had been particularly bad, with three unsavoury characters – Deano, Nelly and Thommo – coming through the ranks into year eleven. Unluckily for Billy, these were the three morons that had taken a dislike to him and took great pleasure in making his life hell. Most of the teaching staff was counting the days until this trio of scum left school for good, which would be in just a few weeks time after the exams had finished.

Born into a dysfunctional family situation, in which violence and drugs were a way of dealing with everyday life, Deano had arrived into a world without the slightest chance of living a normal life and quickly headed down a seriously disastrous road. A smooth, skilled liar who was a badly broken sociopath and the chances were that it was too late to put him back together again. Deano was only five years of age when his father had begun a life sentence for murder. Uncles and cousins were involved in, and convicted of, robbery and violent crimes on several occasions. His Mother had no chance of controlling him. A tragic and pathetic alcoholic who would readily supply him with an alibi when the police came knocking, which they did on a regular basis. Deano had spent time in a variety of foster homes where he went even further downhill after being the victim of physical and sexual abuse. It wasn't an excuse for his behaviour, some kids are just born evil, and Deano had grown up a monster – vicious and hate-filled.

Deano and his two partners in crime, Nelly and Thommo, belonged to a gang who went by the name of 'The Subway Rats'. The three of them were at the younger end of an organised 'pyramid' where the men at the top never got their hands dirty, they decided who went where, and when, and who did what. They supplied the boys with designer clothes, watches, and top of the range mobile phones. Deano, Thommo and Nelly looked upon them as 'cool' friends, they looked after them, whereas they were too dim to realise they were being abused and were the most visible and vulnerable at the bottom of the pyramid.

The bottom tier of the gang was a feral pack loose on the streets of the notorious Shorevale estate and, to a large degree, kept the local constabulary in business all year round. When one of the top members did get caught and put away, then a younger member would be upgraded and would move up the ladder.

However, there were many decent folks who lived here, but they had become hardened and worn down by the relentlessness of their lives. This led to apathy, distrust, and silence, and so the police had lost the war to an oppressive force of occupation. An army of pushers, traffickers, binge drinking, prostitutes, petty thieves, muggers and all the low life associated with a criminal underworld. Witnesses? Nothing ever stuck people turned a blind eye. As soon as the witnesses and victims found out that the Subway Rats were involved, they tended to become very forgetful. Therefore, the gang continued to operate beneath the noses of the law, taking great pleasure in wasting their time and driving them nuts.

After dark, the Subway Rats had nothing to do and plenty of time to do it in. They roamed. Spoiling for action, anxious for excitement, anxious for kicks, anxious to make people's lives as uncomfortable as possible. The Subway Rats were solely responsible for making their chaotic, broken-down council estate a virtual 'no-go area'. Surprisingly, no director of housing, no architect, or council planner lived in these heartless canyons of bleak 1960's design.

If the price were right, any one of the gang members would kill their own granny and then steal her pension book. They caused misery and despair to the community with behaviour ranging from drunken vandalism, intimidation to out and out criminal activity. So brazen and sure of themselves were they that frequent acts of violence were carried out in public as a message to the locals that they are to be taken seriously. Dark humour helped. If you were to ask a resident, 'How was your day?' They'd say it was fine; nobody has mugged or stabbed me.

Deano and his two chums had started as relative minors on the fringes of the gang. The 'street soldiers' tasks would be retribution and intimidation against people who had crossed the gang in some way, or fetching and delivering low-level street drugs on their BMX bikes. These minor wrongdoings served a valuable purpose during their 'Apprenticeship'. The senior gang members had taught them how to break into homes and perform other various criminal acts. But it was Deano who had soon made a reputation for himself. One of the older gang members had had a big fall out with a couple in a neighbouring property. They had had the audacity to ask him to turn his music down as it was disturbing their sleep pattern. He knew that the couple absolutely adored their pet cat and so he had instructed Deano to get rid of it to teach them a lesson. Obviously when the act took place he would be out of the area and surrounded by witnesses. Deano thought it too easy just to get rid of their pet. He would get rid of it in 'Style'. Therefore, he had hunted down the animal, took it to a disused factory site, doused it with lighter fuel, and set fire to it. Unblinkingly he had watched the animal squeal and writhe in agony as it slowly turned into a blackened piece of charcoal. And then as a pièce de résistance he had stuffed the poor creatures' ashen skeleton through the couple's letterbox with one of the gangs 'Business' cards – a black cross on a white background. He had found the incident so thrilling that he had repeated the act several times on other animals, and absolutely savoured the moment. His rise up the ranks was guaranteed. Fire was to be his trademark. Administering pain, to people and animals, gave him a great deal of pleasure.

  The drug business on the Shorevale estate was a drive through business. Deano's exposure to the gangs' values and beliefs soon became accepted as normal. His strong desire to impress was exploited by those around him and it soon earned him the title of 'Street boss' when, at the tender age of fifteen, he had set up an elaborate operation of obscenely young lookouts and handlers. They would continuously change their locations throughout the night and early hours. Planners had made the task dead easy, designing a maze of balconies, walkways, playgrounds and hidden green areas, which were the perfect environment for Deano and the other gang members to do their cowardly business. Deano was becoming noticed and respected by the top brass.

Everything was obtainable for Deano. It was so easy for someone who was prepared to go to any lengths and is totally lacking in scruples. Being a member of the gang didn't only mean kicking the shit out of someone, it also meant learning what was about to go down in the neighbourhood and figuring out how best to take advantage of it. For himself, obviously. It all came so naturally to him.

One incident had gained Deano a lot of credibility within the ranks, when a 'Job' offer arose. It was a way of making a big name for himself.

Just short of a year ago, there had been a tragic event on the estate. The gang had targeted a single, divorced man, living alone in a ground floor bedsit, just because he had accidentally pranged one of their BMW's. Firstly, they had spread malicious rumours about the man being a paedophile. His windows had been broken several times and spiteful, sexually graphic graffiti daubed across his door and walls. A short time later, Deano, Thommo and Nelly had attacked the man whilst he was out watering a hanging basket. He managed to break away and get back inside and barricade himself in. Late that same evening, petrol had then been poured through his letterbox and consequently it had taken hold so rapidly in the hallway, that escape from the resulting fire was made impossible. The man died from horrific burns. Strong rumours had circulated that Deano and the other two had been the perpetrators of this heinous act. Deano and his 'associates' had swiftly been rounded up and questioned. Then they would be released and then picked up again, released and picked up. The message was clear; the police thought they knew more than they were telling, but they hit the proverbial wall of silence and no charges were ever brought. For his part, Deano was presented with a Nike tracksuit. A gang member had suggested, tongue in cheek, that because Deano had been paid for the job, he could now perhaps change his nickname to 'Hitman'. Deano had studied his nails, sniffed through his nose, and said calmly, "Well, it's just another day at the office." He was on a high. It was a pre-meditated and calculated killing. It was the stuff of movies. Deano was heading toward the premiership of rogues whose deadly lore made them household names.

Acceptable behaviour contracts, dispersal orders and ASBO's were sneered at and treated as part of their way of life and were shrugged off accordingly. Deano knew that he was virtually untouchable, he knew full well that he could get away with anything because everyone was afraid to stand up to him and the gang he was part of. Having already amassed 114 criminal convictions and breached his ASBO no less than 19 times, why worry?

Even at the tender age of eleven when he, Thommo and Nelly had entered Boreley Hill Sport and Community High School at year seven, they were bad tempered, cruel and heartless, and they had got a damn sight worse now that they had arrived at year eleven. All three had served several fixed term exclusions but they were street smart, knew how to play the rules to their advantage, and did just enough not to be placed at special schools. 'Ha! The bored dispirited adolescent with nothing to do what would you expect?' bleated the do-gooders. But why bother going
to school at all? Although they could find plenty of 'sport' in the evenings, they found their days were quite boring. It was so much more fun coming into the school sporadically and causing as much bad feeling and disruption as possible. There were also rich pickings. They had a lucrative protection racket on the go, which was a nice little earner. Computers, laptops, mobile phones, and handbags tended to disappear on a regular basis. They made sure that everyone knew them and would remember them for a long time to come; their names and misspelt filth adorned every notice board, corridor and toilet block in the school.

4

He had sat on the bathroom floor for twenty minutes or so when he was brought back from wherever he had been by a sharp rap on the door. Mrs. Crabtree wanted to know if he was OK. He mumbled a yes and she retreated back downstairs.

Billy threw back the bedroom curtains. Fifteen years ago, the vista would have included deciduous woodland, acres of softly rolling farmland and Cannock chase forest in the far distance. Occasionally he would catch sight of deer going about their business, but now he took in the idyll that was Lidl's rear delivery bays.

He stumbled back into the bathroom where he stuck his nose under each armpit in turn, crinkling his nose; he smelled bad. He had not shaved for days. He couldn't give a shit.

Today was the first day of eight weeks of exams and they had to start and finish at precise times during the day. So, Billy had to spend the first hour of his shift in the school's sports hall methodically placing out two hundred and fifty-three desks and chairs in neat rows. By neat rows, Billy knew that Mister Connelly, the exam officer, *meant* neat rows. *Exactly* one desk space between the one in front and the one behind and *exactly* one desk gap to left and right. Rules are rules after all. *Twat.* Pain, despair, and inadequacy. Billy felt they were a little bit easier to control when he put on a public face and concealed them behind a mask. Until the inevitable happened and until the time came where he could think of a quick, painless end, work would be his only salvation. He would keep busy and carry on working from early morning until late to take his mind off things. It stopped him mulling over what lay ahead. From the moment he woke up until he went to bed, he went through the motions of living when all that he really wanted was to stop existing entirely. Everything he now did seemed futile, but It got him out of the house and away from his Mum for the day, and to some extent keeping busy kept his mind away from the gnawing pain that was his constant companion.

Billy felt immense weariness come over him after his stint in the sports hall and so decided that he had earned himself a cuppa. His workroom was a small oasis of calm amidst the noise and bustle of school life.

His lips and mouth were still smarting from the bleach incident, so he had taken along a jar of Vaseline and a bottle of his Mothers mouthwash. Whilst waiting for the kettle to boil, he smeared Vaseline onto and around his lips, and decided it would be best using the mouthwash after his cuppa.

As he was pouring hot water over a teabag, there were several loud, rapid thumps on the workroom door. It startled him enough to make him spill hot water over the work surface, which in turn splashed over his trousers. "Fuck it!" A dark crescent spread around his crotch extending half way down each thigh, which he dabbed vigorously with paper towels.

Billy was still swearing under his breath when he opened the door. Craig 'Deano' Dean filled the doorway. Nelly and Thommo, Deano's ever-present 'sheep', appeared at Deano's shoulders.

Deano was a shade under six-foot and a smidgen under twelve stone - a kid in a man's body. Pale, hollow cheeks dusted with freckles, eyes like glass marbles, close-cropped red hair and a sharp, chiselled nose. Teeth that were as crooked as a Spanish footpath, but they were rarely seen. Deano never smiled in fear of exposing dark places between his teeth. The only exception he made to this rule was when he was causing distress to someone, deriving sick satisfaction from the upset, pain, and/or terror he elicited from his victims. Big, red pustules adorned his entire face, if there had been a monthly magazine dedicated to acne,

Deano would have made a creditable centrefold. Although still only a few weeks shy of his seventeenth birthday, he displayed an angry red 'battle' scar that ran at an acute angle through his left eyebrow.

Deano's eyes were somewhere in the shadows of his baseball cap. He slowly raised his head; Billy had never seen such extraordinary eyes like them before. They were small, perturbed, and bottomless and they glared at Billy warily; they had nothing in them, nothing at all. Billy narrowed his eyes and looking into Deano's black holes it was obvious that he was under the influence of something illegal. In this present climate, it didn't shock Billy that drugs were readily available in school. He would have been more shocked if you could get a decent education.

Deano sneered on one side of his mouth; there was a short glimpse of brown teeth against grey gums, already the early signs of the junkies' mouth, even at this young age Deano was rotting. There was about him a sense of contained feral evil, something inhuman. His head dropped to one side and his eyes roved slowly from Billy's feet to his hairline. The look resembled the look you would wear when picking up something dead in between two fingers.

"Pissed yerself have yer, Crabby?" Deano asked contemptuously in a tone that was guaranteed to agitate. Again, he smiled on one side of his face and chuckled; it was not at all a friendly smile, it was a smile of utter malevolence and the sound he made was more chilling than if he had had a temper tantrum.

The 'sheep' bumped fists and sniggered wickedly.

Neil 'Nelly' Dunn was painfully thin and was just sprouting his first sparse facial hair. He wore his greasy hair long, tucked behind his ears. A silver stud pieced the bridge of his nose. He had such large front teeth that his mouth was permanently open, twisted into an evil reptilian grin. A lad who always looked shifty, as if he had done something illegal and wasn't sure that he had got away with it yet.

Thomas 'Thommo' Thomson was chunky and had slits

for eyes. His face was permanently scrunched up, as though he had been licking piss off a nettle. His forehead was forever furrowed by the bewilderment that was his life. Although both lightweight compared to Deano, here was an increasingly worrying example of today's youth, craving notoriety and status from the gang culture in which they had been reared, finding living on the very edge of society strangely appealing.

Some kids, like these kids, are just born evil and this trio had grown up as vicious, hate-filled monsters with stone cold hearts.

Billy swallowed hard, attempting to keep his emotions in check, maybe accept it as part of the job, but deep down the anger was simmering. This piece of shit had the effect of creating the most intense emotions of anger and frustration and Billy would dearly have loved to smash his fist into Deano's face and remove that smug grin.

Billy took a quick glance down at the lower half of the door – black rubber scuffmarks adorned it. Inhaling and exhaling as normally as possible, trying to calm himself, he breathed in slowly through his nose and then inflated his cheeks. "It could be said that kicking my door is an act of infantile rage, Mister Dean but I suppose you or one of your friends here didn't actually do it, now did you?"

Deano emitted a short laugh, a low heartless noise that chilled Billy's spine. His eyes held a dead stare and they were far away, the pupils almost invisible. He seemed to be staring dully past Billy to somewhere else. His skin so pale as to be almost translucent, muscles aggressively tensed his body language had defiance written all over it. He smiled but there was no humour in it. "Nah, not me, crabby," he said, chewing gum exaggeratedly. "Look, man, I've forgot my locker key, I want it opened, *now*," he insisted with an edge of anger in his voice. He scratched at his left ear; on the back of his hand, Billy noticed, was tattooed the cross of St. George underlined with the slogan 'White Pride World Wide'. Underneath it, a small English bulldog and across his knuckles 'E.D.L.' crudely written in black ink – obviously self-inflicted. There was a small black cross at the base of his thumb, obviously another crude attempt by Deano and a blood tipped dagger disappeared under his sleeve.

Billy felt a surge of anger as adrenaline spiked through him; his visage was a mask of grim fury. He wanted to shout at Deano, scream at him and shake him until he saw sense. Training had told him not to buckle under any invective but to smile gently and be positive. That was easier said than done in Mister Dean's case. All staff knew that his rages were uncontrollable when he was pushed; which didn't take a lot.

Billy's fists were balled at his side, the knuckles turning white. He took a big drag of air through his nose and then released it, his nostrils flaring with the strength of his breathing. He cleared the knot from his throat. "Mmm," he went. "Three things need to be addressed here, Mister Dean. Firstly, I'd appreciate it if you would address me as either Mister Crabtree or Sir." Billy was using an even tone to put forward the image of being in control. "Secondly, after attending this school for five years now, you will be aware that baseball caps are not to be worn inside the building." Embroidered in yellow cotton on the front of Deano's sky blue cap were the letters 'NY'. Billy guessed that in Deano's case the letters stood for Neanderthal Yob. "Finally, I don't do *anything* for *anybody* without a please or thank you. Now then, young man shall we start again?"

Deano's two bookends traded glances and cackled. Somehow, their laughter made them seem even more menacing.

Deano raised a ginger eyebrow and emitted a harsh, jarring laugh. He thrust a beefy finger into Billy's face as his own face darkened alarmingly. "Look, crabby..." spittle flew from between his lips as he hissed out the words. He pointed at his cap, "this is just my lid, man it ain't no fuckin' bomb, y'nah wha' I mean? Anyway, you're just a fucking shit-shoveller, you're nuffink, man, so get my locker open now, twat." He was trying to instil fear, ever the smart-arse in front of his mates.

Billy had a short vivid vision of himself slamming Deano's head against the concrete wall until the back was a bloody mess and then ripping out his black, worthless heart. He really needed to restrain that impulse. He gave his head a quick shake and bit into the inside of his lip; it took considerable effort to stifle a round of expletives.

"Mmm, proper little Peaky Blinder, aren't we? You really do work too hard at being as unpleasant as possible don't you, Mister Dean, eh? You're certainly a master at making people's lives a misery."

Deano contorted his heavily acne-scared face into a grimace. "It's a skill, man, and well worth the fuckin' effort," he retorted.

Thommo gave a laugh a hyena would have envied. He said, "Nice one, man." He put his palm in the air for Deano to high-five it and Nelly elbowed him, clearly impressed with what they perceived to be an hilarious remark.

Billy had slipped his hands into his overall pockets, the better to curl them into unseen fists. For many years he had disappeared behind a wall of controlled rage, which always loitered just beneath the surface. He took in and then let out another slow breath – the anger in his voice was just at the edge of his control. "Listen, young man I have a number of tasks to perform during the day which I have to prioritise, *if* time permits, I will see what I can do." Anxiety had caused his voice to go up an octave; his throat was tight with the obvious effort of control.

Clenching and unclenching his fists, fighting to keep control of
his emotions.

Billy closed the door politely, but firmly. Shutting the door in their faces was a childish victory but a tiny victory none the less. Not smashing Deano in the face with a fist had almost exhausted the last reserves of his willpower. The door was subjected to numerous blows with what sounded like heavy boots and he heard a stream of invective that gradually turned to raucous laughter. The trail of sound dwindled into silence as the gang turned and made their way down the corridor.

Billy needed to let off steam; he clenched his right fist and punched the door hard several times. The pain that shot through his hand and up his arm was like an electric shock. He clamped his teeth tightly together determined not to cry out, flapping his fingers in front of his eyes making sure nothing was broken. Billy turned and sagged against the door and slowly slid down into a crouch. He lowered his face between his knees and wrapped his arms around his legs.

There he sat hunched and useless. Broken. Powerless. Ineffective.

For how long he'd been there, he didn't have a clue. He opened his eyes slowly and blinked rapidly. As he glanced down, he spotted a white, blank business card in between his feet that had been slipped under the door. He picked it up and turned it over. On the reverse was simply a black cross, the same cross that was tattooed on the back of Deano's hand.

Eventually he raised his head and rested it against the door. "Bastards," he mumbled, putting his good hand to his forehead and mopping away a film of perspiration. He twisted his head back and forth, trying to relax the knot of muscles in his neck. Eventually, suppressing the ever-present ache that bored through him, he ambled over to the sink where he turned on the cold tap. Placing cupped hands under the torrent, he lifted handfuls of cooling water to his face until his head cleared. After wiping his face with a paper towel, he used it to wipe the greasy mirror, which hung above the sink. What he saw there was the shell of the man he once was. He could almost see the desperation oozing out of his pores.

How do people handle the mental side of taking their own lives? Just how low do you have to be to walk in front of a train or throw yourself off a tall building? He slumped down heavily into his chair and leant his head on the headrest. He was oh so tired, but it wasn't the sort of tired where you could go to bed and have your recommended eight hours.

After a few moments he rose and walked slowly over to his workbench; his head sagged forward. He placed his hands palm side down on the bench and released another long slow breath. *Why am I delaying the inevitable?* His mouth turned into a tight slit and he rubbed at his lower stomach, trying to ease the pain. A wave of nausea swept through him; he was barely keeping his stomach and bowels in check. Death would now come as such a relief. Above his head was a racking system adorned with an array of tools: Saws, screwdrivers, files, drills, but the one that caught his eye was a craft knife. He lifted it from its retaining clip, pressed his thumb against the steel button and the blade slid out. It glistened wickedly. Unblinkingingly and unemotionally he placed it against a protruding vein on his wrist and closed his eyes; his stomach quivered pathetically as the urge for self-destruction became more vital now than ever. He slowly breathed in through his nose then breathed out sharply, ballooning his cheeks. He quickly slid the blade across his wrist and gradually opened one eye and glanced down - nothing. He repeated the process this time with a little more pressure. A single droplet of blood appeared. *No, no, no, too slow, too messy, do I really want to lie on this workroom floor and slowly bleed to death? Shit, I wish I were a little braver.* He threw the knife down, it skidded across the bench, and the blade embedded itself in a cupboard door.

Billy flopped back down in his chair and again he lost time and many minutes passed with only distressing thoughts washing over him. He was shaken by a sharp rap on the door. He inflated his cheeks. *Oh no, not those three bastards again.* He sprang to his feet and flung open the door.

"Now look, I've told you...ah, good morning Sir," Billy said sheepishly. He sent him a smile; it was not reciprocated.

Mister Clune, the Headteacher - BEd MSc - placed the back of his hand against Billy's chest and pushed him gently to one side, letting himself into the office. Mister Clune was long in the face with a prominent Adams apple. Due to his addiction to anything sweet and sticky he sported a belly you could have plumped up and got cosy on. An overactive thyroid gland had caused his eyes to protrude from their sockets, which gave him a bug-eyed appearance. His hair was a silver mass of tight curls giving him a clown-like appearance. Obviously ammunition to the kids' taunts; they had christened him with the unflattering nickname of Co-Co – though not to his face, never to his face.

Although the glass in the workroom window was frosted, the Headteacher stood in front of it as if gazing out. His posture was ramrod straight with a military bearing, which made him seem taller than his actual height. From the rear, his hair looked like birds had been nesting in it. Billy bit his upper lip as, even in his current state of mind, he found a giggle developing.

The head clamped his hands behind his back and after a few moments he addressed the window acidly, "Now look here, Mister Crabtree I have just had three rather irate young men almost battering my door down. They have informed me that you have refused to open a locker for one of them?" The head was the kind of man you would notice in a crowd – if only by his hair. He had presence and exuded confidence, a man who was secure in who he was and radiated an aura of success.

The Headteacher turned and caught Billy yawning. It occurred to him that Billy had the rumpled look of a man who had been missing sleep; he spotted an open bag of sweets on the desk and broke out into a smile. "Ah yummies...may I?" He enquired.

"Help yourself, sir," Billy said, blithely pointing towards the confectionery.

The Headteacher plucked a toffee from the bag, removed the wrapping, rolled it up between forefinger and thumb, and slipped it back inside the bag. He turned his back on Billy.

Billy said to the back of the Headteachers head, "Well I'm sorry, sir but they came here..."

Mister Clune spun round and waved a dismissive hand, his lips set in a determined, tight slit. "I haven't got time for all of this, Mister Crabtree," he said, glaring at him with Bush-Baby eyes; he rammed balled fists into his hips. "I delegate people to take the load off, yeah? The finance officer deals with finance; the I.T. manager sorts out the network, the business team manager sorts out...whatever, you, Mister Crabtree sort out locker keys, yeah? I've got much more important matters to be getting on with..." he gabbled on about the problems and pressure he faced daily. Teachers low morale, governors who hadn't got a clue what went on in a school, parents whose little Johnny or Julie were little angels and who wouldn't do anything like what he or she had been accused of, it was somebody else's kid who was a bad influence, probably one of the nutters from the Shorevale council estate... "I'm up to my ears in it at the moment what with the OFSTED inspectors here tomorrow. Now, Mister Crabtree go and sort this out, yeah?"

The pressure inside Billy had been building. It was bad enough the kids' treating him as a punch bag, but it was a travesty when even the head wouldn't back you. Billy fought to retain his composure. His cheeks were engorged red with a nearly uncontrollable anger. He stuttered, "Yes...but..."

"*Sort it*, Mister Crabtree. I know that some of the kids here are challenging and we have our fair share of problem pupils, but we need to be positive, I can't walk round with you every day holding your hand...good day to you." With a wave of a hand, Billy was 'dismissed,' and slamming the workroom door behind him, he was gone.

5

The despair that the thought of the day brought to Billy was so overpowering that he felt physically sick. In fact, another wave of queasiness hit him; he lurched towards the sink, bile surging into his throat and mouth.

He tore off a length of kitchen roll and dabbed his mouth. He felt deeply depressed; a great weight bore down on him. He just wanted to sit down alone and get his head straight, which in fact he did do for several more minutes. Then, collecting his thoughts, Billy sucked in deep lungs full of air as he lifted the lockers master key from the key safe. He begrudgingly tramped his way through the music corridor and into the reception area. As he passed the reception office, he could hear the hurried dance of fingers across a keyboard. A voice chirruped through the open sliding glass windows. "Morning, Billy."

Billy did a 'U' turn and approached. Mrs. Westwood, the receptionist repeated, "Morning, nice weekend?" She smiled at him and, keeping eye contact, continued pecking away at her keyboard.

Oh! That smile, the kind that made Billy want to sing out with happiness. On many occasions, Billy had passed this window, sometimes not even going anywhere in particular, it was just a chance to glance at her. He feared she would return his glance and leave him blushing and stuttering. Often, he would lurk in the reception area in an agony of longing, listening to her voice and occasional laughter. He had passed her in the corridors many times and as soon as she came into view, his mouth would dry up. When he tried to say a cheery hello, it came out as a humiliating squeak. On many occasions he had got very close to asking her out, but he knew that the rejection would embarrass him so much that he would probably have locked himself away in his workroom for weeks in an agony of regret. Although a loner, the desire for intimacy had always been there and especially with this woman. Her scent surrounded him, tormented him, a smell in which he would have loved to immerse himself.

Janet Westwood was on the wrong side of fifty and gathering speed. The years though, had taken little toll. She had a tranquil beauty and the light in her eyes still danced with sparkle and vitality. She certainly looked after herself and was always well presented. Her hair had doubtlessly been assisted by a professional and coloured a deep auburn; it was thick with a natural wave. When she smiled, she revealed a truly magnificent set of her own teeth. Billy had admired her from afar for many years, surprising himself that he still had the capacity to be attracted to a woman. He was therefore unfamiliar with the feelings that he experienced for her each time they were in proximity. Alas, he never could pluck up the nerve to take things further; he could not handle the embarrassment of a refusal.

Hi-ya, Jan, have I told you how absolutely, amazingly beautiful you look this morning? Is what he wanted to shout out.

Janet's late husband had been an outdoors type, she had once explained to him. He didn't drink or smoke and would be classed as a relatively fit man, indulging in back-packing, mountain biking and even the odd marathon, but almost three years ago she had watched him wither and die of prostate cancer. She had grieved, obviously, but after a while, when the loneliness had crept in, she had thrown herself into work and so her job and career had become her life. Perhaps she could see her husband reflected in Billy's face. A face that looked as if it had endured terrible hardship or been on hunger strike.

"Hi ya, Billy," Esther called out over Janet's shoulder.

Esther was the business team managers' assistant. She

was a good deal younger than both Janet and Billy, but she was a sturdy woman of quite unattractive disposition. Billy found her funny, outspoken on occasions, and warm-hearted. Her figure was slackened by the contours of pregnancy. Sadly, she had been last in the queue when good looks were being given out. Having virtually no chin and large sticky-out ears they were a great source of amusement to the kids who had christened her 'Wing-Nut'. She wore her hair short, which was fierce ginger, or as she preferred to call the colour, 'African sunset'. She had a scary taste in eyebrows that she had plucked out and re-applied with thick black pencil. A white, V-neck blouse framed a silver necklace from which dangled an eternity ring bought for her by her husband.

When Esther had been employed by the school just short of four years ago, the two women had hit it off instantly, and had become close friends. Esther had rescued Janet from reclusive widowhood following her husbands' early death by insisting on them going out on occasional evenings or the odd shopping trip. To Ester's right, stuck to a filing cabinet, a sticker proclaimed - 'You don't have to be mad to work here, but it helps.' On her desk a crisping house plant.

Billy leant on the windows wooden surround, both palms flat. "Hello, ladies and how are we today?" he asked jovially, although the permanent dark heaviness around his eyes didn't exactly exude happiness.

Before Janet could open her mouth, Esther called to Billy, "When you have time, Billy, could you have a look at this for me?" her chair was supported on plastic castors and she had propelled herself smoothly across the small room. She pointed blithely over her shoulder at a half-opened Venetian blind. "It's buggered, the damn thing won't go up or down," she said.

"You know the rules, Esther," Billy said with a smile, "make out a maintenance slip and pop it into the box and I'll prioritise it. And by the way, that plant of yours could do with a bit of a drink."

"Mmm."

Janet had been staring up at Billy for the last few seconds; her lips parted slightly. Every time she saw him, he seemed that little bit greyer. She knew it was impossible, but it seemed to her that new lines were etching themselves into his face almost hourly. There were shadows under each of his eyes. The eyes themselves were like those of a dazed, haggard stranger. Nevertheless, that didn't stop her liking him. She wasn't quite sure why, perhaps it was the hurt she sensed in him, bubbling just below the surface. He was shy, yes but she liked that. He was always polite and well mannered, which was a rare commodity these days; she liked that also and had recognised over some time that he was a man worthy of her respect.

"We're both fine, Billy," Janet said in a soft voice that had a faint hint of a West Country accent.

Billy thought that Janet's voice was seductive in the most innocent way. When she spoke and smiled, it made *you* smile and while he listened to her, he tended to stop thinking about anything else.

Janet emitted a sigh and then continued with undeniable sincerity, "It's you that I...erm, *we're* concerned about, Billy."

Billy had been so deep in thought watching her moist lips moving he couldn't answer her in fear of prematurely ejaculating.

She's right. What with all the weight I've lost, the ever-present stubble, and the continued greying and thinning hair, I can barely recognise myself sometimes.

Janet smiled warmly and looked deeply into his solemn eyes. "Billy, you do look tired and preoccupied lately, love. You need feeding up; perhaps I could cook you something, mmm? One evening maybe?" she placed her hands-on top of his. A couple of faint lines appeared across her forehead. "What on earth have you done to your hand?" She enquired.

"Erm, well, had a bit of a fall-out with a door...long story."

She nodded thoughtfully. "Riiiggghhhttt, OK, well about this meal then?"

"Yeeesss...great." He flushed, and his heart rate

inexplicably increased as he felt the strings of a powerful emotion that he wasn't at all familiar with. Billy lowered his eyes momentarily and slowly slipped his hands from underneath hers. "Yes, well, we'll do that...yes." He took the locker master key from his pocket and dangled it in front of her face. "Must dash, I'm on a mission." Then he disappeared amongst a wash of cries from a throng of jabbering kids.

She knew that most men hated to admit that they had any problems and tended to keep them bottled up. She sensed that Billy was hurting and putting up a tough exterior.

"I don't know why you keep trying, Jan it's obvious he's not interested," Esther said; she was filing her nails: "You're gonna have to corner him somewhere and stick your tongue down his throat before *he* gets the message."

Janet's jaw drooped. "Esther, *really*."

Ester's brow furrowed; she announced suddenly, "You know, I've just had this very strong craving for cucumber smothered in tomato sauce!"

Billy made his way down through the sixth form common room; a short cut to the year eleven social area. He made a mental note to return later and remove some graffiti that he had spotted on one of the walls. Who was shagging who, who was gay and one student who was apparently copulating with his dog. The student in question had obviously tried to scrub out the offending remark but without success. The barmy author had even signed his name. It was bad enough the sixth formers' indulging in graffiti, what annoyed him even more was the atrocious grammar and spelling.

When Billy arrived at his destination Deano and his two chums were waiting for him and they began sniggering amongst themselves as he approached. Deano wore a wild, gloating smirk and his eyes bored into Billy, daring him to look away.

"Ha! Had a bollocking off Co-Co have we crabby?" Deano jeered. A ruthless and unfathomable hatred exuded from his eyes. "Has he had you across his desk and smacked your little arse has he, ay? I'll bet you *really* enjoyed that, ay?" He elbowed

Nelly and Thommo and they laughed on cue.

Why don't the three of you go and play on the fucking motorway?

Billy's visage remained deadpan although he was gritting his teeth so tightly it was almost audible. The irritation was crawling up his neck and so he took in a deep breath and let it out in slow exasperation. "You need your locker opening, Mister Dean, which one is it?"

Deano looked left and right and threw Thommo and Nelly a conspiratorial wink. A wolfish grin spread across his face. The grin was like a carnivore curling back its lips. "Nah, it's too late now, crabby I only wanted a pen." Deano didn't need a pen, or want a pen, and It was probably a year or so since he had actually held a pen. "Got fed up waiting for ya, so I nicked one off that fat ginger-headed kid." He blithely pointed in the direction of the student.

As Billy turned the kid in question lowered his eyes.

Billy puffed out his cheeks. Continuing his efforts to exercise self-control he said, "Why on earth are you always trying to be so awkward, Mister Dean?"

"I ain't fuckin' *trying*, crabby it just comes natural, man." Deano hissed.

Deano licked his forefinger and chalked up an imaginary notch on an invisible scoreboard; the goons at his shoulders sniggered their approval. Nelly's appearance seemed to Billy to be even more grotesque than usual as he chomped open mouthed on a piece of gum. With that, the three of them strolled menacingly towards Billy and loomed over him.

"Mister Dean," Billy said, "can I give you some advice. Life is a very precious thing. There is not an endless supply of it. I must admit that I have totally wasted my life and you are doing exactly the same, albeit in a different manner. If you were to put the same amount of time and energy into doing something positive..."

Deano sniffed violently through his nose and spat. The green, egg sized slime landed in between Billy's feet. He then took a piece of gum from his mouth and stuck it on Billy's forehead. The two sidekicks buckled up with laughter. As they passed, the three of them dropped a shoulder and 'accidentally' bumped into Billy knocking him back slightly. Billy clamped his teeth together.

You three wankers.

"Mister Dean," Billy bawled, "I would appreciate it if you would clean up this mess."

Nelly turned and tried to emulate his 'hero' by spitting, but it came out like a wet fart and it dribbled down his chin; he ran a sleeve across his mouth. He said, "Fuck off, crabby that's your job, you're the shit-shoveller."

All three buried their hands in their pockets as they lounged out of the social area with contrived swaggers. They burst through the external door and out into the quad. Deano, Thommo, and Nelly again creased up into loud, uproarious, and mocking howls of uncontrollable laughter, playfully punching, kicking and pushing each other and bawling out profanities. Billy watched them as he took a tissue from a pocket and began removing the gum from his brow; he deposited it in a nearby waste bin.

From the far end of the quad came a year seven boy who was late and running to his lesson. Deano cracked the back of his head with an open hand and then spat in the kid's hair, which he then ground in with the palm of his hand; again, they laughed raucously. Then a year nine girl, bag over one shoulder, books tucked under her other arm appeared. Deano pinned her against the wall by her shoulders, Thommo lifted her skirt, and Nelly began fondling her breasts. She struggled violently and screamed out. *Easy targets, that's all these bullies can attack.* Billy moved towards the door and as he opened it, they released their restraining hold on the girl. Nelly raised a clenched fist, middle finger extended. The girl screamed obscenities at them, one suggesting that they were a bunch of wankers, which Billy totally agreed with. The gang sniggered some more and then disappeared through the far door with Thommo bringing up the rear. As he trailed the other two through the door, he turned and suggested, by means of a hand gesture, that Billy was also a wanker. The girl ran past Billy, tears cascading down her face. He asked if she was OK, but she didn't answer, she didn't stop, and she stormed down the corridor.

Billy realised his jaw ached from clenching his teeth so hard and for so long. He emitted a long, audible breath. He was useless. If he were to utter another word, he just knew that he would explode. The dull, disappointing reality was that he couldn't do anything. All he could do was watch the jeering threesome with defeated, hunched shoulders. *What the hell has happened to my England?* A sense of isolation and loneliness pressed down on him.

Ground please open up and swallow me right now.

The incident had put Billy in a fractious mood. He was cocooned in an aura of blackness, and was to spend the rest of the day in a pain-induced haze.

6

That evening Billy had gone to bed early as usual.

On arriving home and even before he had taken off his coat, his Mother had begun driving him nuts twittering on about re-decorating the kitchen, painting the front door, where shall we spend our holiday this year, Weston-Super-Mare perhaps? Ivy, her best friend has been diagnosed with a prolapsed womb… just a few months ago, when he was a different man, he would have joined in, taking some interest in her days events and she in his. Now, he couldn't be bothered. The whining irritated him immensely. He explained to his Mum he didn't feel too well, and went straight to his bedroom.

Lately, Billy's world was his bedroom. It was sparse, containing a scarred double mahogany wardrobe, a dilapidated armchair draped with clothes that needed washing and ironing, a small round coffee table on which lay well thumbed magazines and three mugs which contained cold dregs of coffee. (The table was once destined for the skip because the headteacher inexplicably needed a square one) At the foot of the bed a three-drawer pine unit on top of which was perched a portable TV set. He guessed that he might be the only person left in the country who didn't own a flat screen TV. They were the types of furnishings that charity shops threw out. On the walls, pink roses twisted and snaked their way up green ivy. The Wallpaper was beginning to peel in places, not that that was of any interest to him. Every surface was grey and feathery with dust, but what did that matter? No one ever came up here to see it.

The room had a sad quality: it was a room where nothing

happened except for the passing of time. Nothing to shout about, but it was his private little haven, a haven where he spent his time ageing rapidly.

He went to his hi-fi and wondered, like he did every time he used it, what the hell a graphic equaliser did? He slipped a Neil Diamond vinyl album from its sleeve, wiped its surface with an anti-static cloth, and put it on low. Owning some of Neil's later work would have been nice, but Billy had never got round to purchasing a CD player.

Billy lay supinely on the bed with his eyes closed, trading the yellowing artexed ceiling for empty darkness; he tried to clear his mind of negativity but failed. There were too many things swirling around in his head. He felt very weary and a little sick. After a short moment he sat up and fluffed up his pillow, resting his back against it. The record had ended, which he hadn't noticed and couldn't remember half the tracks he'd listened to. He turned on the TV looking for distraction and hoping that its flickering images would hopefully take his mind off his problems. Quickly he surfed the channels, and something would catch his attention for a few minutes giving him a brief respite from his worries, but mainly all he found was crap, endless programmes that said absolutely nothing. Programmes designed just to fill airtime, doom and gloom and nothing had the power to grip his attention.

He had read a couple of pages of a Tom Clancy novel, and then tried to settle down into some sort of sleep. Sleep was a barely remembered luxury. He had taken a couple of painkillers and waited for them to kick in. Meanwhile, he had heard his Mum come upstairs and then noticed, through the gap under his door that the landing light had been turned off.

Billy screamed.

He woke with a jolt after living a recurring nightmare. He had plummeted from the highest point of the school – the squat tower that took fumes away from the boiler house – and just as he was about to hit the concrete floor, he would wake bolt upright in a cold clammy sweat. The same nightmare kept playing repeatedly until finally the intense vision had fled, leaving him wide-awake in a foetal ball with thoughts that were jumbled and haywire. His throat was raw from the scream. He poured himself a large whisky and downed it in one. Then for a couple of hours he had lain on his back in a state not unlike death itself, trying to make sense of his life – or lack of it. Then he'd drop off again to wake shortly after in tears after a re-run of his nightmare. Eventually, he gave in and turned on the bedside lamp. He stared wide-eyed at the ugly ceiling and began to count down the minutes until dawn.

His mind settled on the day's events and especially the growing problem with Deano and his sidekicks. He was quite certain that if he were to confront them individually, they would probably shit themselves.

Cowards, that's what we're turning out nowadays, cowards. Anybody can play the tough guy when there's a gang behind them.

All that Billy had left now was the past, not that there was much of it. For weeks he had lain up here hour after hour amongst the forlorn furniture dipping in and out of unexciting memories. His fears and joys, emotional needs, doubts and hopes were his to explore without anyone else's advice, guidance or sympathy. He placed both hands behind his head, intertwining his fingers. He opened his eyes. The artexed ceiling would have been fashionable forty years ago.

The cane, that's what's needed, it needs to make a come-back. The muscles at his temples twitched.

Billy's mind drifted back to the varying types of corporal punishment that had been generously and sometimes undeservedly applied to varying parts of his anatomy when he was a young boy at school. A slipper, a ruler across the knuckles and a rounders bat, but he had only been caned the once. His memory locked onto that one occasion.

It was just shy of his fifteenth birthday, about a week before bonfire night. He and a couple of mates had been roaming the streets larking about indulging in innocent devilment. Just kids being kids. Egging each other on to knock on doors and run away or jumping over privet hedges. One of the lads had a couple of bangers in his pocket and dared Billy to push one through someone's letterbox. Billy had argued against it, but when the pair had taunted him with their incessant chicken impressions, Billy capitulated and like an idiot, he went ahead and did it.

A neighbour had witnessed the incident. She had recognised one of the lads and had reported the incident to the school.

It didn't take too much detective work to find out who the other two lads were. A couple of days later the three of them were ordered onto the stage after assembly. They were given two options. They could argue their case – which would have been unwise because the woman who had witnessed their prank would have been called into the school to confront the trio. In those days, the word of an adult would have been enough to prove their guilt. In that case, they would receive twelve strokes of the cane for lying and wasting the heads time. If, on the other hand they were to admit their guilt and apologise, they would be 'rewarded' with only six strokes of the cane. Anyway, they admitted their part and the Headteacher ordered them to lower their trousers. In turn, they were held by male teachers across the heads desk and were subjected to six strokes of the cane. The pain inflicted was bad enough, but the embarrassment and shame of it in front of a sniggering whole-school assembly lingered to this day.

The school then felt it their duty to inform the boys' parents, where the second wave of punishment was meted out. Billy's parents were livid. His father was furious and struck Billy a hefty blow across the face with the back of his hand. That was just for starters, the main course consisted of him removing his belt and lashing Billy across the back of his legs and backside right over the weal's that had formed from the caning. At the time, Billy felt that the punishment that he had received by both the school and his father was way over the top and he was extremely bitter about it for years to come. However, as he got older and looked back, it had had the desired effect. Billy was never to receive any form of corporal punishment for the rest of his school life, and he now felt that the punishment fitted the crime because in the end, it did the trick.

Did I do it again? Like fuck I did. Now that worked, if Deano and his mates had to face that they'd cry like little babies and piss their pants. Nowadays there's no deterrent; Deano, Thommo and Nelly are hell bent on inexorable progress to disaster with nothing standing in their way.

Billy's teeth were firmly clamped together and his thoughts continued. *And what do we owe this gang culture to with their shit attitude, knives and guns? Parents, blinkered do-gooders and no retribution. What the hell are their parents doing to make them act in this way? Don't they care what their kids are doing? Now in my day we were nurtured and taught right from wrong from day one. What the hell has gone wrong? Kids demand designer gear and get it; all that does is promote greed. They use foul language in front of their parents – is it me or has my England gone mad? Deano and the other two little shits know the human rights act inside out but don't know their human responsibilities. If I reported them to the police for some misdemeanour, they'd shrug their shoulders and tick them off, but if I drove down the street without car insurance, they'd jump on me from a great fuckin' height. The only people wringing their hands are the fuckin' Solicitors. I wish I were a bloody Headteacher I'd change things. I'd teach them some bloody manners and the buggers wouldn't answer back. Even kids as young as seven are being excluded from school for attacking teachers. We have a generation coming into high school that has no understanding of discipline or accountability and no respect for authority. They never have to take responsibility for anything. Who teaches them this lesson? The fucking parents, and as soon as anything upsets their little cherubs, they're banging on the Headteachers desk blaming other kids, the teachers, the system, anything or anyone but themselves. Any excuse for appalling behaviour. 'Oh! Johnny's got Attention Deficit Hyperactivity Disorder'. 'Oh! Emma suffers with Emotional Behavioural Difficulties'. 'Oh! Trisha suffers with schizo-affective disorder.' 'Sorry, Harry just can't be blamed, he's bi-polar.'*

'Sorry, our little Tim suffers with de-personalisation.' 'Sarah's not to blame; she has a dissociative identity disorder,' or any fucking disorder that's the flavour of the month. Nicked a car? Oh, he was abused as a child. Done a burglary? Oh, he was abused as a child. Rape? He couldn't help himself he was abused as a child. Any excuse for behaviour that is inexcusable and sometimes criminal. Well I could soon cure the little shits of that.

Billy realised that he'd been grinding his teeth together so hard that his jaw was aching.

His mind was yanked back from its wandering as he felt a telltale twinge in the pit of his stomach. *Oh, Christ here we go again.* He glanced across at the clock beside his bed; the red figures glowed 1: 51a.m. *My god I've been up here almost seven hours.* He reached over to his bedside cabinet where he kept his painkillers and tipped the required dose, i.e. two, into his palm. He stared into space for a few seconds then added another tablet, after all what harm could it do him now? He swallowed the pills with a glass of water. As he reached out to replace the glass onto the cabinet, it hit him. Like a sword passing slowly straight into his midriff. It was pain he found difficult to comprehend. It stabbed him, burned him, and screamed in its intensity. He dropped the half-empty glass onto the floor and clutched at his stomach. Perspiration leaked into the small of his back as he curled up into a foetal position desperately struggling to master the pain. Salt water flooded his eyes as he began shaking uncontrollably and his chest heaved. The pain was so great that he thought he could not possibly survive it. He clutched at his pillow and buried his face into it to muffle his convulsive sobs.

Billy Crabtree endured long, oh so long waves of sickness, waves of loneliness, and waves of pain that had no description.

Then, it was an hour later.

The painkillers had finally kicked in although he was still left with a dull ache in his lower abdomen. Cold perspiration soaked him. Billy couldn't even muster the energy to yawn and keeping his eyes open had become impossible, but still sleep would not come. He tossed and turned as he played his boring mundane life through his mind again like an old silent newsreel that didn't make sense. He sat up and propped himself against his pillow again, hugging his legs, with his chin cradled between his kneecaps. Then he would stare into the blackness, weeping. Dawn was a long way away and negativity swamped him: Guilt, Unworthiness, Sadness, and Morbid Thoughts. He could hear a gentle rain falling onto the roof tiles. He cursed the restless thoughts that filled his mind and held sleep at bay; he was probably in for another long night without sleep, but it did come eventually.

However, it was very short lived.

Billy had had enough. Slipping on his clothes, he quietly made his way downstairs where Sophie greeted him as if he'd been away for a month. He pulled the living room curtain to one side to check on the weather. The rain had stopped so he donned a light jacket. He clipped Sophie's lead onto her collar and quietly closed the door behind him.

He'd only been walking for about fifteen minutes when he came upon a car parked with its engine running. It was a black Subaru Impreza with full body styling kit; all the windows were blacked out. As he neared, he noticed the passenger window was down, and the passenger was thrumming his fingers on the wing mirror to some tinny crap that the youth of today mistook for music. Tattooed on his left hand was the same black cross that Deano, Nelly and Thommo wore. Billy glanced at his watch; he could just make out 3: 42 a.m. courtesy of a nearby street light. *These buggers are up to no good.* When he had drawn level, Billy took a glance inside. Although the passenger was wearing a baseball cap pulled down low over his eyes Billy could make out the fact that he was of mixed race; the driver was white and was wearing a multi-coloured beanie. The passenger flicked a cigarette end onto the pavement just in front of Billy. This spooked Sophie who began barking furiously and reared up at the car door making both youths jump back in unison.

The passenger jumped out of the car. "What in the name of fuckin' shit are you doin', granddad! Get that fuckin' mutt outa' my face, man before I stick a fuckin' knife in it."

"I – I'm sorry," Billy stammered, "she's not normally like this…"

"Yeah? Well, fuck you and your fleabag dog. Get outa my fuckin' zone, man else I'll cut you both up." He slipped his hand inside his leather jacket as if going for a weapon.

Billy hurried on his way. Within seconds, and immediately to his right, three mountain bikes appeared from an alleyway; all riders wore hooded tops. They skidded to a halt by the driver's door; Billy backed against a garden gate and disappeared into the shadows formed by privet hedges. He could here garbled chatter and then laughter. One of the riders glanced furtively to left and right and handed a small rolled up bundle to the driver who in return handed a small package back. The driver switched on the cars courtesy light and began counting what looked like banknotes. High fives were exchanged all round, someone shouted, 'laters,' and they headed at speed back towards the alley. As they gathered pace the wind caught the lead riders' hood and it slipped off. Billy took a sharp intake of breath as Deano sped past with no doubt Nelly and Thommo in close attendance.

7

There was a short torrential downpour and Billy was totally soddened by the time he got back home. He placed his clothes over a radiator and freshened himself up in the bathroom.

He took up his usual night-time position – that of lying on his back staring at the ceiling. His heart was still thumping against his ribs after his encounter with the drug dealers. He was shocked that this sort of thing was going on in his area – something else to lie here worrying about.

Eventually, he managed to drift into something approaching blessed sleep. At some stage, he must have turned off the bedside lamp, and then he woke again in a panic, not knowing where he was in the darkness. It was pitch black because he was trapped in a tangle of blankets and he struggled to free himself. He switched the lamp back on. The first thing that struck him was a headache that felt like a concussion. Sunlight streamed through a chink in the curtains, taunting his bleary eyes. His first thought – *what time is it?* Then, *what day?* Then, *why do I give a shit?* Glancing at the bedside clock it would be another hour before the alarm went off. Finding the motivation just to get out of bed was hard enough. For a moment he lay silent, and then swung himself up, sitting on the side of the bed. He lurched to his feet, donned his ragged tartan dressing gown and then slumped back down. He surveyed his bedroom. This room had eaten into him of late; he could literally feel the walls clawing at him, sucking in on him. It would be yet another day of drifting through life and floundering in his own solitude.

    The feeling of darkness that he was so familiar with was trying to slowly descend and envelope him. His life was without purpose or meaning, plagued by a feeling of guilt and a sense of worthlessness. The sinister gloom within him was blacker than the disease itself. Billy fought back the impulse to retch. Hugging his knees, he began rocking slowly back and forth, breaking out into soft sobs.

8

And then, a little before six, Billy snapped into a bleary consciousness. He was lying at ninety degrees to the normal sleeping position, his feet dangling on one side of the bed and his head lolling over the other side; he was still wearing his nightcoat. It was raining yet again and it sounded foul, spattering against the window and drizzling its misery and deepening his sense of gloom. He was clutching his pillow to his chest and realised he had had barely two hours of quality sleep. His bedside lamp was still burning and the book that he had been trying to read lay open where it had fallen.

Throwing open the curtains, he stood for a few moments watching rivulets running down the window and through it the bleak, graffiti-daubed loading bays of the supermarket. He collapsed back onto the bed stretching his arms above his head and extending his legs as far as he could to work out the kinks and knots. Shortly, he swivelled and sat for a while with his feet resting on the cold vinyl floor. His toes curled reflexively. A pair of slippers lay somewhere close by, but he just couldn't be bothered to look for them. Instead, he stood slowly and painfully. The stretching exercises had done little, he felt just as wrecked as he had feared. His body ached, and his temples throbbed, so he swallowed several painkillers with the aid of a glass of water, which he had refilled on one of his many trips to the bathroom during the previous evening and early morning. The bedclothes had slipped or been kicked to the floor. His whole body was rigid and heavy.

After showering, he had just enough energy left to brush his teeth, which made him feel sick. Looking in the mirror Billy noticed the first vestiges of old age in his pale, puffy face. He wasn't in the mood for his Mother and so skipped breakfast and left the house before she had risen.

The heavy rain had eased to light drizzle. Reaching the school, there was already a gaggle of cleaners milling around the main entrance.

"We've been stood here for a good fifteen bloody minutes, we're soaking wet," one of them chirruped from the rear of the crowd.

Billy buried his clenched fists into his hips. He sighed through his nose. "Who said that?"

A flabby, tattooed arm shot in the air exposing a full thatch of armpit hair. "I did, so fuckin' what?"

"And what time is it now, exactly?" He said sharply.

They shot each other vacant glances as if Billy had asked them their opinions on inter-galactic warfare.

He slipped back the sleeve of his coat. "Well, I'll tell you ladies what the time is shall I? The time is now precisely six fifty-eight, meaning that I am in fact two minutes early. You said the same thing yesterday and the day before that and the day before that and no doubt you will say the same fuckin' thing tomorrow."

"Oooohhh, sorry for being born," said one.

Billy sighed heavily as he opened the main entrance door with his master key and the cleaners filed in close behind.

Billy turned. He closed his eyes and ran a palm across his forehead. "Look, you do this *every* bloody morning! How many times do I have to tell you? Wait outside until I have turned off the alarm system!"

"What's your problem, Billy, wrong time of the month is it?"

Again, the remark came from the back of the crowd and relative safety.

The girls burst into fits of giggles.

Billy tut-tutted loudly and left them there while he sorted out the alarm.

Apart from Billy's day-to-day set duties, he was also expected to dabble in minor maintenance projects. This could involve for example putting up shelves in a cupboard or classroom, assembling flat packed furniture, repairing or replacing locks and door closers etc., etc. These tasks could be requested by the teaching staff on maintenance forms, which they could fill in with their requirements and leave in the reception office. Billy would then collect them first thing in the morning, take them back to his workroom and prioritise them whilst enjoying a leisurely cup of tea.

This morning, that is exactly what Billy was doing and one work slip caught his eye, it read: - our environmental pool is looking a bit shabby, any chance of removing a few weeds for me and perhaps a bit of a tidy round? It was signed by a Miss. Gutteridge, one of the science teachers. *Mmm, the rain has stopped and the suns out, it could turn out to be a pleasant day out there; I think I'll spend an hour or two out of harms way on this little project.*

The furthest point West from the school buildings, beyond the school playing fields and tennis courts, was the environmental area. This consisted of approximately a quarter of an acre of trees, shrubs and plants, which was used by the science department for study. Also situated in this small wooded area was a pond, which was used by the kids for 'Pond dipping.' This enabled them to study pond ecology and the life cycles of invertebrates as part of their curriculum.

After finishing off his tea and a few biscuits, Billy made his way to the boiler house. Here, in one corner, he kept an array of garden tools propped up against the wall. He picked out a shovel, a trowel, a pair of secators and a pair of shears. Then, after picking up his wheelbarrow from the skip area, Billy began his lengthy trek to the environmental area.

On arrival, Billy had already built up a bit of a sweat, so he removed his jacket and hung it from a branch. He dug his fists into his hips and surveyed the area. It was littered with cigarette butts, most of them floating in the pond; some of the kids had obviously been using the environmental area as a smoking den. It was an ideal spot, as far away as is possible from the prying eyes of the staff and the CCTV system. Billy set about the task in hand. Any branches that were over-hanging the pond he trimmed back heavily and piled them into his wheelbarrow. After that little task was completed, he dropped to his knees onto the concrete paving slabs that surrounded the pool. He began firstly to pull out the smaller weeds with his fingers and then he attacked the larger ones with his trowel.

Billy was quite enjoying the peace and quiet of this sun-dappled spot. Time slipped by unnoticed, the bell had already sounded for mid-morning break, but it was barely audible at this distance from the school. He would normally have a cup of tea at this time of the day, but he had been so carried away that he didn't notice that he had already missed ten minutes of his break time.

As Billy pottered about on all fours around the edge of the pond whistling a nondescript tune, he just happened to glance into the water and caught the black shimmering reflection of two, maybe three heads. One of the silhouettes shifted and moved forwards and a shadow passed over him. He made to look round and caught a shape in the periphery of his vision, but it was already too late. He felt something against his backside, a foot perhaps, and suddenly he was flailing around in the murky depths of the pond. It took him a few seconds to re-orientate himself, but he managed to haul himself to his knees. He was panting heavily, and it took him some time to get a good foothold on the muddy bottom. When he did manage to get himself upright, he was knee deep in freezing dirty water with a lily draped around his shoulders. He had also taken in a couple of mouthfuls of the slimy water and he began choking; bile filled his mouth. This developed into a coughing fit, which lasted a good few minutes. On recovering, he quickly turned through three hundred and sixty degrees, but whoever the perpetrators were, they had already slithered away unnoticed. Billy hauled himself out of the pond and removed the weed and pond life from his pockets and clothing. Then, he removed his work boots and emptied pond water from them. *Bastards! I'll find the bastards who did this, although I already have a good idea who was behind it.* He gathered together his tools, placed them on top of the branches and weeds in his wheelbarrow and squelched his way through the trees and shrubbery and out onto the playing fields.

The problem he now faced was that he had a long trek across the playground, which was still full of kids letting off steam during the break time. He'd only taken a few tentative steps onto the playground when one kid spotted him and within seconds waves of the little buggers surged forwards and formed a gauntlet of finger pointing, jeering, cackling hyenas. Their laughter, shouts, and squeals of delight abraded his nerves and sparked in him a deep anger. Billy felt that it was the longest walk that he had ever made. On the edge of the playground, which backed onto a service road, stood an empty litter bin surrounded by sweet wrappers and discarded half-eaten sandwiches. It was chained to the fence as on occasions, like most of the bins dotted around the school, it had gone walkies. On one such occasion, a bin was actually found on the third-floor roof of the maths department. Sitting on the bin was Deano; his two accomplices stood either side.

"Hey crabby!" Deano called, "Been for a swim, have yer? You should feel at home in water what with a name like crabby." He smiled sardonically.

Nelly and Thommo exchanged smug grins, nodding their approval.

Billy approached Deano and thrust a finger into his chest. He needed to bite his bottom lip to stifle an expletive. "You did this," he spat, "you three deliberately pushed me into the pond, I'll have you for this you little…"

"Whoa, think you're hard d'ya Crabby?" Deano sniffed.

"The only time he's hard is when the year seven girls push

SCHOOL'S...OUT...FOR...EVER

past him wearing short little skirts." Thommo wasn't normally forthcoming with humour but the other two found that quite hilarious.

"Nice one, Thommo." Deano high-fived him, and then to Billy: "Now look, Crabby, there's no need to chuck a mental, man," he growled, "You can't lay heavy shit like that on us, man." He slid off the bin and towered over Billy; his eyes were cold and unflinching, a curl of hatred distorting his lips. "We've been hangin' out and chillin' here for at least twenty fuckin' minutes, ain't we, guys?"

Nelly and Thommo nodded in unison.

"Well they're bound to say that..."

They moved menacingly to stand either side of Billy. He felt like the filling in a sandwich.

"...I'm going to report this to the Headteacher, and you'll be in serious..." he cut short his sentence, suddenly realising that he was making a bigger fool of himself than he already was. *Serious what?* Billy sagged at the realisation of what a stupid and pathetic remark he was about to make. The three thugs began rocking with laughter, and Deano threw himself dramatically across the waste bin in mock hysterics.

Deano turned and jabbed a beefy finger into Billy's face. "I am you're enemy, man, go and hide 'cause Deano don't take prisoners." He had obviously overdosed on violent American gangster movies.

Deano then snaked an arm around the shoulders of both Nelly and Thommo and they sauntered away slapping and pushing younger kids out of their way.

The experience painted a dull sheen of desolation in Billy's eyes. He made his way to the boiler house where he locked himself in. He stripped naked and donned a pair of old overalls, then hung his soiled clothes around one of the three boilers to dry.

Billy stayed there for the rest of the day with only negative thoughts for company and in desperate need of clean clothes, a shower, and more painkillers. He felt the urge for the toilet on one occasion, but couldn't be bothered to leave his hidey-hole; he pee'd into a watering can. *It's warm in here; it'll have evaporated by tomorrow.*

A short time after the school bell had sounded Billy crept out of his hide and made his way to his workroom. He was weary, exhausted, and mentally battered from the trauma of the day. Another day had ended; he was still alive and unable to justify his survival.

No one had missed him.

9

That night Billy slept surprisingly well, without experiencing a recurrence of the previous night's problems.

The next morning, he had pottered about the school for a couple of hours and on entering his workroom to pick up some tools, the telephone was ringing. He answered it and swapped a few pleasantries with Janet before she informed him that the head would like to see him at 10:00a.m. sharp. It was a rare occasion that Co-Co had requested the presence of Billy and it set the nerves jangling. He wondered what the head would want with him, was he up for a reprimand? Had Deano concocted a story to get him into trouble? He couldn't think of anything that he'd done wrong. He hoped it didn't involve more paperwork. There was virtually no paperwork involved with the job when he first started. Now, there were rows of shelves jammed with Health and Safety issues and procedures for this and that. Billy couldn't remember if in fact he had opened any of them.

Billy had busied himself for a while keeping a sharp eye on the time. At 10:00a.m. precisely Billy was sitting facing the heads closed door. He had already acknowledged and followed the instruction that was pinned to it: - 'Please knock once and wait'. Minutes passed in a profound silence. After what seemed like hours, Janet tapped Billy on the shoulder, which startled him out of his daydream. She informed him that the Headteacher would see him now.

"You what?" Billy said in amazement. "He's phoned you to come and tell me to go in? Can't he open the bloody door himself? Has he got a broken wrist or something?"

Janet stifled a giggle into the back of her hand and returned to her office. Billy rapped the door lightly and a voice pronounced in a regal tone, "Come!"

Come? Do I look like a fuckin' dog?

Billy entered. It was not an office that exuded warmth. Not much to look at: a row of filing cabinets, a large desk sporting a dull mahogany veneer, four chairs surrounding a square - not round - coffee table, and some cheap and bland framed pictures probably bought from Ikea. *A bleak and bland office, a bit like Co-Co himself.* Billy observed.

The Headteacher had taken up the Headteachers' stance, i.e. hands clasped behind his back and he was gazing out of the window. His collar was a little too tight, rippling the back of his neck. Billy approached the desk, pulled out the chair and sat down. The seat was low enabling Co-co to look down on whoever was seated there from the comfort of his much taller leather-backed swiveller.

"Take a seat if you would, Mister Crabtree," the Headteacher said to the window.

"Erm, thank you, sir," muttered an already seated Billy.

The Headteacher turned on his heels and sat behind his desk. He leant back and rested his elbows on the arms of the chair and then folding his hands in front of him, rubbed the balls of his thumbs together in a circular motion. "Now then, Mister Crabtree…"

"Billy," Billy said.

"Yeah, Billy, indeed. Now then you will be aware, Mr… erm, *Billy* that tomorrow is a very important day for the school what with the visit of OFSTED. Now then, when your…" he drew quotation marks in the air with his fingers … "Ladies come in tomorrow I want you to take them to one side and impress upon them that I want a little more elbow grease. I want the school to be spic and span and sparkling, I want the school to look like it's just been taken out of the wrapper, a brand-new building, no dust, dirt or cobwebs anywhere, do I make myself clear, Billy?

Billy gave a crisp salute. "Yes sah!" he said in a tone

dripping with sarcasm.

"Mmm, indeed," The Headteacher went. "*Anyway*, Billy, I have some exiting news for you. Starting next term, we will have Academy status. There will be big changes, Billy, which includes your department. We will be bringing you into the twenty first century. For example, a computer will be installed in your workroom connected via the internal network…" he drew quotation marks in the air with his fingers again… "The Intranet, as we call it, and also we will be appointing a Site Supervisor…"

"A Site Supervisor? Why would you do that?" Billy said folding his arms tightly across his chest.

"Well, the Site Supervisor will take some of the pressure off, Billy. He or she will be responsible for Health and Safety matters, dealing with contractors, insurance's, fire regs…"

"You mean someone will come in on a much larger salary than mine and do exactly what I'm doing at present and have been doing for the last twenty odd years?"

The head sighed through his nose. "Look, it will leave you to concentrate solely on maintenance issues *and* we'll be giving you a posh new title! Senior Site Technician, what do you think of that?"

Billy sat impassive and didn't flinch. "Senior Site Technician is a grade lower than what I'm on at present, so obviously I'll be taking a drop in salary…wee-ha and whoopee-do!"

The head sighed again. "Your present hourly rate will be frozen for one year, Billy so that there'll be no immediate effect on you financially."

Billy knew that he would definitely not be here in a year's time, but it still narked him. He stood, leant forward, and placed both hands palm side down on the desk. He said deadpan, "Excuse me, sir whilst I die of uncontrollable excitement."

Co-co shook his head very slowly and then perched his chin on steepled fingers. He said coldly, "Please close the door as you leave would you, Mister Crabtree?" He spun his chair round

ANTHONY ASPREY

to face the window.

10

After Billy's morale-destroying meeting with the head, he made his way back to his workroom slamming doors behind him as he went. On entering the telephone was ringing. He pondered about whether to ignore it and have a cup of tea or pick up and answer. He was glad he decided on the latter because there was a medical situation that Janet wanted him to attend. As Billy was fully trained in first aid, he was kept quite busy during the school day although on most occasions it was only to deal with minor cuts, bruises or sprains.

In front of the reception windows were three chairs, specifically placed for waiting visitors to the school. This is where Billy was expecting to find his patient. On entering the reception foyer Billy had found no one waiting for him and so he stuck his head through the open reception window.

"Hello, Jan," Billy said, "where's the patient then?"

Janet glanced over Billy's left and then right shoulder, her brow creased very slightly. "Well she was there a minute ago; perhaps she's made her own way into the medical room."

"Mmm, maybe." Billy strolled over to the medical room, which was diagonally opposite the reception office. He poked his head through the door. A young girl had perched herself on the edge of the medical bed. Her bleached hair was lank and bedraggled. She was stick-thin, her features angular. Two metallic dots pierced both nostrils and further piercings adorned her ears. The face was pale, and her eyes encircled with thick black mascara, but the one feature that really caught the eye were her huge front teeth. One of her shoes lay on the floor.

Clasped in one hand the ever-present mobile phone. Billy had seen uglier kids - but not many.

"Ah! The patient," Billy said jovially. Something 'pinged' in his head. "Are you related to Neil Dunn by any chance?"

She sniffed, "Yeah, man he's my brother, wanker ain't he?"

Indeed he is young lady and just as ugly.

The girl wrapped her cardigan across her chest and folded her arms tightly.

It was stipulated as part of Billy's training that he should never put himself in a one to one situation with a student as this could lead to all sorts of unwelcome and unfounded accusations. He decided to ask Janet if she could come and stand guard whilst he treated the girl.

"I'm just going to fetch some help, I'll be back in a tick," he said brightly.

The girl grabbed at her leg and whimpered, "No, don't go, help me, man, I'm in agony." She chewed gum exaggeratedly.

Billy thrummed his chin with his fingers, "Wwweeeell, it's highly irregular...OK." He closed the door. "Now then, what have we been up to then young lady?"

The girl shrugged with the indifference of a bolshie sixteen-year-old and slowly raised her shoeless leg, "It's my ankle, I've twisted it, I think it's fuckin' broken, man."

"OK, I know it may be a little sore, but let's watch our language shall we young miss?"

She rolled her eyes and tutted quite audibly. "Whatever, granddad." Each time she spoke it was with a sigh.

Billy took a nearby chair and placed it in front of the girl. He took the girls leg half way up the calf and, raising it slowly, rested the ball of her foot on his knee.

The girl screwed up her face, "Ahhh!" she squealed, "be careful it's killin', man."

"Weeelll, let's have a quick look then shall we? And what's your name young lady, eh?"

"Toyah, crap name ain't it? I hate it," she said, blowing a bubble with the gum. It burst leaving a gossamer skin across her chin.

"It's a beautiful name, Toyah. How did the accident occur?"

"Erm...well...erm...I slipped, man, just sort it, I'm in agony."

"Manners don't cost anything you know. Now then, can you wiggle your toes for me?" Billy said, smiling.

The girl complied as she picked gum from her lower lip and chin.

"Was that sore at all?"

Toyah nodded as she lazily wrapped a strand of hair around a finger.

"Well it's obviously not broken...it's odd there's no swelling or bruising...mmm, I'll tell you what we'll do, I'll go and fetch you a bag of ice and we'll sit you down in reception for fifteen or twenty minutes and see how you get on, OK?"

"Mmm."

Well we are a great conversationalist aren't we, young lady?

Billy moved his chair back against the wall. "OK," he said, "I want you to slide off the bed and rest your good foot on the ground for me."

Toyah slid forward and Billy put a hand under her armpit to take some of the weight. Her mobile phone rang. She glanced at the display and abruptly terminated the call. Billy suggested he put it in his pocket until they returned to reception, but her face collapsed and she bawled, "Nah! Don't fink so, man."

He grabbed her shoe and with his help, she hopped back into the reception area where he sat her on one of the chairs. He entered the office, took from the fridge an already prepared bag of ice, and returned to the girl.

"Here you go, young madam hold this against your ankle for a while and if the pain subsides then you can return to your lesson, if not see Mrs. Westwood and she'll make arrangements for you to either be taken to hospital or go home is that ok?"

"Yeah, s'pose."

Well thank you, Mister Crabtree, thanks a fucking lot.

Billy entered the reception office. "Proper little prima donna," he whispered to Jan, who stifled a chuckle into the back of a hand.

Billy requested the accident book, which Jan handed to him. Then leaning through the hatch, he took the girls full name, year, and form and entered all the details concerning the incident into the accident book. He then returned to his workroom.

The incident with Toyah had taken his mind off his meeting with the head and he had calmed down considerably.

Billy indulged in a mid-morning cup of tea and biscuits.

11

Billy had had quite a busy few hours and it was just after 2 o'clock when he finally sat down for his lunch. He had barely prised the lid from his lunchbox when the telephone rang for the umpteenth time that day. *Not a-bloody-gain, one day I'm gonna have me the dinner hour that I'm entitled to.* He let it ring, and ring, and ring, but the incessant noise seemed to get louder and more irritating; eventually he picked up the receiver. Janet informed him that the Headteacher would like to see him in his office a.s.a.p.

"What again!" Billy snapped, "I don't see him from one week to the next and…"

"I'm only passing on the message, Billy," Janet interjected.

Billy closed his eyes and massaged the middle of his forehead with his fingers. "Yes, yes OK, sorry, Janet bad day I'm on my way."

Billy took a bite from his sandwich, replaced it in the sandwich box, and then made his way to the Headteachers office. He stood in front of the door, chewed the last remnants of what remained in his mouth and swallowed. He then knocked on the door and went to sit in the waiting area but this time the door opened before he could take his seat.

"Billy, come in, come in," the Headteacher said brightly.

As Billy was ushered into the room, two earnest looking men were already seated. One, Billy recognised as the Deputy Headteacher and next to him a man who Billy had never seen before. There were strong emanations of one of the more macho aftershaves.

Both men had a clipboard perched on their knees. Billy shot a glance at the deputy heads clipboard; he'd been doodling aimlessly on it. Lines and squiggles with no apparent meaning, but in the one corner he did make out a sketch of a set of gallows with a noose around a matchstick mans neck. When the deputy head caught Billy looking, creases appeared on his pitted forehead, and he drew the clipboard to his chest.

Billy smiled but his face bore such deep melancholy lines that no one noticed.

The Headteacher pointed blithely towards the two men. "Right then, Billy you obviously know Mister Graveney the deputy head…"

Billy nodded his head pleasantly at Mister Graveney and said, "Afternoon, Alan." He wore charcoal trousers and a white shirt, open at the neck. A brown leather flying jacket rested on the back of his chair.

"…and this gentleman here, Billy is Mister Inderpal Chandra, Mister Chandra is on the board of governors."

Mister Chandra did not look up; nor did he greet Billy or acknowledge his presence. Billy was somewhat upset by the man's lack of manners, but he kept his smile. He had been around long enough to work on the premise that ninety percent of what most governors thought they knew or said was crap.

The head was also annoyed at the lack of professional etiquette and so feigned a cough into the back of his hand. Mister Chandra glanced up and the head flicked his eyebrows in Billy's direction.

Mister Chandra went, "Mmm?" With a smile Billy classified as false. Then: "oh, yeah, good of you to come, Mister Crabtree." Some people may have mistaken that for sincerity. He then stood. He was short and thickset with a puffed-chest stance like an athlete. He wore a smart black suit, a tie with alternate grey and pink horizontal stripes. Still studiously avoiding eye contact with Billy, he held out a hand for a shake, which Billy grasped; it didn't live up to Billy's expectations. Although the man's hand engulfed his own, it felt quite soft and limp, and it had obviously never indulged in manual labour. *Definitely not an athlete*. Billy's hand returned soaked and he surreptitiously wiped it down the leg of his trousers.

"How-do," Billy said, and then continued: "Well this is a bit of a gathering, what am I supposed to have done, murdered one of the kids?" Billy laughed weakly at his own joke; the Headteacher gave him a smile no thicker than the blade of a Stanley knife. The other two men wore forbidding expressions indicating that pleasantries were not on the cards.

The Headteacher offered Billy a seat and then busied himself at a small coffee machine. The two other men had apparently already been served with a coffee each.

"Coffee, Billy?" the Headteacher offered in a jovial tone although he sported a fixed expression and tight lips; he seemed tense.

"Erm, no, not for me thanks." Billy said.

The head then offered a plate. "Biscuit?"

"No."

Billy's eyes roved. Directly in front of him were several shelves that he had put up about four Headteachers ago. They were now bowed under the weight of document boxes and files. The desk supported mounds of paperwork.

The Headteacher sat at his desk; he looked typically phlegmatic; he pushed his bifocals up so that they rested on top of his head and then took a swig of coffee. Co-co smiled - or pretended to. "Ahhh, now then, I have had to call this emergency meeting, Billy because a bit of a delicate subject has arisen," he began, not wasting any time on social niceties. "I had a year eleven girl in here earlier with her head of year, erm…" the Headteacher looked in his glass case and his forehead wrinkled slightly.

"On top of your head, sir," Billy said.

"What?"

"Your glasses, they're on top of your head." *Jeese, these brainy types have got no common sense.*

"Damn, how stupid of me." He slid the pair of bifocals

down his face, resting them on the tip of his nose. Referring to a sheet of A4 in front of him he continued, "ah, yes, a certain Miss Toyah Dunn?" He removed his spectacles and chewed on one of the arms. "Apparently you treated her sometime this morning for an ankle injury, yeah?"

Billy forehead crinkled slightly, and his eyebrows drew together; he had a vague feeling of unease. "Yeeesss, I did treat a young girl this morning by that name...what's all this about, sir?"

The Headteacher feigned a cough into a clenched fist, trying to think how he could carefully articulate the next few words. A deep vertical worry line appeared between his large round eyes. "The young lady in question seemed quite distressed whilst she was in here earlier, Billy. She claims that during the time she spent with you in the medical room you made, erm, improper suggestions, and advances toward her?"

A cold shiver ran across Billy's shoulders and his face crumpled. He glanced at both Mister Chandra and Mister Graveney; Mister Graveney lowered his eyes and Mister Chandra held his cup of coffee to his face, he was still wearing a forced smile and his eyes, visible above the cup, were slightly narrowed.

Billy sat forward, giving the head his full attention. "I'm sorry, sir I don't follow you," he said in a voice that was not at all steady.

The Headteacher heard the edge in Billy's voice but wasn't certain if it came from anger, fear or perhaps both. He dropped his glasses onto the desk in exasperation. He then rose from his swivel chair, clamped his hands behind his back, and stood facing the window, looking out at a grey May day. "The girl in question has told me that whilst the two of you were in the medical room, Billy you took her leg..."

"Yes, and?" The words a whisper, the lines on Billy's forehead intensified significantly.

"...you took her leg, Billy and you ran your hand up her skirt and..."

Billy should have guessed something like this was coming

SCHOOL'S...OUT...FOR...EVER

after they had greeted him with such bland politeness. He drew a shallow, shaky breath; for a moment, he couldn't think straight, his brain rejecting what his ears were hearing. Billy saw the heads lips moving but heard no sound and so missed most of what else the Headteacher was saying; his brain seemed to have shut down after he heard the words '...ran your hand up her leg...'

Billy slammed a fist down on the desk for emphasis. "No! No! This is all bollocks," he blurted, "I'm sorry, Mister Clune but this is all crap..." he flicked his eyes back and forth among the three men, trying to gauge what was in their minds but they were busy studiously regarding the walls, careful to avoid Billy's eyes. He felt slightly light-headed, slightly disconnected from the world.

"OK, Billy calm yourself, yeah?" the Headteacher said. He held a hand up in a defensive gesture as if trying to fend off an attacker. "I am feeling pretty sanguine about this situation, I am all for the old saying innocent until proven guilty, Billy but we have to investigate, this is a serious matter, we have to hear both sides of the story, yeah? Now then, Billy I must be seen to be neutral in this matter. Therefore, Mister Chandra and Mister Graveney here..." he said, waving a hand blithely in the direction of the two men, who suddenly found the floor at their feet very interesting, "...will concern themselves with a thorough investigation. What I would like to say though, Billy, off the record, is that our Miss Dunn seemed to become quite agitated when I asked if she would like the police to be involved. Therefore, I am thinking that perhaps...*perhaps* she may not be telling things as it is. So, would you like to break for a while? Perhaps you would care to contact a union representative?"

The room was silent for a moment and heavy with tension.

Billy was very tempted to shout out 'Go fuck yourselves,' and storm out of the room but the moment quickly passed when he realised that may be taken as a sign of guilt. "No, I haven't done anything wrong so that won't be necessary." His voice trailed off into a sigh of utter dejection. Head bent, hands in his lap. He swallowed hard, his composure starting to fracture. A trickle of sweat cut a slow, cold path down his back. Etched across his face, there was bewilderment, hurt feelings and disappointment. He pushed himself back into his chair hoping he could disappear into the furniture. Without looking up he muttered, "I can't believe this, why would she say these things? I was there to help her and nothing else. Christ I've been here twenty-three years and nothing like this has ever happened, check my record Mister Clune."

"No, no there's no need for that, Billy," the Headteacher reassured him. He sat back down behind his desk, leaning into the table and knitting his hands together, his favourite thinking position. After a short moment he took a tissue from a box inside a drawer, and began to polish the lenses of his glasses. "Let's go through it from the top, shall we? Tell us *exactly* what happened, Billy."

Billy gave a short account of what had happened and then the subsequent question and answer session lasted for over half an hour; it seemed a lot longer to Billy. During the proceedings the head continually jotted things onto a pad, his forehead supported by his left hand, elbow on the desk. He sat back in his swivel chair for a brief spell, pushing the tips of his fingers together, allowing Mister Chandra and Mister Graveney to take the lead in the questioning. And many questions followed. Billy felt that he was being grilled like he was a murder suspect. Each man in turn throwing question after probing question at
him in quick succession, a whole barrage of them, his every stuttered answer subjected to a fierce cross-examination. They added complications, changed circumstances and generally did all they could to confuse him. You have never been married have you, Billy? Have you a girlfriend at the moment? What's your view of some of the girls who come to school wearing very short skirts? Have you any friends? Why don't you have any friends? Points were repeated several times, points which Billy

had already answered; it seemed that they were determined to force Billy into making a mistake, trying to catch him out, but he tried to answer each of them truthfully. Wasn't he in enough internal, emotional turmoil and pain as it was?

Billy experienced a whirlpool of emotions. He was angry, defensive, and embarrassed and found himself, on occasion, closing his eyes and blanking out what they were saying. He raised his eyes hoping for support from the Headteacher, but he avoided Billy's gaze by picking up his mug and looking into it to see if there was anything left, knowing that there wasn't.

Billy's mouth was a tight slit turned down at the corners like a tragic mask. The eyes were hooded, the shoulders hunched, head bent forward his gaze fixed on the Headteachers desk. He glanced up; the head was stretched back in his swivel chair now, fingers knitted behind his neck exposing Billy to his sweat-stained armpits.

Billy's lower lip was trembling, in fact, the feelings he was experiencing were so intense, his whole body began to shake; he closed his eyes tight shut and drew his shaky hands up over his face; he felt emotionally raw. His ears pounded rhythmically with his racing pulse. Surely, no other person in the world felt the desperation that Billy felt right now? It was support he needed right now not this officious whining.

Billy heard a feigned cough. He looked up. Mister Graveney had been speaking to him. "Are you listening, Billy?"

Billy cupped a hand to his ear, "Sorry, what did you say?"

Mister Graveney continued, friendly one minute, angry the next, accusing Billy of being vague, uncertain or hesitant with his answers. Billy's eyes were smarting as words punched him from all sides – friendly, furious, and cruel. He understood the intention; they wanted clear and definite answers. When they had finished with him and satisfied that no more could be gained by continuing, the Headteacher dropped his glasses onto the desk and pinched the bridge of his nose. He then rose and perched on the edge of the desk, one leg planted on the floor and the other dangling; he placed a friendly hand on Billy's shoulder.

"I *will* get to the bottom of this. This incident will be investigated thoroughly, Billy," the Headteacher said, in a calm and quiet manner.

A heavy silence settled over Billy. He could see their mouths moving but the sound seemed muffled as if he were being grilled under water. He sat silent and rigid, finding it difficult to follow any train of thought and was desperately trying to process everything that was being said but caught only half of what was being thrown at him. He shook his head vigorously several times then looked up at the Headteacher, his glassy gaze remote and uncomprehending. After an eternity, that was perhaps just thirty or forty seconds, he took a deep breath, "Sorry? I think I missed a whole piece of conversation just then."

"I said this thing will be investigated thoroughly, Billy. As we speak, the girl is with two senior teachers who have had special training to handle these situations and if she is lying then they will break her down. In the meantime, can I ask as to why you entered the medical room alone with this pupil? You of all people should know the rules concerning these sort of situations, Billy."

Billy dropped his head into his hands. "I know, I know, but she was in obvious discomfort what was I to do? I was just trying to help. Christ, no wonder you can't get any staff trained up as first aiders, this is all done voluntarily you know, I ain't doing this for my health." His voice seemed distorted to his own ears, like an echo.

By now, all three men were leaning forward, straining to catch what Billy was saying as he spoke in an almost strengthless whisper.

"You know the rules, Billy you fetch help, you know that." The head picked up a biro and chewed the end. He then passed a box of tissues over the desk. Billy took one, dabbed his eyes and then blew his nose.

The head continued, "We will have to review our procedures; it will have to go to the next governors meeting in a couple of weeks."

The room began to spin slowly around him now. Billy felt a chill and so drew his arms across his chest, hugging himself. He breathed deeply, trying to keep calm, trying to clarify the situation. He didn't seem to hear the rest of what was being said, his thoughts were too scattered, much too distressed. He pressed the heels of his hands into his eyes and tried to shake his head free of all the questions. Then he'd had enough. He looked up suddenly, his teeth clenched. One of the men was saying something but he interrupted him in mid-sentence. "And what if this girl had cut through an artery? Do I stroll around the school looking for help while she bleeds to death?"

No one answered. Billy looked from one man to the other but was met with blank stares; the governor and deputy head continued scribbling down notes. Mister Chandra continually consulted a large multi-faced wristwatch of the sort that you could rely on at twenty fathoms; boredom beginning to show on his face he obviously needed to be somewhere else. Billy balled his fists and leapt to his feet, his eyes fiery and defiant. "Where is she now? Let me talk to her I'll soon make her…"

"Billy there is a procedure to these matters," Mister Clune interjected; Billy flopped back into his seat. The head had discarded the biro and was now sucking the arm of his glasses, his face anxious. "…and the procedure is in motion. In the meantime, I can't see any reason to suspend you."

Billy shot to his feet again and, placing balled fists on the desk, he leant forward, their noses almost touching. "Suspended? I should fuckin' think not, on the word of this lying cow?"

The Headteacher pinched the bridge of his nose between forefinger and thumb; he released a diminutive sigh. "Look, Billy, I know you're angry, but this thing must take its proper course. I want you to go home now and try not to worry; the truth will out in the end, yeah?"

Suddenly Billy's poise gave way and he again slumped back down into his chair. His palms were damp and cold: he blotted them on his trousers. He massaged his temples with the fingertips of both hands.

Already a man at rock bottom, he bent forwards in his seat and began crying with deep, convulsive sobs. A string of saliva ran down his chin and dropped into his lap. The mere act of speaking had wasted him.

The three men shot each other quick, awkward glances, at a loss at what to do to help. After an involuntary adjustment to his tie, the Headteacher once again rose from his swivel chair. He circled round his desk and snaked a friendly arm around Billy's shoulder.

"Come on, Billy, get yourself home, yeah?" This rare show of civility arose purely from awkwardness; he felt unsure how to act in this situation and seemed genuinely sorry for the position that Billy found himself in.

Billy tried to stand but his legs had lost all power. He pushed against the armrests and with a helping hand from the head, managed to heave himself up. Both men turned and started for the door, the Headteacher still with his arm around Billy's shoulder. Billy felt that the head had used his first name too often and now his personal space had been invaded; he felt uncomfortable, this was all false, the head had never acted in this manner before.

On reaching the door, Billy hesitated with his hand on the knob. Then he half-turned and straightened his shoulders; he looked like a man teetering on the edge of a breakdown. Grinding his teeth in indignation he said, "I can't believe this, why me, ay? Why me?"

After the door had been closed, Billy raised a middle finger; he knew it was futile and childish and it didn't make him feel any better.

Billy shuffled along the corridor feeling defeated and very very alone.

12

Yet another little piece of him had been destroyed. It was if the last vestige of life had been snuffed out.

I could quite easily be the most insignificant man on the planet.

Billy had returned to his workroom and had spent a few uncomfortable minutes hunched over the sink. He had bought up everything he had eaten and drunk that day until his stomach was completely empty, and all that was dribbling out of his mouth and down his chin was stinging bile.

A mental fog hung over him; the inside of his head was a raging torrent of confusing thoughts. His shoulders were slumped under the weight of defeat. Dispirited. Beaten. He collapsed into his chair and ran splayed fingers through what little hair he had remaining. Time momentarily seemed to be suspended for him now. Inflating his cheeks and resting his head on the back of his seat, he ran his palms slowly down his face and began sobbing again. Billy's whole body seemed deflated; his mind was like a washing machine on spin cycle as thoughts whirred around his brain. *I must end this soon.* The darkness of the worst of his moods spread throughout his body. *I have enough on my plate without all this shit to contend with.* Billy ran a sleeve across his eyes to mop them then, rising from his seat, he shuffled over to the sink where he tipped away a cold cup of tea and swilled out the cup under the hot water tap. Then he took a half bottle of whisky from his bag and poured a very generous measure into the cup, which he swallowed in one. He swilled the cup out again and placed it upside down on the draining board. Stooping slightly Billy ran the cold water and, cupping his hands, splashed some onto his face. He rubbed hard; hoping the friction would invigorate and return some of the colour into his cheeks. He stared for a while at his reflection in the smeared mirror. His skin was dull and seemed to have a greyish, pale tinge; he was haggard, and his lifeless, aching eyes seemed to have no purpose. Billy thought he wore the visage of a corpse that had lain in water for a long time. Although his stomach was now completely empty, he didn't feel at all hungry. *Soon*, he promised himself, *it must be soon; I'm just going through the motions of living*. He moved closer to the mirror looking perhaps for a tiny spark of hope – none was present.

Billy spent a few minutes tidying the room, although he had no real heart in it. Then he placed his sandwich box in his bag and put on his coat. As he left the room, he glanced back and thought of all the happy years he'd spent in there. Enjoyable years, up until his illness Billy had enjoyed what he did and there are not many people who can say that nowadays. He flicked the light switch and closed the door. As he made his way down the corridor, a voice called out.

"Hello, you there, caretaker-chappie."

Billy's mind was on other things and although he heard the voice, it didn't register.

"Hello, just hang on a mo if you would."

Billy stopped, and half-turned. Ms. Carroll, one of the P.E. teachers was bounding towards him. *Caretaker-chappie? Is that what she just called me? Daft cow.*

Ms. Carroll, and she insisted on the Mzzz, which speaks volumes, was a charmless, rigid woman with 'hockey' knees. She had a flat, shiny red face, which seemed so popular with P.E. teachers and thick black eyebrows, which looked like one long eyebrow running along her brow. She held a sports science degree, which to Billy was equivalent to winning an egg and spoon race.

"Now then, Mr..." she clicked her fingers several times as a prompt.

"Billy," Billy said.

"Indeed, terrible with names." She guffawed equinely.

"Well that's understandable, Mzz, I've only been here twenty-three years."

Ms. Carroll had no concept of sarcasm.

"Just a reminder, erm…"

"Billy."

"Indeed, just a reminder that I will be taking a party of sixth formers up to Snowdonia on a camping lark the day after tomorrow, we'll be leaving in the evening about sixish. I have booked one of the schools mini-buses for five days so if you wouldn't mind awfully giving one of them a spring clean it would be appreciated. And if you would check the tyres and have it fully fuelled as well, is that OK with you?"

"It's all in hand, Mzz, it's in my school diary." Billy tapped the side of his nose with a digit and winked. "Nothing gets past Alan."

"Oh, thank you, Alan you're an absolute brick. Must dash." She turned, walked a few paces, stopped, and then half turned. Placing a finger on her chin she said, "I thought you said your name was…oh, I see." She gave a perfunctory smile to acknowledge that it was a joke and then 'Gazelled' down the corridor.

Cow. Billy thought.

Reminder to oneself – never get old. She thought.

Billy shuffled down the corridor and out onto the car park. As he approached his car, he began fumbling in his bag for his keys. On finding them, he slipped the appropriate key into the door lock. Then he noticed that on the drivers' side there was a deep, wavy scratch that ran from the rear wing right up to the front bumper. He ran his fingers along it. *Bastards! I know who…* Billy caught the sound of cackling and jeering coming from somewhere. He spun round. To his right, about twenty metres away, was a low wall that separated the high school from the primary school. Perched on the wall were Deano, Nelly, and

Thommo. Deano had his arm slung around a young girl and on narrowing his eyes Billy recognised her as Nelleys sister Toyah, the girl he had treated for the 'alleged' sprained ankle. *How could I have been so naïve? It had been a set-up, no doubt Deano being the perpetrator. An evil and deliberate attempt to get me suspended or even sacked.*

Billy dropped his bag to the floor. "I know that *you* are responsible for this, Mister Dean, and you're going to pay for it," Billy bawled as he pointed blithely at his car. He clenched and unclenched his fists.

The gang was already off the wall and sloping away, mocking and ridiculing him under the knowledge that they were the untouchables. Deano glared at Billy savouring his appalled expression.

"Come back here, I want a word with you lot."

Billy began walking towards them, but he knew that his present energy levels would not allow him to break out into a slow jog and he struggled to keep up with their rapid pace. The gang steadily increased the distance between them.

Billy continued to call after them. In one sentence, he used the word 'Cowards', which hit a nerve in Deano and prompted him into action. He spun and ran at Billy and in what seemed like just a second he was on him. Deano arched his back and spat violently into Billy's face; saliva formed a sticky web over Billy's eyes. He quickly ran a sleeve across his face and when his vision had adjusted Deano was already back with the others who were laughing raucously. They indulged in fist-bumps and slapping him on the back in a congratulatory manner. Billy continued calling out to them but all he got in return for his efforts was a variety of furious expletives and obscene hand gestures, even the young girl had a fist raised, the middle finger extended.

The veins at Billy's temples puckered up into knots; this was certainly testing the limits of his self-control. Weariness seemed to drift over him in a drab cloud. He inwardly chastised himself for being weak and fearful and he wilted perceptibly. If someone were to touch him right now, he felt he would just disintegrate.

Billy stood in silence for a moment, wrestling with his emotions. Eventually he retrieved his bag and trudged dejectedly back to his car feeling that, if he had a gun at hand, he would have no qualms about mowing the lot of them down. He unlocked the car door, but when he grabbed the door handle, his hand closed around something that resembled the viscosity of honey. He instinctively snatched his hand away. He heard snorting hollow laughter in the distance. Turning, he noticed the gang had stopped and was facing him, looking on curiously. On inspecting his hand closely, it was coated in white goo. Billy's brow puckered slightly, it triggered a prickly wave of dread in him. An alarm bell was telling him what it *might* be; when he offered his hand up to his nose, it was confirmed. He felt his throat constrict, his clean hand flying to his mouth. He dropped his bag, threw himself across the wall, and began vomiting in huge spasms. When the heaves subsided, he wiped his soiled hand on a nearby grass verge. Billy then sat on the wall and ran a sleeve across his mouth. *Bastards, lousy, filthy, rotten bastards. Only someone with a very sick and depraved mind could have masturbated on the door handle.*

The gang stood watching him, giggling and mocking. After a couple of minutes, Billy stood and as he did so, he broke wind. He felt a warm stickiness spread out in his underpants and then slowly trickle, like molten lava, down both legs. The emotions of the last few days rushed to the surface and Billy leant over resting his hands on his knees. He sobbed uncontrollably.

"Are you ok, Alan?"

Billy glanced up. Ms. Carroll was strolling towards her car holding a briefcase. On seeing her, the gang turned and hurried away.

"Go away," Billy snarled without parting his teeth.

"Charming, I was only…"

"I'm ok, Mzz, probably something I ate. Thank you."

"Very well…goodnight, Alan."

When she had got into her car and driven off, Billy collapsed to his knees, weeping with impotent despair.

It would surely be a blessing now if the evil inside him that wanted him dead would take him right there and then. Shortly, he stood. Grief and rage battled inside of him as he trudged solemnly back to his car.

From a distance, Deano and his sidekicks were still watching with gloating relish.

13

Billy dropped like a boulder onto his mattress, but despite feeling totally knackered he knew that sleep would be a distant prospect. Another restless night was on the cards because a familiar rage was boiling just beneath the surface. Apart from the marked increase in the level of pain he had to endure, Deano and his mates were at the forefront of his mind. How would he deal with them? How could he make them see? Although, why should he? He wasn't going to hang around much longer so why lie here tossing and turning worrying about scum like that? When he did eventually manage to nod off, something brought him back from the space that he'd been occupying. He thought he heard a voice calling out his name. A gentle, pitiful voice. *Shit! Is that the next stage, hearing voices in my head?*

"Billy, BILLY!"

No, it was his Mother calling out to him. Billy sighed heavily and glanced over at the clock, it winked back at him 3:14a.m. He swivelled over the side of the bed and searched the floor with his feet, but his slippers were nowhere to be found. He didn't bother to look for them. Pain shot through his back and legs as he stiffly rose to his feet. He grabbed his dressing gown from the bedside chair and then made his way along the landing. The laminate flooring was cold, and his toes curled up involuntarily to the unwanted stimulus. He tapped gently on his Mothers' door with the knuckle of one finger and she invited him in. she was sitting up in bed, her misshapen fingers laced together across her lap.

"What's the matter, Mum?" Billy sighed, "Can't you sleep,

have you seen the time?"

Mrs. Crabtree's visage resembled that of a puppy from a toilet tissue advert. "I'm sorry, Billy but I've had one of my little accidents again." Due to her deep embarrassment, her voice was barely a whisper. She pulled back the bedclothes to reveal a large wet patch covering both the sheet and her night-dress.

Billy pinched the bridge of his nose; he felt absolute despair. *As if life couldn't get any worse, if there is a God, then why does he hate me this much?*

Billy held out a helping hand and she took it. "OK, Mum get yourself to the bathroom, freshen up and change your nightie, I'll get a fresh sheet from the airing cupboard."

"I'm sorry, Son, you're such a good boy, Billy I'd be totally lost without you, thank you darling. I'll bring a glass of water with me and take another sleeping pill; you know what I'm like once I'm awake."

Yes, I do fucking know!

Mrs. Crabtree pulled a clean fresh night-dress from a three-draw chest and then shuffled off to the bathroom. Billy fetched a clean sheet from the airing cupboard. He ripped off the damp sheet and placed it in the wash basket, which was kept on top of the landing. He returned to his Mothers' room and replaced it with the new crisp white one. Then he sat, hunched, on the edge of his Mothers' bed staring at the floor waiting for her to return. He blithely picked up his Mother's medicine bottle from the bedside table and absentmindedly read the label. Diazepam – may cause drowsiness. *May cause drowsiness? There's a good fucking chance of that considering they're sleeping pills.* Billy sat bolt upright, and his eyes widened. *That's it! It's been staring me in the face all this time. I'll take a handful of these with the half bottle of single malt that I have left from Christmas and Bob's your uncle.* Billy quickly removed the lid and poured a generous amount of the tablets into his palm. He replaced the lid and slipped the capsules into his dressing gown pocket.

On his Mother's return, she once again apologised. She took a sleeping pill with the water that she had returned with and Billy helped her into bed.

"I must get a repeat prescription, Billy," she said, "I could have sworn I had more tablets left than that."

"Mmm," Billy went, and tucked her in. He kissed her on her forehead.

"We're OK aren't we me and you, Billy?" she croaked, "Just the two of us?"

Billy threw her a smile with no humour in it. "Go to sleep now Mum, I'll see you in the morning."

Billy went back to his room, wrapped the Diazepam capsules in a tissue, and put them in the draw of the bedside cabinet. All he had to do now was pick the appropriate time to do the deed. He could have ended it there and then but, after his disastrous attempt with the bleach, he thought that he was perhaps being a little selfish. So, before he picked the time and place, he needed to sort out some form of agenda and put his house in order first. He had a couple of letters to write and he needed to make quite sure that his Mum wasn't left on her own. He lay on his back with his hands behind his head and felt a lot more relaxed and calmer about the situation now that he had found an ideal, pain-free means of escape. In fact, in a very short space of time, his eyelids began to droop and he fell sound asleep.

Billy's well-earned sleep would be short lived; the radio alarm clock would be treating him to the delights of BBC radio two in just over two hours' time.

14

The following morning and Billy woke up feeling as though someone had shit in his mouth and sandpapered his eyeballs. Briefly glancing in the bathroom mirror, he looked a lot older and wearier than he had done the previous evening. Nothing new there then.

Billy skipped breakfast, instead he dined on numerous painkillers swilled down with several cups of coffee; he now felt as good as it was going to get. On reaching the school, his first task was to deal with eighteen very irate cleaners who had swarmed over and around him like ants on a sugar cube. He had passed on the Headteachers' message and they had assumed that he was hinting that they were not doing their job right in the first place. Billy informed them that the Headteacher would be more than pleased to see them if they had any grievances. *That'll serve the twat right, let him deal with them.*

Today, Billy's mood was quite buoyant, he now felt in control of his destiny, and he went about his tasks with new found vigour – that was until he sat down for his elevenses.

The door wasn't knocked so much as battered, causing Billy to virtually jump out of his seat and in the process, he spilt hot coffee down his shirt. He ripped off a length of kitchen roll and began dabbing himself as he approached the door. When he opened it, his heart sank.

"Alright, Crabby," Deano said. Nelly and Thommo were at his shoulders; they seemed to be indulging in synchronised sneering. "Hear your wheels need a spray job, man. I know a bloke who'll do that for yer on the cheap."

It was all that Billy could do to stand his ground; he would dearly have loved just to lash out and break the bastards' nose. He placed his hands behind his back where he could clench and unclench his fists.

"OK, Mister Dean and considering the fact that you and your two Muppets here were the yobs that did the damage, can I assume that you will foot the bill?"

Deano's jaw drooped. He threw his two sidekicks a shocked glance then stepped forward a couple of paces until their noses almost touched. Billy could feel Deano's breath in his nostrils, a stale odour of unclean teeth and garlic.

"Is that supposed to scare me, Mister Dean," Billy said in a calm voice. He took an exaggerated sniff of the air and screwed up his face. "Have you been sucking someone's socks, young man?"

Deano bared his teeth, turning into an animal ready to eat its kill. His eyes widened, and his face reddened. He sniffed violently through his nose and spat a large greeny into Billy's face.

Nelly grabbed some air and went, "Yyyeeesss! Nice one, man."
Thommo sniggered maniacally.

Billy ran a sleeve across his face. His breathing became heavy as adrenaline poured into him, throbbing in his ears. After suffering the ultimate degradation for the second time, he could no longer contain himself; it was all too much as the pent-up emotions caused by months and months of the gangs' taunts filled him with rage. Hate spilled over unlike anything that he had ever known before. Billy grabbed Deano's hooded top just below his chin and forced him backward pinning him against a wall. He didn't have a clue where the energy or strength had come from, but Deano was up on his tiptoes and there seemed to be genuine shock and fear on his face.

A voice behind them, boomed with authority: *"MISTER CRABTREE, WHAT ON EARTH IS GOING ON HERE?"*

Billy slowly turned his head, his face was scarlet, and spittle bubbled at the corners of his mouth – standing behind him was the Headteacher, accompanied by two women and a man. *Shit! The* OFSTED *inspectors.* His grip on Deano slowly relaxed. The change in Deano's expression was ludicrous as he put in an Oscar winning performance. He slumped to his knees like an Italian footballer. His eyebrows shot up in a pantomime of false wounded innocence and distress, clutching at his throat, he coughed and gasped for air.

"Help me, sir, help me," "Deano whimpered to the Headteacher in a piece of pure theatre, "he's gone mental, man, he's trying to kill me, please help me, sir!"

The performance was sickening and grotesque.

The Headteacher strode purposefully toward Billy, his face red and contorted into a thunderous scowl, his eyes wide and unblinking. "Erm, a word with you in my office later, Billy if you don't mind?" He delivered the sentence through clamped teeth.

As the head and his entourage strode away, Billy glanced down at Deano who had pulled his mouth into a repulsive, disgusting smirk. He was thoroughly enjoying Billy's predicament.

15

As it turned out, the head was much too busy and preoccupied to see Billy that afternoon, and so Billy once again found himself sitting outside the heads office the next morning. He entered the office after the obligatory, "Come!" The head was talking to someone on the phone but signalled vaguely to Billy to take a chair in front of his desk. He ended the call with a stiff, "Goodbye". Without acknowledging Billy, he stood and, turning his back on him began gazing out of the window, hands knitted together behind his back. "You know, Billy I don't see you from one week to the next and suddenly I see you three times in as many days."

Billy sat in front of the Headteachers' desk, slightly hunched and was feigning interest in his shoes; he could still see the sickly grin on Deano's face.

The Headteacher turned and walked over to his desk. Nailed on smile and stiff posture. There was no hello or handshake; he placed his open palms on the laminated top and leant over. "What the hell do you think you were playing at, Billy?"

Billy felt as if he had travelled back in time and he was at his old school, trembling in front of the Headteacher being accused of some misdemeanour and no doubt, the cane was to follow; he took in a deep breath. "What was I to do? He spat in my face, sir…"

"We have to show control, Billy," the Headteacher cut in, "we cannot afford to go around beating up on the kids!" He combed his hair with his fingers, sighed loudly, and then flicked a piece of lint from his lapel.

"Sir, anything else I could have handled, but spitting in my face was the ultimate degradation and anyway it wasn't just this one incident," Billy protested, "it's been building up for months."

The Headteacher sat down behind his desk, facing Billy; he picked up a pen and clicked it continually, drawing the ballpoint in and out; he sighed quite audibly. "Look, Billy off the record, yeah? I know Mister Dean and his two so-called friends are little shits..."

Billy's eyebrows crept up his forehead.

"...and I would dearly love to meet our Mister Dean down a dark alley believe me, but we are the ones who set the standards, we have rules of decorum, we do *not* retaliate no matter what. There are procedures in place to deal with any situation, although they are not working the way I would prefer. I expel pupils and then my decision is overturned on appeal. Even the ones kicked out for violent behaviour and verbally abusing staff have successfully challenged their exclusions. My hands are tied; appeal panels are undermining my authority. I think I am best placed to decide what a suitable sanction is, but until the rules are changed, Billy, *you* and I must abide by them. You're from the old school, Billy, and I quite understand that some things are puzzling to you and to be quite honest I respect you for that because some of the old ways worked better than what we have nowadays. We *all* must bite our tongues on occasion, Billy. I was stuck in this office until well after six last night trying to placate the OFSTED inspectors. They were naturally angry and upset at what they had seen, I've told them I'll deal with it in-house and report back. *Anyway*, I've been on the phone to Mrs. Dean, apparently she has washed her hands on her son and I got the impression that she wasn't bothered about what he does or what happens to him. Anyway, Mister Dean has been suspended for one week, Billy..."

"*ONE WEEK...*" Billy laughed, although it came out more like a pained, incredulous shriek.

"Billy, you ought to be thankful that Boreley hill has got

away with this situation so lightly, some parents would have had the claim forms in before the dust had settled. I'm only going to say this one more time, Billy these people will be gone in a few weeks, keep your head low, I do *not* want to be having this conversation again, do I make myself clear?"

Billy nodded gently and went, "Mmmm."

"You may go."

Billy rose and turned to leave.

"By the way, Billy," the Headteacher added, "your Miss Dunn? She eventually broke down and admitted that she had lied about the incident in the medical room. I have given her a good talking to, informing her that her behaviour has been no less than despicable and immoral. She is also serving a one-week suspension."

"Thank you, sir. A weeks' holiday will certainly teach them both a lesson." His tone dripped with sarcasm. "But with the utmost respect to you, Mister Clune, this is all bollocks," his tone now suggesting anything but respect. Billy shut the door forcefully on his way out.

16

"I'll go and make us a cup of tea."

Billy placed his newspaper flat on the kitchen table. "No, you stop there, Mum, I'll do it."

"I'm quite capable," Mrs. Crabtree said, rising awkwardly to her feet, "anyway, it will give me something to do. I've been sat here all day twiddling my thumbs."

"OK," Billy said, "please yerself," and carried on reading his newspaper.

Yet again Billy was just going through the motions. He wasn't actually reading the newspaper; he couldn't concentrate. Apart from having to cope with his illness, the relentless campaign of increasing hostility by Deano and his mates was constantly playing on his mind. *And all over something so trivial.* He sat back in his chair and pushed his reading glasses up so that they rested on top of his head. Billy fingered his chin thoughtfully.

Just shy of a year ago Billy had been summoned to one of the social areas where broken glass had been reported. On arrival, he had found the evil threesome kicking a football around. The floor was littered with broken polystyrene ceiling tiles and several light fittings were either smashed or hanging precariously from the ceiling. Billy had simply asked Deano, Nelly, and Thommo to refrain from kicking their ball around their social area and take it outside. After throwing Billy a barrage of verbal obscenities, Billy felt he had no choice but to report the matter to the Headteacher. They hadn't given him a minute's peace since, and with only a few weeks of term time

SCHOOL'S...OUT...FOR...EVER

left, they now seemed to be cramming in as much mischief as they could. Billy rested his head on the back of his chair and rubbed his eyes with clenched fists. *I think I'll have me an early night.* It made him feel guilty. As his Mum had said, she had been alone all day and she would probably enjoy nothing more than a lengthy conversation about Billy's day, but he wasn't in the mood – as usual.

Mrs. Crabtree returned to the table with a tray on which was placed almost an entire tea set. Matching china cups, saucers, teapot, milk jug, and sugar bowl. She placed it in front of Billy.

Billy sighed. "Why go to all that trouble, Mum, huh? A couple of mugs would have done, look at all the washing up you've created."

She tutted. "I've told you before, son, if something's worth doing, it's worth doing well. Drinking tea is an art form. You can stick your tea bags, there's only one way to..."

"OK, OK, just pour it out, Mum." Billy removed his specs from his head and pinched the bridge of his nose. "I think I'll take mine upstairs with me, Mum. I'm going to bed; I've had a difficult day."

Mrs. Crabtree's eyebrows moved towards the ceiling. She nodded slowly. "A *difficult* day, you say? Well why don't we have a chat about it? It'll help to get things off your chest, don't you think?" She was almost pleading, she wanted to talk, and she wanted company.

Billy released a rush of air through his nose. "I'm not in the mood, Mum, I'm going..."
Billy's sentence was truncated when a dull thud came from the lounge area. He instinctively took hold of his Mum's wrist; tea slopped from his Mums cup into the saucer, and from the saucer onto the table; she didn't notice.

"What was that?" Billy said.

"What was what, dear? I didn't hear anything." She took a few faltering steps until she was standing behind him. She stroked his head gently as if she were stroking Sophie. "You're looking a little tired and peaky lately, son is there something wrong, mmm? Anything I can..."

There it was again, yet another dull, heavy thump. This time Sophie shot out of the kitchen and Billy followed her into the lounge. Sophie reared up, rested her front paws on the window ledge, and began barking furiously.

By this time, Mrs. Crabtree had entered the room. Billy said, "There's somebody out there, Mum I'll go and take a look."

Mrs. Crabtree grasped at Billy's elbow as he passed. "Don't go outside, Billy you never know who it might be."

Billy nodded thoughtfully and had second thoughts. Instead, he drew back the curtains and leant into the bay window. On the left-hand pane was what looked like mud spattered across the glass. He squinted and peered out into the gloom through the central, clear pane and saw nothing at first, not until his sight adjusted to the darkness, and then he saw movement. He counted three silhouettes outside. All wore dark clothing and scarves covered their noses and mouths. Two wore hoods, the third a baseball cap. One of the shadowy figures moved closer to the house and set off the outside security light. He froze for a few seconds like a rabbit caught in car headlights. It was all that Billy needed to make out the tell-tale acne and the scar running through the figures left, ginger eyebrow. *Oh shit, they've found out where I live.* The figure stooped and took a large stone from the front garden rockery. As he lifted the rock behind his head, Billy dropped down below the window ledge bawling, "Down, Mum, get down!"

Billy heard a muffled scream from outside, "Kiss this, Crabby you old cunt!"

The rock came crashing through the window showering Billy with shards of glass; it carried on its journey smashing into the television set which imploded with a dull boom.

Mrs. Crabtree screamed and dropped behind the settee.

Billy jumped to his feet. "What the fuck..."

He made towards the front door, threw it open, and strolled as briskly as is possible in a pair of slippers up to the garden gate. Sophie had followed him and was barking at whatever had disappeared into the gloom. Glancing to his left and right, the street was deserted.

"I know who you are, you bastards," Billy screamed into the darkness, "I'll get you for this, don't you worry."

He leant with both hands on the gate and bowed his head. He had felt that it was impossible to sink any lower than he had been, but now he found himself floating in a dark nothingness, very alone and isolated. *This is getting out of hand; they're getting more and more brazen.* He hooked a finger under Sophie's collar and led her back down the path. Reaching the house, he was met with yet more misery. Across the garage door was sprayed-canned - CRABBY LIKES IT UP THE ARSE. Billy dug his fists into his hips and ground his teeth together. *It seems that God is continuing his mean streak with me.*

Returning to the house Sophie nestled into her basket, tongue hanging out, panting for breath. Mrs. Crabtree was just replacing the phone onto its cradle.

Her brow wrinkled amongst wrinkles. "I don't understand it, Billy," she said, "I've phoned the police and they said that no one's available at the moment who can deal with mild harassment. The lady has given me this." She held out a slip of paper on which she had scribbled some numbers; Billy took it.

"She said it's a crime number, whatever that means," Mrs. Crabtree was scratching her head thoughtfully. "She said someone will attend as soon as they're available."

Billy cackled freakishly, and tears snaked a path down his cheeks. He ran his palms slowly down his face. "As soon as they're available? Mild fuckin' harassment? Ha! We're just a faceless statistic in a sea of faceless statistics," he said, "What a great fucking country we live in." His voice was not at all steady.

Mrs. Crabtree reached out and stroked his neck; it was wet and sticky. Examining her hand, she found blood. "Oh my God, you're hurt, dear go and sit down and I'll fetch the first aid box."

Billy's wound turned out to be slight. While his Mum dressed it, he finished off his tea to which he had added, with a shaky hand, another two teaspoonful of sugar and a slurp of whisky.

When he felt a little calmer, Billy drove to the school. He let himself in, turned off the alarm system, and then made his way to the woodwork department. He cut himself a piece of thick plywood to the measurement that he had taken from the broken front window, and then made his way down to his workroom where he collected a bottle of graffiti remover. By the time he had returned to the house, boarded up the window, and scrubbed the graffiti from the garage door, it was well past one o'clock. It then took him another half an hour or so to calm and settle his Mum into bed.

The adrenaline was still coursing through him, as he lay wide-awake on his back staring at the bedroom ceiling. It wasn't until this moment that he had realised that the graffiti he had removed would want to have been seen by the police as evidence, but it didn't bother him; he didn't want the neighbours seeing filth like that at first light. *This is taking a very sinister course.* His mind fixed on the poor soul who had lost his life in the house fire on Deano's estate. He closed his eyes and tried to gather his unravelled nerves into a tight bundle. *What's next on their list for me, will I also get petrol through the letterbox? So, what do I do now? The schools not interested; the police don't give a shit...*

Three heavy raps on the front door disturbed his thoughts. He slipped his legs out of bed and grabbed his dressing gown. As he padded across the landing his Mother called out to him, but he reassured her, "It's ok Mom, it's probably the police, stay there and try and get some rest."

On opening the door, a dark, masked figure confronted Billy; Deano had returned. Before Billy could say anything, Deano produced what looked like a small, washing up liquid bottle and pointed it towards him. Billy instinctively held up a hand and began turning away. His hand took most of the liquid, but the left side of his face caught some of the splashes. His skin burned and he howled in agony as pain seared through his hand and face. There was hissing and steam as his polyester dressing gown began to dissolve. Billy slammed the door shut and virtually sprinted up the stair and into the bathroom. His first aid training told him what he needed to do. Without wasting time to undress, he stepped into the bath and turned the shower to cold. That is where he sat for the next ten or so minutes. After gingerly drying himself he tended to his injuries. They could have been a lot worse if he hadn't acted so quickly. Inspecting his face in the mirror there were angry red blotches on his left cheek and across his forehead. He felt very relieved that the liquid had missed his eyes, but his hand throbbed like mad. Billy thanked God for his Mums partial deafness; the commotion hadn't disturbed her. He decided not to call the police again, what would be the point? Deano had worn a mask and anyway, he would have half a dozen witnesses to swear he was somewhere else.

   Billy sat in the lounge with the light off and the curtains open. If anyone did return he would see them in advance through the panes of glass that remained. His injured skin prickled like a very severe sunburn. He knitted his fingers together behind his head and relaxed in the armchair as best he could. He felt torn, stark and was drained of all energy. His day had been long; the night would be longer as many hours of sleeplessness lay between him and dawn.

17

Over the next few days, Billy kept his head down. He kept away from the head, and away from reception. The few staff that he did bump into enquired about the angry red weal's across part of his face, and he had quipped that he had had the same blade in his razor for about five years and it probably needed changing. No one got the joke.

The attacks continued on a nightly basis. A couple more windows broken, the door hammered at varying times during the night, shit through the letterbox. Billy assumed that the excrement probably belonged to one of the gang; it surely wouldn't have been so much fun for them if they had just used dog shit. After a couple of days, Billy and his Mum had a short visit from a community patrol officer who took notes and said that she would pass them on to someone higher up the ladder. Billy enquired as to why they had sent round a Girl Guide, which didn't go down too well with 'Sarah' whose other job was a travel agent.

Although Billy had spotted Thommo and Nelly around the school on occasions over the next few days, all he got was whispered, hurtful, and derogatory comments, especially about the condition of his face, which they found very amusing. Billy didn't bite, what would be the point? They were born liars and would just deny everything, and what would he say? 'I've informed the police, they'll sort you out!' yeah, that would really put the shit up them.

Billy had guessed rightly that although they only had a brain cell or two in their heads, they probably wouldn't work independently of Deano and so couldn't put together any kind of mischievous escapades without their 'leader' present. At least things had quietened down at school and so the next few days passed without further incident.

Quiet before the storm?

On certain evenings, Billy was expected to work late to cover school lettings. Two nights a week a karate class hired the sports hall and there would also be the odd parents evening. Tonight, there was to be a dog training class.

On such evenings all that Billy was expected to do was to hang around waiting for the building to empty, undertake a security check, set the alarm system, and lock up. He had had a cup of tea with a *Wagonwheel.* Then, so as not to get bored, he thought he might as well take the opportunity to make ready one of the schools mini-buses for Ms. Carroll, the P.E. teacher. Earlier that day he had popped out to a local garage that the school held an account with to re-fuel the vehicle and check the tyre pressures. He fetched the mini-bus from its designated spot on the car park and drove it to the rear of the school; here he would be left undisturbed. Empty plastic bottles and cans rolled around the foot well. Sweet wrappers and empty crisp packets adorned the floor and seats and chewing gum had been strategically placed so that the next occupants would leave the mini-bus with it stuck to their clothing. An A4 sized laminated sign sellotaped to the dashboard read - *NO EATING OR DRINKING ALLOWED IN THIS VEHICLE.* In the open glove compartment were about half a dozen black bin liners that Billy had put there about a year ago in the hope that they would be used if any of the teachers decided to ignore the sign, which obviously they all had.

Billy would start the cleaning process by collecting the larger items in a black bin liner and then he would hoover the inside and hose down the outside.

The service road led Billy alongside the indoor swimming pool, which was used by the school during the daytime and the town's leisure centre at night. He then turned sharp left and stopped in front of the security barrier gate whose arm was striped in alternate green and yellow luminous paint. To his left ran a high brick windowless wall. This formed the back of the spectator seating area for the swimming pool. As Billy fumbled in his pockets for the security pass card that would lift the barrier, he noticed a figure emerging from the rear of the Design and Technology department further along the road. Leaning through the open window, he inserted his security card into the slot on the post that supported the barrier and it rose slowly. Billy drove through very slowly, probably no more than 5m.p.h. He soon recognised the approaching figure as Thommo. *What the hell is he doing here at this time of night? Probably been up to no good. I'll bet he has something in his rucksack that will end up on E-bay.* Thommo was ambling along with his head bowed low. He was totally pre-occupied, jabbing his thumbs into his mobile phone. *What the hell do they see in those things? They seem to spend their whole lives jabbering into the monstrous playthings and anyway, surely a moron like Thommo doesn't have anything worthwhile to say to anybody?* Glancing at his watch Billy read 5: 03p.m.

It was a chance in a million, but just at the precise moment that Billy took his eyes off the road, Thommo had stepped off the curb without looking to left or right. As Billy looked up from his watch there was Thommo's startled face in the middle of his windscreen. Billy literally stood on the brake, lifting himself off the seat, but not before he heard a dull thud. Although travelling at low speed, there was still a short skid before the mini-bus came to a shuddering halt.

"Oh, sweet Jesus!" Billy bawled, and kept repeating it over and over again, as he fumbled to release his seat belt.

Billy jumped down from the cab; his head was spinning, in free fall. He swallowed hard, not wanting to see what awaited him in front of the vehicle. As he rounded the front, Thommo was rolling around clutching at his leg and screaming. Billy's eyes stayed riveted on the broken boy as relief flooded through him; he was just so elated that Thommo was still alive – but that would soon change.

"You bastard, Crabby," Thommo spat, "you meant that, you tried to kill me you fuckin' bastard. I'll have you for this, Crabby I'll tell 'em you mounted the pavement and went for me, I'll get you the fuckin' sack..." his eyes were wild and bulging, his lips flecked with spittle.

Although Billy could practically feel the anger and hatred radiating toward him, he went into first-aid mode and knelt beside Thommo. "Just lie still and let me look at your leg, son I'm trained in first aid and..."

Thommo knocked Billy's hand away, "Don't fuckin' touch me you peado, we'll sort you out don't you worry we'll be back, we know how to sort twats like you out," he raged. The tendons in his neck were rigid.

As Billy rose and loomed over Thommo, he struggled to rein in his own rage. The corners of his mouth turned down, his lips slightly parted to reveal clenched teeth...then he grimaced and clutched at his stomach as the terrible dark energy returned. Nausea threatened to engulf him, but he forced the sensation back down. Thommo's voice seemed to turn into an incessant, irritating whine. Billy's face collapsed as the sharp pain took over. Cold beads of sweat began to burst out across his forehead, as Thommo continued his pathetic cries of obscene, virulent abuse.

Then as suddenly as it had come, the pain subsided.

There was an instant – a time-stopping freeze – where all of Billy's morals were turned on their head. The decent life he had led was replaced with something else, a short future life wholly different from the life he had lived. It was something he didn't want to see but the moment wouldn't stop, and it would never ever change back. Stress can make people do strange things. Week after week, month after month, year after year Billy had taken crap from kids and teachers alike. Over a long period, he had bottled up this pent-up anger, he had been pushed to the edge of a crevice and now his anger had nowhere to go it was if his head had literally exploded. His breaking point had been reached, raw anger shredded his self-control, and Billy had a hell of a lot of control to lose.

Billy's chest tightened, and his throat thickened. His mind was a jumble of thoughts and fears. A revulsion that was almost uncontrollable surged and boiled in his stomach. There was none of the proverbial 'Red mist' descending. Instead, he felt calm warmth run through him, like when he had just finished a third glass of port at Christmas. In that moment he had changed. Suddenly, he had a sense of absolute clarity unlike anything he had ever experienced. He realised what he had to do. He knew he was going to kill. There was something different and foreign about him, about his eyes, an almost euphoric sense of relief swept through him. His eyes slowly turned owlish and he felt himself float above the pain, detached and as light as air. There was a soothing voice in his head; a message had been planted in his brain. An internal darkness encroached on Billy's field of vision, until he seemed to be gazing into a tunnel. His breathing was deep and slow, and he was beyond anger now; he was in another, calmer place, beyond any rational thought.

Billy exhaled in a long, deep spasm of relief; the corners of his mouth turned upward and the muscles in his face relaxed. A look of determination swept across his features, as if an important decision had been made. He could inexplicably hear his own voice from a distance – 'I'm going to end my life quickly and as planned...*AND I'M GOING TO TAKE THESE THREE BASTARDS WITH ME.*' He felt strong, he felt resolute, and more than anything else, it now gave him the will to fight.

Snapping out of his long existence of morbid gloom, Billy slowly raised his eyes and glared unblinkingly at his first victim. His fear and timidity seemed in that split second to wash away, replaced by a strange peace. The weak, melancholy expression was gone for good. His day had started
in despair as deep as he had ever known it, yearning for death; he now wanted desperately to live. He *needed* to live. Intense anger was the engine of change in him. Rage had changed Billy, bit deep enough to wake him from his long trance of desolation.

Rationality had left him. He had a terminal disease; he could do anything he wanted to. After all, who could punish him more than the punishment he had to endure from his illness and these three bastards? Rules no longer applied. When he eventually ended it all, these three shits would still be around to cause untold suffering if he didn't do something to stop them. If he took their evil, destructive force with him, he would surely be hailed a hero. The untouchables now became the expendables. *An old dinosaur, am I? Past my sell-by date, mmm? They're all wrong, so fucking wrong.* Billy turned slowly, almost robotically, and made for the drivers' open door.

"Don't leave me here, twat," Thommo wailed, clutching at his injured leg. His eyes watered and the tune had now changed to a plaintive bleat. "Do something, call me an ambulance I'm in fuckin' agony, man."

Thommo's outline shimmered then resolved, shimmered then resolved. Billy's unnerving, ever-growing smile almost left spit on his earlobes. "Oh, don't you worry, young Thommo I'll soon get rid of the pain for you," he said, calmly and quietly to himself. His face fixed in an almost eerie repose.

Billy jumped into the cab and glanced around the immediate area - no one about. He also knew that, although there was a camera perched high up on the wall that the mini-bus was parallel to, it was always pointing down at the entrance barrier and so the mini-bus was presently occupying a blind spot from the schools' CCTV system. He took a deep, steadying breath and with a shaky hand, he found first gear and released the handbrake. Thommo froze and his forehead creased. His face became a contorted mask of alarm and he held out his hands instinctively in front of him as if that would be enough to hold the mini-bus back. His mouth fell open and there was desperate pleading in his eyes. The mini-bus crept forward; there was a very short, sharp cry of panic from deep inside Thommo's throat and then there was a slight bump. Billy found reverse and there was another slight bump, forward bump, reverse bump. He applied the hand brake, chose neutral and jumped out of the cab.

Thommo's body was terribly misshapen. His insides were still spilling out and thick, guttural noises gurgled from his mouth with every burst of bloodied spittle. Ribs protruded from his chest cavity and a grey/crimson mush oozed from several cracks in his crumpled, deformed skull. The blood loss seemed to be torrential and unrelenting and the pavement was spattered with gore. Billy loomed over Thommo's lifeless form. Any normal person would have shut their eyes against the dreadful vision, but in Billy's present state of mind he justified his actions as a righteous killing. He stood statuesque and staring as blood emptied out of Thommo, spilling around him. Brain leaked slowly over the tarmac.

Billy dug clenched fists into his hips. "You're looking a bit off colour, young man," he said wide-eyed, "I think *this* would now be an ideal time to call you an ambulance." He smiled wickedly.

Suddenly, as the adrenaline of the situation subsided, he felt himself weaken and pain snapped him into consciousness. His knees buckled, and he folded uselessly to the ground.

Billy's heart hammered deep in his chest, a pounding that seemed to echo all around his body. He dug his fingernails into his lower stomach, and he swallowed a rush of bile. He fluttered his eyelashes a few times as if he had been in a trance, which in a way he had been. Tremors of revulsion now ran through him as he realised that his mind may have shut down for a short while, mesmerised by the horror that lay in front of him, unable to process and make sense of this scene. Another flood of burning bile rose into his throat. He puked tea and a mushy *Wagonwheel* into the gutter.

Billy ran a sleeve across his mouth and began taking in rapid gulps of air. He then slowly rose from the tarmac and, using the swimming pool wall for support, he made his way very tentatively to the leisure centre reception. By the time he arrived, the pain was so great that his face was flushed, and tears had welled up in his eyes. He slumped across the reception desk and blurted out the dreadful situation that had taken place.

The staff listened in stunned disbelief to Billy's garbled account of what had happened. It seemed as if he was genuinely upset for the lad in question, but the tears were purely down to the extreme discomfort he was trying to deal with.

The receptionist called the relevant emergency services as one of the leisure centre lifeguards jogged to the scene of the incident and draped a blanket over the body. The gory scene took its toll. Although trained in first aid, she returned trembling and taking deep, gulping sobs. Work colleagues comforted her and felt she would benefit from some fresh air. They helped her outside and sat her down on a bench. Shortly, she took the opportunity to empty the contents of her stomach onto the paved area.

Back inside, Billy sat with his elbows perched on his knees; someone had draped a blanket around his shoulders. One staff member had plied him with cups of sweet tea; his third was held in his trembling hands, which he used to swill down several painkillers.

Billy's head was bowed low trying to give the impression of a man going through hell. No one saw the corners of his mouth slowly turn upwards.

18

When the painkillers had kicked in, Billy found a quiet corner and phoned his Mum to tell her of the situation that he was in and that he may be a little late. A slight miscalculation, it would be well after ten o'clock before he eventually got home.

The first police officers on the scene had taken a preliminary statement from Billy. Then a little later a certain detective inspector Collins, a large and shambling man with small black eyes and an oval face, questioned him in more detail. Billy's first impression was that he resembled a talking potato, although his outward demeanour and mannerisms suggested that he was a Colombo tribute act. After searching in every pocket for his warrant card, the inspector had unwittingly flashed Billy his Sainsbury's Nectar card as proof of identity. He apologised for being late because he had initially turned up at the wrong school. The inspector was suited up in a white disposable overall supplied to him by the Crime Scene Investigators. He suggested that a never-ending supply of tea and coffee for himself and his men would be appreciated. He interviewed Billy in one of the most monotonous voices Billy had ever heard its lack of intonation having possibly sent most people that he encountered into a deep coma.

The Scene of Crime team drifted around the accident site like ominous spirits, faceless in white suits and hoods. Although road traffic accident sites were generally considered too contaminated to wear protective clothing, on this occasion the inspector had requested it. Fluttering blue and white striped crime scene tape bearing the wording 'police line – do not cross' had cut off the service road. Two uniformed officers guarded the area – one at each end. Floodlights had been erected and a tent had been hastily set up over the scene so that the small gathering of the genuinely concerned, the curious and the ghoulish rubberneckers that mingled quietly by the barrier had nothing to gawk at. They had been drawn to the scene by the flashing blue and red beacons of the emergency vehicles. The body had been examined *in situ* and the Scene of Crime officer was working away methodically photographing and filming the scene to record and document the area from every angle. An ambulance was parked discreetly in the shadows.

After everyone had done their bit, they had all arrived at the obvious initial conclusion – it was a tragic accident.

After getting home much later than expected, Billy poured himself a large scotch and placed it on a tray with his evening meal, which his Mum had microwaved for him. He felt that he had already offered his mother enough explanation about the incident over the phone. He fobbed her off with, "Tough day at the office," and managed a small smile. Billy then took the tray up to his bedroom; he now had a clear picture in his mind of what needed to be done – there was a lot of planning to do.

Billy realised that there would be intense interest in him at school the following day. After phoning the headteacher at home and bringing him up to date about the deeply distressing situation that had occurred a few hours earlier, Co-co had decided that things would carry on as normal as possible. He explained to Billy the chaos it would cause if he closed the school for the day, as most families had both parents at work and it would not give them time to find child minders especially for the younger kids. Also, exams were only a few weeks away and he didn't want to disrupt their studies and revision timetable. And anyway, it was much too late to phone or text over a thousand people to inform them of the situation. The head told Billy to take a few days off but Billy said that it would make him feel worse sitting at home brooding and that he would carry on. Co-co grudgingly accepted Billy's decision and asked him if, when he arrived in the morning, he wouldn't mind keeping the main entrance locked, which overlooked the scene of the accident. He would also appreciate it if Billy could set up a series of signs directing kids and staff towards the side entrances.

Billy was aware of anxiety clamping his chest. Most people would have taken time off, but he felt he needed to turn up for work because he was anxious to get his plan off the ground a.s.a.p. Everyone would be asking questions, and no doubt, he would be seeing the Headteacher again in the morning. He also knew that there might be interest from the local or even the national media. It would be a struggle to keep them at bay, but he would see to it that the Headteacher dealt with any press that may turn up.

Not for the first time, adrenaline was to keep Billy awake well into the small hours. It didn't matter. Billy was a new man; he had a goal, a purpose, something to focus his attention on, something to keep him centred and calm – his strong desire to live. Something had emerged from inside him that he didn't know he had. Something dark and very scary. He had stood on the brink of a black abyss of misery, but now his desire to survive a little longer than planned, was suddenly stronger than it had been for months. He had now convinced himself that his life had purpose and meaning enough to justify continued existence, maybe there was a positive aspect to being completely doomed after all. Revenge was all there was left.

For hour after hour, Billy sat in the armchair in the corner of his bedroom scribbling notes and thoughts into his diary setting about his task with gusto. He searched the dark corners of his mind trying to come up with fates unpleasant enough to penalise the two little shits that remained. He would track them down and destroy them before they had chance to ravage any more lives – including his and his Moms. Finally, he rested the diary in his lap and took a large slug of whisky. On the dresser next to him he had placed a small bowl containing liquid TCP. A large wad of cotton wool lay next to it. Occasionally he would dab his acid burns, and every time he did so, he saw Deano's evil shadowy figure filling his bedroom doorway. The strong antiseptic hurt like hell for a few seconds, but it took some of the stinging sensation away. He combed thin strands of remaining hair with splayed fingers and then rested his head and stared up at the ceiling. He imagined that when he had finally put the other two out of action the people who lived on their estate would be out in the streets dancing under the knowledge that they could begin to get some normality back into their lives. Less hassle, less intimidation and certainly less vandalism. He smiled to himself. *I really hope this starts a trend, I pray that my actions will be the trigger that fires people into protecting themselves.* He visualised vigilante groups being set up by people just like him. People who had behaved and conformed to the rules and at the end of the day had been shit on from a great height. He truly hoped that across the country all the little shits that were plaguing estates like his would mysteriously disappear from the face of the Earth. Billy knitted his fingers behind his head. *It must come. What else is there? The government and police are gonna' do this and they're gonna' do that, but nothing changes. These scumbags are literally getting away with murder.*

Yeah, this plan was going to be his pièce de résistance, one for the books, no one's heard of Billy Crabtree *yet*, but they will. He could almost hear their voices in his head – 'What a fucking hero that Billy Crabtree was, at last, someone who saw sense, someone who was willing to stand up to the untouchable scumbags who are blighting lives up and down the country'. *Bollocks! I wish I'd have thought of this earlier, I could have taken out a lot more of the little twats and made even more lives worth living.* He would never be a victim again. Billy felt his resolve harden even further; he cackled in a freakish manner and had to put a clenched fist to his mouth to control himself.

But it's gonna' have to be quick; I'm gonna' have to hit 'em before anybody realises what's going on. A sudden twinge caught him in his lower abdomen, which disturbed his violent revenge fantasies. He sucked in a breath and held it. He reached for his painkillers and tipped a number into his palm; he had stopped counting them now, what would be the point? He raised his cupped hand to his mouth and swilled them down with what little whisky was left in the glass. Glancing across at the alarm clock it winked 4:21a.m. He grimaced and clenched his teeth. Billy thought the best thing he could do now was to keep himself occupied until the painkillers began doing their job. He drew his knees up to his chest and then, reaching for his pen, he began scribbling more notes into his diary, creating elaborate scenarios that would seal the fate of the two remaining gang members.

Billy revelled in his new-found 'Hobby' - that of planning Deano and Nelly's end – and maybe one or two other gang members if he had the time. He realised that he had crossed some invisible line into an obsession beyond any rationality, but he had had enough and to be frank, he just didn't give a toss.

Billy's life in the last few years was a strict schedule of work and solitude. Every morning he had arrived at his small workroom by seven. From here he would plan his day arriving back home just after five or later depending on what activities were planned after school hours. His tea would be placed on the table as he entered the house. He and his Mother would 'Chat' about this and that - or 'Fuck-all' as Billy would prefer to call it, and then he would sit in his room and watch TV or read a book until he grew tired. A routine that was repeated day after day after day. Lately his mouth had assumed an almost permanently down-turned position, but now things would be different, things were going to change. From this point on, adrenaline and anger would propel him onwards.

Billy's head was swimming with the possibilities that the next few days may throw up. Only one impulse motivated Billy now. He couldn't prevent a slight smile tugging at the corners of his mouth and there was a surge of both pain and adrenaline, which stood side by side in his stomach. His heart was like a machine gun in his ears, pondering the enormity of the task in hand, but also there was the irresistible thought of his impending reunion with Nelly and Deano.

Now, Billy Crabtree had a precise and conscious purpose

for the first time in his life. He had previously lived his life by the book and now? Well, fuck the book!

19

By the time the sun came up and poked its fingers through chinks in the curtains, Billy had only managed an hour's sleep. He had been unable to do anything but obsess about the nearly impossible task that lay in front of him. For most of the night he had tossed and turned, switching on his bedside lamp, making notes, down to the kitchen making coffee, erasing ideas, making more notes, switching off the lamp until he had been rudely awakened by the alarm clock at six; he felt like he had only just nodded off, which indeed he had.

Yet Billy Crabtree awoke feeling more relaxed and positive than he had been for quite a while *and* his bowels felt OK too, none of the gripes that had been plaguing him of late.

Yes, on *this* particular morning he had awoke with some purpose. The depression that had clouded his life for the last few months was lifted and as a result, he had felt somehow whole and alive. The cobwebs had been dusted from his head and made him look forward to the day with some vigour. Yesterday he'd been ready to die, but now he was ready to live. He felt a renewed sense of determination; depression had turned to anger. It was time for him to take control. His mood had brightened enough for him to muster a jaunty whistle; even his reflection in the bathroom mirror seemed different. He normally looked so wan and tired but now his eyes were alive and bright and there was a slight pink tone to his cheeks.

Billy decided to get to work particularly early that morning to avoid contact with any media that may have turned up. He thought perhaps that the story might be investigated under intense media scrutiny. He knew that this was the kind of story that reporters dreamt about and anyone worth his weight would have a field day with the news. However, when he did arrive at school he found things a lot worse than he had imagined. The media circus had already commenced their invasion and was on the prowl. There were cars and vans snaking down the schools' driveway and small groups of reporters huddled together at the security barrier nattering about film speeds and lenses or whatever they tend to talk about. Microphones and cameras were at the ready like rifles. Billy had to abandon his car. He pulled the collar of his jacket up around his face and, with head bowed, walked briskly towards the barrier. TV crews and reporters jockeyed for position as a bouquet of microphones and cameras were thrust into his face. Flashes from their cameras lit up the grey sky. Billy stuck a hand over the lens of one camera and gave it a good shove; he heard a loud click and then a moan, the camera operator spun away holding his mouth.

Television and the tabloids are going to have a holiday with this. I wonder what exaggerated description and spurious shit they're gonna give me. 'BOY KILLED BY CARETAKER IN SPEEDING SCHOOL MINI-BUS!'

"Mister Crabtree are you Billy Crabtree?" one reporter bawled.

Billy struggled to find the right key for the padlock, lines of sweat trickled from both temples. "Erm, no," he stuttered, not averting his gaze from the lock. "I'm the erm, site manager; I believe Mister Crabtree will be taking a few days compassionate leave…now if you'll excuse me."

Questions were shot at him from all directions and Billy deflected them as best he could until finally he managed to unlock the padlock and raise the barrier. He was approached again by one of the reporters.

"Could you tell us where he lives? I'm sure he'd…"

"Definitely not," Billy interjected, "he's probably taken this very badly, I'm sure he wishes to be left alone."

Billy informed the mingling congregation that if they passed the barrier then it would be looked upon as trespass. As they were parked on private property, he advised them to move their vehicles to allow staff to get into the school. Finally, Billy suggested that they ring the reception after eight and ask if the Headteacher was available for comment.

"Do you know I've seen more of you lately than I have of my own wife?" the Headteacher laughed feebly at his weak joke. He was leaning forward, forearms on his desk, hands clasped. "What on earth have you done to your face?"

"Ah, erm, splashed myself with bleach. What am I like?" Billy thought he'd abandon the razor gag, as it got no response.

"Dear oh dear, we'll have to look into the health and safety aspects of the dangerous chemicals that we store on site. Anyway, Billy, tell me, why the hell did you come into work this morning?"

Billy sat hunched, feigning interest in his nails. He coughed a couple of times, trying to sound as pathetic as he could. "I thought it best, sir, no good sitting at home dwelling on what happened and getting all worked up." *I hope that sounded low-key enough.* Then he resumed, "I've had a restless night, you know? If I'd have done this, if I'd have done that..." he dramatically slapped a palm to his forehead. "God, he just stepped off the curb and..."

The Headteacher left his swivel chair and skirted his desk. He placed a friendly hand on Billy's shoulder. "OK, old man, I know, I know. I did come out to the incident last night but by the time the news had trickled through everyone had gone home. Anyway, I do wish you would go home, why don't you take a couple of days off, yeah?"

Billy was finding this acting lark a lot more difficult than the previous evening; at least then he had the pain to bring tears to his eyes. He insisted that the best thing he could do was to keep himself occupied and busy.

The Headteacher sat on the corner of his desk and loosened his tie. For a number of seconds, he studied Billy with beady-eyed compassion. "Right then, Billy, but you just take it easy, yeah?" He slipped back the sleeve of his jacket to expose his watch, "I'm sorry, Billy, you'll have to excuse me, I've got a press conference to attend, see if we can't get rid of these media wolves pretty sharpish, mmm? I'm quite certain that the sensationalist tabloids will blow this story out of all proportion, but I'm sure this incident will only be in the public eye until a bigger story comes along. In the meantime, it may make life a little easier if you refer any interested parties directly to me."

If you insist. Billy nodded, the gratitude evident in his eyes. He rose solemnly, thanked the Headteacher, and held out his hand; they shook hands firmly. They had spoken almost as equals for the first time, was the thought that entered Billy's head. As Billy closed the door behind him, he leant his back against it. He rubbed his hands briskly together and the corners of his mouth turned towards the ceiling.

Billy made his way towards the reception area and stuck his head through the open sliding glass doors.

"Morning, Jan," Billy chirruped.

Janet averted her gaze from her computer screen and slipped her glasses up from her nose, resting them on top of her head. The moment she looked into his eyes, she saw a different Billy Crabtree. Instead of the troubled, dark visage that was normally present, he was smiling brightly, his vigour fully restored, and it was if a light had been turned on behind his eyes.

"So," Billy said rubbing his palms together, "this drink we were supposed to be having, doing anything tonight?"

Janet felt her eyebrows rise involuntarily; she could only stammer, "Er, well, no, no I don't think so...what's happened to your face..."

"Splendid, jot your address down on a piece of paper and I'll pick it up later, shall we say half seven, eight?"

"Erm, well yes, but..."

"Excellent, we'll have a bite to eat somewhere, OK? You choose. See you later then."

Billy was gone.

Esther called, "Jan, Jan, call him back and ask him about the incident last night!"

Janet shot up out of her seat and leant through the window. "Billy, about last night..." her voice fell away and was lost amongst the decibels of raucous laughter, tinkling voices and braying outbursts from the kids who, at that time, were in the middle of changing lessons.

Janet dropped back into her seat and swivelled round. "Well what on earth was all that about?"

Esther raised meticulously plucked eyebrows, held out her hands as if checking for rain, and shrugged her shoulders. "Well, he certainly seems to have taken it well, Jan."

Billy returned to his workroom to wait for the inevitable visit from Mister Dean, which, for the first time, he was actually looking forward to.

20

He didn't have long to wait.

Billy barely had time to boil the kettle when there was a staccato of almighty thumps on his door. He could hear the unmistakable muffled ranting's of Deano and his one remaining henchman. Billy glanced up at the clock. *8:37a.m.? That must be the earliest that Mister Dean has ever attended school.*

It had taken a while for the story to filter through the town and Deano had only heard of Thommo's fate earlier that morning. Each person in the chain who had received a message had added their little bit of exaggeration to the story. The original text of 'Thommo has been involved in an accident with the school mini bus and crabby was the driver', now read on Deano's mobile phone, 'Crabby has murdered Thommo.'

As Billy opened the door Deano took a step forward and jabbed a dirty, well bitten fingernail into his face. Deano froze Momentarily because for a second or two he hardly recognised him. Although a good deal shorter than Deano, Billy now seemed taller, a military bearing, hard-muscled, fiery-eyed, hard-faced, and determined. The corners of Billy's mouth were also turned up slightly, which Deano did not like at all.

"Can I help you, gentlem…" is all that Billy managed, as he stared up Deano's nose.

"You killed our mate, Crabby," Deano spat through clenched teeth. A flame of demonic, crazed hate and revenge flickered in his eyes. "You are so fuckin' dead, Crabby, dead… dead…dead." He punctuated each word with a slap across Billy's face.

Nelly took a long suck on his cigarette, stepped forward, and blew smoke into Billy's face. He gave Billy a chilling, lopsided grin.
Billy didn't flinch. Nelly glared at Billy with the same interest as two boxers give each other at weigh-in.

Billy crossed his arms in front of his chest; his stare was clear and intense. Then, very slowly, a smile began to spread across his face; and this is why. A lilting voice was singing in his head: - *You're going to die, you're going to die, eee-eye-adio, you're going to die.*

Deano began breathing heavily through his nose but as he went to speak again, Billy piped up, "Now look here, Mister Dean, let me tell you the true order of events. It was a complete accident, your friend walked out in front of the mini-bus; I just didn't have time to brake. Now then, Mister Dean whilst you are here I would like to inform you that I hate you. I hate everything about you, you revolt me, and so does your ugly friend here who has obviously fallen from the top of an ugly tree and hit every ugly branch on the way down and now needs to go into an ugly clinic. Scum like you are the dregs of my England. So, if your dumb, goofy friend here and you, you freaky, ginger headed, brainless little shit would care to fuck off somewhere and indulge in some serious self-harming, it would be much appreciated." Billy smiled and flicked his eyebrows a number of times. He no longer felt harrowed or afraid and cackled mockingly.

Deano and his sidekick both stood stony faced and statuesque with their lips slightly parted. Deano's eyebrows disappeared under his baseball cap. They had never been spoken too like that in school before because the rules stated that it wasn't allowed to talk to them like that, only *they* could talk to people like that. It was a foreign language to them. Most of the teachers *thought* it but they had to stand there biting their tongues and just take it. Most kids demanded respect but never reciprocated it.

The pair of them wore the visage that one might expect to

see if presented with the complete works of Shakespeare written in Swedish.

Nelly fluttered his eyelashes and shook his head. "Yeah, well, but you're still a fuckin' dead man...ain't he Deano?"

"Yeah," Deano agreed, "I'm gonna see Co-co about this, you'll get the chop for talking to us like that."

Billy gave out a short sharp shriek and slapped a hand to his mouth. "So, you're going to tell the Headteacher are you? Don't you normally set fire to people who upset you?"

The brows of both boys creased in unison.

Again, a finger appeared in Billy's face. "I've told you, Crabby that weren't me, but you, you're gonna get another fuckin' visit..."

"Another visit? Oh, so it *was* you who threw a brick through my window and left me with this present?" Billy was pointing at the angry pink blotches across the side of his face and forehead.

"Ay? Look, man you are dead fuckin' meat, d'ya hear me? Dead." and he spelled it out just to drive the point home, "d - e - d, dead."

Billy grinned and hoisted a thumb. "Well I have to agree with you there, Mister Dean. I am a dead man, and the sooner the better." He guffawed loudly.

Deano's face collapsed; he was totally bewildered. "You're fuckin' nuts, man." He and Nelly began to back away, "Be seeing ya soon, Crabby," Deano said, but he sounded very unconvincing.

"Yeah, soon, man," Nelly echoed.

"Can't wait, look forward to it," Billy said and waved them off.

As they strolled away, Nelly, in an act of sheer bravado, turned and flicked his cigarette butt at Billy but it dropped short. He then formed his fist into the shape of a gun, closed one eye and let off an imaginary shot with a "ppeeeooowww!" Billy grabbed the 'bullet' out of the air, put it in his mouth, and pretended to chew it. Nelly frowned and twirled a finger next to his temple.

Billy waved again, blew them a kiss, and closed the door. He leant his back against it and grabbed some air, "Yeeesss! That felt soooo fucking good," he muttered to himself.

Then he squeezed his eyelids tight and doubled up as a stab of pain hit him; he clutched at his lower abdomen with both hands. *Oh bollocks, here we go again.* Billy slowly slid down the door, fumbling in his pockets for painkillers. The pain was so intense, he couldn't move. Desperate for a glass of water, but he couldn't get to the sink, so he chewed them and swallowed the bitter goo. There he stayed for long minutes, the pain persisting in agonising waves.

The teachers, who met in the staff room early each day for the morning brief, resented the negative publicity that the tragedy involving Thommo would undoubtedly bring on the school. On the other hand, the kids in the playground revelled in it; many had congregated around the school gates where the media were camped in the hope of seeing a glimpse of themselves on the evening news bulletins.

Billy kept himself away from everybody.

The Headteacher had arranged the press conference in the schools' lecture theatre. Given the choice he would have picked eating raw pigs' liver over holding this particular press conference what with the reputation that they carried. Nasty little people, he thought, shit stirring for a living, making up stories for a quick dollar. He had done this kind of a thing on a previous occasion but in a much better climate. A famous premier league footballer had visited the school a couple of years previously to open the new multi-function gymnasium and synthetic football pitch. Reporters and a TV crew had attended on that occasion and he had found being in the spotlight quite enjoyable. Things were different this time. Awkward. He couldn't stand the thought of facing all those flashing cameras and everyone shouting at the same time. He knew he couldn't avoid it though; a student from the school was dead. He could quite easily have asked the deputy head to handle it but that would be the cowards' way out. No, it was his duty, his job.

As the last reporter filed into the room, he put himself centre-stage and gestured for quiet. The room fell silent; dozens of pairs of eyes were fixed on him. He decided to make it brief. Firstly, pleading to the media present that Mister Crabtree, and indeed the school, be left in peace, he wanted as little disruption as possible what with the exams just starting. He explained in effect what they already knew – that the incident was a complete accident. Their presence, he felt was a distraction to the kids and the sooner they left the better. When he was finished a burst of questions rained down on him like over-excited, bellowing schoolchildren as they realised the briefing was over.

The Headteacher stood up. "Not now, ladies and gentlemen," he said, raising a palm to quieten them and then leaning forward with an expression heavy with gravitas he announced, "please, I ask only that you respect Mister Crabtree's and indeed the schools wish for privacy. I'm quite sure you would receive better information if you were to camp outside the police station that is dealing with this matter. I have nothing else to say, thank you and goodbye."

Silence rained for a few seconds then one reporter shouted, "Can we speak with the driver of the mini-bus? Is he in school today? Have you spoken to the boys' parents?"

This motivated the other reporters into action, who riddled the Headteacher with questions trying to squeeze out a few drops of information, but by now he was already off the stage and arrowing through them with his head bent low. Wearing a tight smile, he hurried off towards the safety of his office, bawling out the occasional, "No comment."

21

That same evening Billy was working late due to an activity taking place in the lecture theatre. He had locked himself away in his workroom all day, only popping into reception on odd occasions to peek at the CCTV screen where one particular security camera covered the front gate. He was relieved to see that the media had begun to thin out after lunch; they were probably already losing interest because the school was on lockdown and they were getting no information whatsoever.

The story would soon dry up when they had wrung every drop of drama out of it. It was probably sensational news now, but tomorrow they will hopefully move on to other scandals. Staying hidden away had given Billy the opportunity to scribble more notes into his diary and make final adjustments to his plans. He was continually crossing out certain items and making amendments, this needed to be perfect and work first time; there would be no room for errors.

There were very few people left in the school when Billy finally emerged. Cleaners were still dotted about and the odd teacher who preferred to stay behind and mark the kids work rather than take it home where they might encounter distractions.

Billy stood outside the Headteachers office with his master key poised. He took a furtive glance to left and right and then let himself in, locking the door behind him. He headed for the far side of the office where he tugged at the chain that was situated at the side of the window blinds until they were in the closed position, and then he flicked on the table lamp that was perched on the desk. The head was smiling at him from a photo frame. He was standing behind a handsome blond woman who was seated with a child perched on one knee. Billy assumed to be his wife. *She's fit, much too young, and attractive for Co-co. What the hell does she see in him?* On the other side of the desk a young man in cap and gown. Obviously, his grown up son by the look of the tight curly hair that protruded from under his mortar. There were other framed photos obviously taken several years apart, one of which was a much younger wife and infant.

Burying his fists into his hips, Billy's eyes roved. He spotted the coffee machine. *Why not?* He checked the water level and flicked it on.

Framed certificates and diplomas from prestigious universities took up one wall of the office. Two plaques for badminton victories. A bank of grey filing cabinets lined another wall. Billy scanned the labels on the front of each until he found the ones that he was looking for - pupil personal details. He felt there had to be a clue locked somewhere inside these cabinets that would give him a spark of inspiration. The first cabinet was marked with a hand written sticky label A-E. *Ah, that's where we'll find our Mister Dean.* He pulled out the top drawer and started rifling through the file holders where he found the one that he was looking for, Craig Bellamy Dean. Billy chortled. *Bellamy! Jesus his parents certainly had a sense of humour.* Billy sat himself down at the Heads desk and adjusted the table lamp so that it was shining directly down onto the folder. Unsurprisingly it was the thickest one in that

particular cabinet. No wonder, there was page after page of complaints from teachers and disgruntled people who had had the misfortune to cross his path. Billy pulled out a page from the front of the folder that was dated the same week that Deano had joined the school in year seven. It involved an incident in which one of the boys' toilets was flooded. The senior teacher who dealt with Deano at the time had remarked about his attitude even at this early stage in his school life and had written at the end -

Mister Dean, I feel, will be one to keep an eye on in the future. Billy shook his head slowly from side to side and smirked to himself.

After spending a good few minutes going through Deano's file, it was obvious to Billy that time after time Deano had fallen through societies net. His lifestyle was almost exclusively criminal. He lived outside of civilised society and anyone who had the misfortune to come across him was quite happy to turn their back on him. The notes contained a good amount of information. There was lots of suspicion there if you read between the lines, but Billy found nothing that might have helped him in his quest.

By now, the coffee machine was gurgling a happy tune, so Billy spooned a teaspoonful of sugar into a mug and poured the hot coffee over it. He opened the door to the mini desktop fridge, took out a carton of semi-skimmed, and sniffed its contents. The milk was just turning so this was to be Billy's first ever black coffee.

He replaced Deanos file back in the cabinet and fingered through the rest of the files until he pulled out the one concerning Neil Dunn. This one turned out to be almost as thick as Deanos. Billy took Nelly's file over to the desk and sat himself down. He took a loud slurp of his

drink and nodded his approval. *Not bad.* He thumbed through several pages, sucking in the odd breath or tut-tutting at the antics that this yob had been involved in. One particular handwritten sheet of A4 caught his attention. The date on it was about nine months old, and it was signed by Mrs. Dunn. Billy put down the file and read the paper with some interest.

The letter concerned a particular misdemeanour that he, Nelly, had been involved in with, surprise surprise, a certain Thomas Thomson and Craig Dean. Apparently, a certain teacher had upset the three of them because she had had the audacity to tell them to be silent while she was trying to teach her class. A little while later, they had decided to put a brick through her classroom window. Luckily, the classroom was empty apart from the teacher in question who was marking papers. The missile had missed her by a wide margin, but she had been showered with fragments of glass; the outcome could have been a lot worse. The school policy was that any pupil found vandalising the school would be dealt with accordingly, but also the parents would be sent an invoice and would be expected to pay for any repairs. Apparently, the school had invoiced the parents of the three youths in question, expecting each to foot a third of the bill. Billy ran his finger down the letter missing out certain paragraphs that were of no interest to him. Mrs. Dunn described the fact that she was a single parent...blah blah blah...couldn't afford it...blah blah blah...I can't control him, he worries me sick...blah blah blah...he's always running away and there were nights and weekends when he just doesn't bother coming home at all. ...*That's it! He's next.* Billy closed the file. *More likely than not Mrs. Dunn, who seems to be beyond caring, won't give a toss if he goes missing, it's unlikely she'll*

even bother to inform the school or the police about his absence for a while at least. That'll give me time to plan and then deal with our Mister Dean.

Right, next item on the agenda. He took out his wallet and placed his Visa card on the desk. He then swivelled to his right and turned on the Heads computer. The blue screen lit up the room, Billy hoped that it wasn't visible from the outside. He clicked on Internet Explorer and then entered the Amazon website. In the search box he typed in the gadget that he thought perhaps would come in handy on one of his escapades – and found several, but one caught his eye - £99.95p + free delivery in 3-4 days, or £12 p&p for next day delivery. *I cannot believe that you could buy one of these without a licence!* He entered his name and address then his credit card details. He thought it was well worth the extra so clicked the box for next day delivery. *Incredible.*

Billy steepled his fingers in front of his face, sat back in the Headteachers' chair, and began swivelling slowly from side to side. The corners of his mouth turned towards the ceiling and he cackled quietly to himself. He was really looking forward to pursuing this matter with utter commitment.

22

At the far end and to the right of the restaurant as you entered there was a small kidney shaped bar. To its left doors leading to ladies and gent's toilets. Spaced out along both sides of the walls are tables in double rows. Most are occupied. There is one family. The father is attempting to coax one of the two boys to finish his meal, pressing home loudly the amount that it has cost him. Couples in varying stages of their relationships. At one table, two girls facing two boys, late teens, very noisy, their table littered with the remnants of a drinking spree. Bottles of cheap lager, another thing Billy hated about the youth of today – swigging beer from a bottle, an affectation too far. *Or am I getting old?* Single couples who are jabbering and giggling away merrily to each other, the long term married couples, not talking, looking bored and blithely inspecting the décor. Tastefully done in creams, browns and the odd splash of burnt orange. Original framed oils with price tags on them from fifty pounds upwards scattered about the walls. Ubiquitous sitar music droned on in the background. Unluckily, the waiter had sat Janet and Billy down at a table behind the four teenagers. He apologised to them when they asked to sit somewhere else, but the other tables were booked. He handed them each a menu and left them to ponder.

"Well come on then, tell me about yesterday's accident!"

Janet was sitting opposite Billy in the Indian restaurant of her choosing. Billy's eyes were dark and spoke of lost sleep, whereas Janet's eyes were wide and sparkling and were restless to know exactly what had happened. Billy took a sip of water.

"Not much to tell really," Billy said, wanting to play the situation down, "the lad just stepped off the curb without looking, there was no way I could have avoided him."

"Mmm," she went, "he was in a bit of a mess from what I heard."

Billy sighed, albeit there was a grin on his face. "Look, Jan, it's taken me months and months to pluck up the courage to ask you out, I'm sure you don't want to hear all the gory details, not when we're just about to eat anyway."

Janet *did* want to know, but she took Billy's point and dropped it, and anyway the waiter had approached and asked them if they cared to order. Janet rattled off what she wanted and Billy, having never been in an Indian restaurant in his life, said that he would have the same. He knew that he would suffer greatly later after eating spicy food, but he was out with Jan, and that was all that mattered. *That she should spare a first glance, let alone a second on a man like me is incredible.* He couldn't believe he was actually sitting here with her; he was already obsessed. The thought of just being out with someone different instead of Tuesday night bingo with his Mother would perhaps help him unwind and forget his problems for a little while.

He had stared at her for perhaps a little too long, holding her eyes with his own.

"What?" she enquired, smiling.

Billy couldn't tell her that all he was thinking about was sex and for the first time in…he didn't know how long… he actually had a very welcome restless groin under the table. He smiled and shook his head slightly, "Nothing."

Billy studied her some more. She looked younger tonight, courtesy of an extra half-hour spent on her make up. Her glossy lips were parted slightly, her hair a mass of semi-waves. *What the hell had inspired her to take a shine to me?*

Before he had left the house, Billy had hoped that with the chemical assistance of caffeine capsules, and a multivitamin pill swilled down with a litre of Lucozade, he could remain awake and alert. He had also popped a number of painkillers and hoped that that little cocktail would see him through the evening. He could also pop to the loo a little later and top himself up with a few more painkillers if necessary. The main task, though, for this evening would be to try to ignore the nausea that was now constantly churning his stomach.

Billy was quite happy and relaxed. He had dropped his Mum off at her friend Ivy's house for the night and had told her that he would pick her up later. Although if things went the way he was hoping, he would be making a telephone call with some excuse for not collecting her and would pick her up early the next morning. She had stayed there before so Billy assumed there would be no problem. The house was empty and if Deano decided to pay a visit this evening, at least she would be out of harm's way.

A grating laugh rose up from one of the male youths at the table behind them. Raucous and loud, fading quickly into the more moderate giggling and banal banter of his companions. Billy turned his head and threw the perpetrator a glare that would cut a paving slab.

Janet sat with both arms on the table, palms face down. "I like it here, nice and friendly, I come here with Esther on occasions, and we have a good chin-wag."

Billy grinned; he wasn't here, he was back at Janet's house undressing her.

Janet frowned slightly and for the second time she found herself saying, "What?"

Billy reached across and laid a hand on top of her hand, his eyes never leaving hers; he was mesmerised. Could this be a whirlwind romance? No. He knew how this was going to end, but that time wasn't yet; it didn't matter what he said or did, she was going to end up getting hurt and he hated himself for that. Billy had let go of his dreams many years ago, but now he had this one last chance. *Enjoy it while it lasts, Billy.* "I'm sorry, you look incredible tonight and it's very distracting...Mrs. Westwood, you are an amazingly beautiful lady."

Janet coloured slightly, something she hadn't done since she was in her early teens. She suddenly found her fingernails of keen interest.

She cleared her throat. "Well, Billy Crabtree, aren't you a dark horse…"

He reached across, took her chin lightly in his hand, and tilted her head up to reach his eyes. "It would be very easy for a man to be enamoured with such an attractive woman like you, Jan." Billy's grin spread from ear to ear.

Janet fanned her face with a hand. "My God, Billy, have you been eating a dictionary? I don't even know what that means!" She shook her head gently from side to side. "Well, you sometimes go weeks without even saying a word and now…well, you *are* full of surprises, Billy. You are a true gentleman. You really are old-fashioned sometimes, but I like that."

Billy grinned, "There's been a side to me that's been dormant for too long, Jan, and now I want to live it up a little. I'm not a believer in love at first sight, Jan, but it struck me like a bolt of lightning the first time I set eyes…"

Billy's sentence was truncated as the waiter arrived with complementary poppadum's and assorted dips, and a good job too; he was beginning to get a little carried away. He rained himself in a little and they continued chatting, mainly about school life and the people that worked there.

The main course came shortly afterwards on small silver trays and the waiter laid it out neatly and methodically. "Enjoy," he said, and disappeared back into the kitchen through two ranch style swing-doors.

Janet billowed her cheeks. "My goodness we'll never eat all this. Mind you, you look like you could do with feeding up, Billy Crabtree. People are genuinely worried about you; you don't look at all well."

He smiled. "I'm OK, just getting over a dicky stomach that's all."

"Mmm, let's tuck in then, I'm starving, Billy I can hear my tummy growling quite loudly."

He did, and he savoured every mouthful. He scolded himself inwardly; this was something else that he had missed out on. Where had he been? He had a deep longing to get to know Janet in the shortest time possible.

Billy continually refilled his plate, which Janet loved. She had finished long before Billy and when he did finally collapse back in his chair puffing and panting, she arched an eyebrow.

"What?" Billy said.

"I take it you like Indian food then, Billy?"

Billy's cheeks were rosy, which they hadn't been for many months. He smiled broadly.

There was an annoying little tune being played out behind them and then one of the male youths began venting his displeasure into his mobile phone.

"Alright, mate…you what?…what do'ya mean, he ain't got the money?…you *are* fuckin' jokin'…you tell that bastard to pay up or I'll kill the cunt, do'ya hear me?…yeah…yeah…well, I don't give a shit where he gets it from, I want it tonight, yeah?…OK, later, man." There was the sound of the phone crashing into glasses or bottles and then, "Bastard!"

Billy sighed heavily through his nose and formed his lips into a tight slit.

Janet raised her eyebrows. "Sign of the times I suppose," she said.

Janet drank white wine, Billy sipped only water; the fact that he was driving being the excuse, but he knew any amount of alcohol would set off the darkness inside him. They stuck to superficial topics. As Janet got more and more tipsy, she began to realise that Billy Crabtree was indeed a very nice man. She found him to be talkative, knowledgeable, and interesting and she told him so. Likewise, she made him laugh and found that they had a lot in common. No one had ever sat down with him and talked like this before; she was very easy to talk to. She chatted engagingly and he loved the simple enjoyment of her company and found she was one of the rare people he had met over the years that radiated uncomplicated pleasure. He asked questions that were genuine and listened with interest to her answers.

Billy didn't want to whine on about his past mainly because he didn't have one. The fifty-eight years of his life could be summarised in less than a minute, so he began talking easily about very little. Titbits of conversation, inconsequential scraps, the films he liked, the few places he had been to and the places he would love to go to and the books he enjoyed reading. Quiet small talk about the area where he lived, art, history, food, although he knew very little on any of the subjects. He chatted as amiably and interestingly as he could, and she seemed pleasantly relaxed. It surprised him that the talk flowed quite easily; he was normally a yes or no man. She took her turn and Billy listened while she talked incessantly. Obviously, the alcohol had loosened her tongue, but it made her even more endearing to him.

Billy didn't want Janet to make her excuses and leave as other dates had done in the past. Or should that be date? Therefore, he thought he'd try a few jokes and tall stories. He light-heartedly told her of the time when he had been preparing himself to be the first man on the moon, but he had gone down with a bad cold and Neil Armstrong had to take over at the last minute. The time he was about to be signed by Manchester united but failed his medical because his penis dangled below the legs of his shorts. The fact that Carol Vorderman was one of his ex's and he had taught her everything she knew about maths. Janet exaggerated a roll of her eyes after each tale, but she smiled genuinely and laughed throughout.

"Have you met the new member of staff yet?" Billy asked, straight faced.

Janet frowned slightly. "No, I'm sure I'd know if we had taken on new blood, Billy."

There was a glint of amusement in Billy's eyes; he smirked. "Well apparently he's got no arms and legs and no torso...he wants to be known as 'The Head'."

Janet slapped the back of his hands. If she hadn't had so much wine she would probably have giggled at his poor attempt at humour, but instead broke out into riotous laughter. When she had composed herself she said, "You know, Billy, you look so much younger when your eyes are alight."

Billy reached over and caressed her face and she in return leaned in closer feeling a vehement sensation course through her. He took up her hand and stared into her trusting blue eyes feeling...what? *Intense, deep love that is what I'm feeling.* He felt good, comfortable and for a moment, all his troubles were over the hill and far away. He said, "You look incredible tonight, Jan."

One of the teenage girls' who was seated directly behind Billy, slid her chair back and it caught his chair quite sharply, he jumped slightly and tutted loudly. As she stood, she cracked the back of his head with her elbow. Although she apologised, she began laughing behind a clenched fist. Her three friends also found it most amusing and muffled giggles could be heard.

Billy sprang to his feet. "Yeah, very funny," he said, deadpan. "Try and be a bit more careful, huh?"

"Oooooowww," went one of the lads, the comment dripping with sarcasm.

The waiter returned shortly and cleared the table. Billy ordered another drink for Janet. He leant forward and placed both his hands on top of hers.

"I usually find it very difficult to approach women to ask them out," Billy said, "I suppose I've just got into the habit of closing myself off and staying in my own little comfort zone, I think the embarrassment if I got turned down would be unbearable."

"But you asked me out?"

"True, but things have changed, I've realised that life's too short."

"You're not wrong there, Billy."

Billy took a sip of water, "I was always very envious of Mike," he said, gazing directly into Janet's eyes. "When he used to come and pick you up from work I always thought to myself what a lucky man he was to be taking you home."

She lowered her eyes and then raised them again. "Mike

was a nice guy, buutt…"

"What?" A couple of shallow wrinkles appeared across his brow.

Janet's inhibitions were now lowered by a significant degree, her tongue a little looser. She raised her head to look at him, resting her eyes on his, a warm, relaxed gaze. "Wwweeelll, he was always very predictable, you know? He attended his union meetings on Thursday. We would go to the same pub and sit in the same seats on Saturday. We took our holidays in the same caravan park every year, he would roll on top of me every Sunday morning then roll off…" she slapped a hand to her mouth. "Oh, God what am I saying, sorry, Billy it must be the wine."

"No probs," Billy said, guffawing loudly.

"But, he was a very brave man. He was healthy and fit, but his cancer had been relentless, he fought and fought and fought and in the end, it turned him into boney scraps. It had taken him over two years to die, Billy." She gazed into a spot just above Billy's head.

That's exactly what's NOT gonna happen to me.

A few grains of rice landed on their table and then a few more, some of which hit Billy's left ear and dropped onto his shoulder. He heard one of the girls behind whisper, 'Stop it,' and then there was muffled laughter. Billy was struggling to quell the rising tide of anger swelling in his stomach. He half stood but Janet wrapped his hands with her own.

"Leave it, Billy," Janet said, "it's just not worth it." She smiled warmly, and a cluster of faint wrinkles appeared at the corners of her eyes.

Billy dug his nails into his palms, sighed heavily, then gave a thin smile and sat down. The anger didn't leave him; it was simmering, lying just beneath the surface. "Go on, Jan what were you saying?"

"Don't get me wrong, he was a good man, Billy and I do miss the company."

"Well, you've got company tonight. I've really enjoyed

being with you, Jan. I just can't believe that you said yes when I asked you out.

I just love how down to earth you are, nothing pretentious. You're so pretty, so full of life, so much personality, and such an infectious laugh..."

Janet fluttered her eyelashes, "Oh you're so right, Billy..."

He laughed. "I think we may have to take out a window to get your head out of the restaurant the way you're carrying on."

She picked up a desert spoon and began turning it between the thumb and forefinger of each hand. "Look, Billy this may sound a bit old hat but I'm the type of person who isn't bothered that much about how a person looks. I like the quality of your chat, your humour, your politeness, and manners. These things seem to be out of fashion nowadays."

This feels so very comfortable, as if we have been doing this for years.

The time slipped by easily as they chatted. It was as if their table was the only table that was occupied. He found something about her voice intoxicating; he could listen to her all night and never tire of hearing it, although as she was talking he wasn't taking everything in because he couldn't stop thinking about sex. This wasn't surprising really after all his years of unplanned and unwanted celibacy. She was incredible, and he was obsessed, all he could think about was getting back to her house and...

A coaster flew past Billy's right cheek and landed on the floor; he chewed his bottom lip. Seconds later a small piece of naan bread skimmed across the top of his head, catching Janet's right shoulder and dropping into her lap. This time there was a roar of alcohol-fuelled laughter from behind.

Billy's scalp prickled, and he could actually feel the adrenaline and fury starting to trickle into his bloodstream; he swallowed against the unease that was now churning inside his stomach. He calmly patted the corners of his mouth with his napkin, clapped his hands on his knees, and stood sharply. Once again, Janet went to grab his hands but this time he snatched them away. In one deft movement that belied his years and health, Billy was spinning on his feet, fury sweeping through him in a wave that gave him strength he'd never experienced before. Clamping the nearer of the youths by the shoulder with one hand and grabbing a handful of his shirt collar in the other. He yanked him to his feet and his chair skidded out from underneath him. A couple of inches shorter than Billy, stockier, glazed eyes, close cropped blond hair and a series of overlapping silver ear studs. The two girls stayed put, his friend made to stand but was shoved back into his seat by a couple of the waiters who had approached having watched the drama unfold. Janet emitted a mousy shriek and jumped to her feet, slapping her open palms to her cheeks. All eyes were on Billy.

"Listen, son," Billy spat into the youths' face, "we have come out tonight for a quiet meal, not to be bombarded with scraps of food. There is not one person in here apart from your three ignorant friends who want to listen to your drivel and filth all night. Either sit down and shut the fuck-up or get out."

The youth was either red faced due to embarrassment or the fact that Billy had clamped his hand so tight around his shirt that his windpipe was restricted. Spit dribbled from one side of his mouth. When Billy released him, he staggered back and collapsed into the chair that one of the girls had retrieved and slid underneath him.

The youth rubbed his throat. "Wanker," he whimpered, "it was just a joke, man."

The waiters, who had now been joined by two more of their work colleagues, insisted that they pay their bill and leave. Billy remained standing, facing them; fists dug into his sides, not wanting to turn his back on them. The two males – mumbling obscenities - threw some cash onto the table. Billy glared at them unblinkingly as they made to leave. When the party reached the door, Billy closed one eye and shot the mouthy one through the temple with a hand that he'd formed into a gun. Billy then blew away imaginary smoke from his 'smouldering' fingers.   As the youth opened the door, his top lip curled back into a sneer and he made a hand gesture, which resembled throwing dice.

Billy was upset, *very* upset. *With a little more time, I could have added him to my list.* He sat down heavily and, inflating his cheeks, took a moment or two to collect his mental footing.

Janet's eyebrows were raised, and she was grinning. "Well, hasn't *someone* been watching 'Death Wish', proper little Charles Bronson aren't we?"

Billy smirked and held a fist out to Janet, his knuckles facing her. Janet winked, touching her fist to his.

Billy adjusted his shirt collar and jacket. "Mmm, well, I hate 'em, Jan, kids today." He leant forward. "Who the hell do they think they are, ay? They just can't go out and enjoy themselves without making someone's life a misery." He sighed heavily.

"You should have ignored them…"

"No no no, never," Billy fumed, prodding the table with a digit. "We have got to stand up for ourselves. Nine times out of ten they turn out to be cowards as you've just witnessed."

"Mmm, but if that lad was the tenth one, you could have been in serious trouble, Billy."

Billy grinned. "It's over with; let's get back to us, shall we?"

The waiter approached them and set down two glasses of white wine. "On the house. I'm so sorry for that little…"

Billy offered the waiter his palm. "Not your fault, mate sign of the times…and thanks for the drinks."

Janet fumbled in her bag and held out her mobile phone. "Would you mind taking our picture?"

"Of course."

Billy scraped his chair round until he was next to Janet and they placed their heads together.

"Say chutney!" the waiter joked.

For another half an hour or so they continued to swap small parcels of their lives. Just mundane things, like the recent weather and colleagues at work who they liked or disliked. Billy told of his laziness at school and then later at college, the couple or so years that he was totally absorbed with his train spotting,

Janet rolling her eyes and feigning an exaggerated yawn into the back of her hand. Janet's obsession with gymnastics growing up in Herefordshire, her first meeting with Mike. Nothing difficult, no ghosts in the cupboard.

Billy's cupboard was so full of ghosts that he needed fitted wardrobes, but he obviously wasn't going to tell Jan about his plans.

Janet slew back the last of her wine and finished off Billy's also. A daft smile spread across her face; Billy noticed that her eyes seemed to be working independently. She was slurring her words now and was leaning towards him far enough for him to be concerned that she may well fall into the table.

Billy raised one eyebrow. "I think we need to get you home, Mrs. Westwood."

During the journey back to Janet's house, they gabbled on about this that and the other, mostly inconsequential nattering. Billy hung on to every word she spoke; he drove on and listened intently, he loved just listening to her. Billy turned into Janet's quiet street, Victorian houses with neat front gardens. When he pulled up outside her house, he killed the headlights and turned off the engine. He slew round to face her.

Janet's head flopped to the one side and she wrinkled her nose.

"Thank you, Billy Crabtree," she drawled, "I've had a really great night…I know you've probably heard the cliché a hundred times on the tele or in movies, but would you like to come in for a coffee?"

Billy took her hand and he kissed the back of it gently. "No thanks," he said with a broad smile.

23

A sad frown lightly puckered Janet's forehead. She looked at Billy with a half-amused, half-shocked expression on her face. Was he joking or being serious? It wasn't the response that she had expected. Her mouth dropped open, but no words came out.

"No, I would not like to come in for a coffee," Billy repeated, and he snaked an arm around her neck pulling her closer. He kissed her gently on the cheek and took in an inebriating flowery perfume. Her proximity made his blood run heated through his system. "But I *would* like to come in and make love to you, Jan."

Janet's jaw drooped a little more and her eyebrows rose. If she had been sober Billy would probably have received a hefty slap across the face, but both her eyes and mouth slowly turned into tight slits. "Well, Billy Crabtree, you're certainly full of surprises tonight." She smiled, "Coffee," she insisted, and let herself out of the car before Billy had the chance to skirt the vehicle and open the door for her.

As they approached the house, the sensor on the security light picked them up and it burst into life, bathing them in a yellow glow; Billy noticed the debris of dead insects through the globes frosted glass. A few moths circled, the distorted shadows of their wings swooped across the white UPVC front door. Whilst Janet fumbled in her bag for the door key, Billy took in a long slow breath to ease his nerves. He rolled his head around a couple of times to loosen the knots and he gazed skyward. The night brought clouds and no stars.

Janet led them into a long hall and then turned

immediately left into the lounge. She flicked on the light.

"Just sit yourself down Bil…"

Janet's words were cut short because Billy had spun her round by the shoulder and he was kissing her, drinking her in. Gently at first, then hard, as though she might slip away from him, but she did not fight, she kissed him right back. Her handbag dropped to the floor.

Janet drew away and they held each other's eyes. She raised an eyebrow.

"What's wrong?" Billy whispered.

She smiled and prodded the end of his nose with a finger, "I *said* coffee."

"Later."

He kissed her again, this time slowly backing her up against the lounge door. Billy was awash with all the sensations that he had read about in his Mothers' Mills and Boon novels: sea crashing in and out, fireworks bursting in his head, bands playing. He brushed the underside of her breast and followed the curve up. Janet caught her breath as he encircled them and started kneading gently. They grabbed at each other in some sort of emotional desperation. He undid a couple of the buttons of her blouse and slid the fabric over her shoulder, cupping her, squeezing gently, fingertips tracing her. She quivered as he unbuttoned her bra and explored the rigid nipples, his fingers skilfully stimulating her. She unbuttoned his shirt, her heart felt like a sledgehammer in her chest as hot blood spiked through her.

Janet experienced a moment of panic. What did she think she was doing? She inhaled sharply and pulled away again. "Billy, Billy," she gasped, "we're acting like teenagers, this is too quick, too soon…"

He smiled broadly. "No, it's not," he whispered, and then he pulled her toward him, her breasts pushing against his chest. They kissed hard, a kiss so full of need that they were lost in it for a long time, fuelled by loneliness and lust, making up for the long desperation of times spent isolated in their own small environments. It wasn't gentle, it was about wanting, craving. For Billy especially he had many years of dammed up passion to unleash and any negative thoughts that still lingered were lost in the sensations that flooded him - and Janet was *not* complaining.

Billy put heavy pressure on her with his thigh against her groin. She writhed against it, her hips moving at a slow rhythm, her breath coming in gasps, her body moving involuntarily. She grabbed his head and forced it lower. He kissed her nipple, licked it, took it in his mouth, and sucked it, she whimpered. He covered her face with kisses his penis rigid against her, and then suddenly it wasn't his penis against her groin it was his hand, she grabbed his wrist. Billy expected his arm to be wrenched away, but instead she pressed it to her. His thumbs were inside the knickers, they were down at her ankles, and then his fingers were inside her. When she came, it was violent, and she squeezed Billy's hand tight to keep the fingers inside her, straining for more. She fumbled at his trousers, but Billy was impatient and did the job for her, she touched him, it was hard and hot and she wanted it inside her. This was all too much, she twisted and arched and cried out. He took a buttock in each hand and lifted her as if she was stuffed with feathers and he was inside her. Thrusting her repeatedly against the door, his rhythm quickly increasing until he was slamming into her. He was forcing himself to think of less erotic things – the stalling tactics that he had read about to try and delay an early release. His mind fixed improbably on Alastair Stewart reading a news item about the spiralling cost of crude oil in the Middle East, but he was snapped back as once more she fell over the edge, spiralling into a delicious orgasm. Billy thought, *oh! Sod it*, and his desire broke quickly, too quickly in a flood of release, there were waves of colours and loud rushes of blood through his ears – he slowly lowered her to the floor, panting, and kissing her gently. Her eyes fluttered open; it took a few seconds to focus and she rested the back of her head against the door and sighed.

Billy's breathing was ragged; he took a step backward.

"Was that a sigh of contentment or disappointment?" He wheezed, backhanding speckles of sweat from his upper lip.

She nudged him gently and smiled, "What do you think? Oh, Billy I've never felt anything so intense, I feel so…ravished."

"You make it sound dirty," Billy said.

"Oh, it was, it was, but so fantastic." Janet's cheeks were rosy and hot; she poked him in the chest with a finger. "You, Billy Crabtree are *so* on my naughty step."

"So, that's sex is it?" Billy grinned, "It's much better with two people."

Her brow wrinkled slightly. "What do you mean? You're not trying to tell me that was you're first time, Billy?"

He formed his lips into a tight slit and raised his eyebrows. He nodded gently. "Mmm!"

Tears appeared at the corner of her eyes, "Oh, Billy, you poor…"

"No, don't." he wiped the tears away with his thumb. "It was well worth waiting for and I just can't wait for my second time. Coffee?"

She smiled warmly, "Mmm, that sounds good, or perhaps something a little stronger while we recover, huh?"

Billy nodded enthusiastically.

She smiled, "I'll see what's in the fridge."

After they had dressed, Janet returned with a drink each. She threw open the patio doors and they moved out into the garden. A two-seater wooden bench whose varnish was peeling sat on a small slabbed patio. The evening was dark velvet. Janet savoured her white wine, Billy nursed a beer.

Janet breathed deeply, "Oh that air feels so good, I feel as sober as a judge now. It makes a pleasant change to sit out here with company, I normally come out here with a book until the light fades, and sometimes feel I'm the only one around for miles. I miss having a special *someone* to come home to. I really miss being wanted, Billy." She sighed, "I sometimes sit here for hours just listening to the night."

Listening to the night? Billy cocked his head. There was

remote ambient sound: somewhere a high-strung dog was yapping; a steady thump thump from a rock concert that was taking place in the towns football stadium; a couple of cats that were falling out somewhere; starlings fighting and squawking to get the best perch in an immaculately clipped row of Leylandii.

Billy said, "I've never actually done this before, it's amazing what you can hear...the neighbours' tele's a bit loud."

"Yeah, the walls are paper thin. Sometimes when I lie in bed I can hear sounds that remind me just how long it's been since I've had...well, you know." The light from the living room illuminated Billy's face.

"Billy Crabtree, I do believe you're blushing".

Billy didn't say anything; instead, he studied the slabs.

She placed a hand on top of his, "I like that in a man, Billy. I was just thinking, I'm really glad you're here although we don't really know much about each other yet."

"I think I know you well enough, Jan."

"Do you?"

"Yes. You're intelligent, you're kind, a great sense of humour and beautiful. I know little about your past, but I don't think that's important. I never knew you then all that matters is the person I've come to know."

Janet drew her arms across her chest, which offered little protection against the chilly night air. Although the days had been quite warm, the nights had been pretty cool. Billy thought that if he had been wearing a jacket he would have removed it and placed it around her shoulders, just like he had seen Clark Gable do in a film once. Instead, he suggested that they move back inside.

Billy said, "I've never thought of doing anything like this, Jan, I seemed to have missed out on so much."

"Well, we'll just have to do something about that won't we?"

As Janet closed the patio doors behind them, Billy gently lifted her chin with a finger and kissed her. "You know, Jan, I must have done something right to deserve this...I think I'm

ANTHONY ASPREY

going to love you for the rest of my life."

24

They hadn't made *love* in the living room; they had got what they needed from each other. *Now,* in the bedroom, they were making love. Throughout the night and into the early hours their lovemaking became insatiable. He craved it, couldn't get his mind off it. An unquenchable, frantic desire for her. He was alert to the signals she gave. For her size she was surprisingly strong, but gentle. Passionate, but not aggressive. Billy also was tender and hungry at the moments she desired. Janet thought that their lovemaking should have been set to music. In between, they had lain in each other's arms chatting. Their conversation had ping-ponged between laughter and almost tears as their feelings poured out. As for Janet, she had never, in all her life, been with a man so attentive, passionate and caring.

Billy rested his head against her shoulder and tucked his legs against hers. Sliding his hand up her hip, he found her hand on her stomach, which he covered with his hand. He buried his nose in the nape of her neck and luxuriated in her hair; he couldn't be any closer to her if he tried. For the moment, he felt no worries whatsoever. Far away from it all. He felt comfortable and warm in this bed, even serene and tranquil in these unfamiliar of surroundings. For the first time ever, his life had meaning. He was needed. This is what it feels like to really love someone. He felt like he had a purpose. *I've really enjoyed being fussed over by this beautiful woman; it is a fantastic sensation.* He listened to her shallow breath next to him, the comforting sound that he had longed for for so many years, and the sound that he had resigned himself to never hearing.

Billy thought, *I am dating. Me. Billy Crabtree.* He could not believe it. *Janet has talked my head off about books, films, TV programs...all sorts and, although I've loved every second, I ain't got a clue about any of it. Where have I been?* His smiled in the darkness. For so many years, all he had had were fantasies and daydreams; now, unbelievably, he was lying next to the real thing. His eyelids were drooping now, the room going in and out of focus until he had finally succumbed to a rare deep slumber.

It was to be short lived.

Billy was woken sharply from his unconscious state by a muffled moaning. Still with his eyes tightly closed, he patted the mattress next to him only to find that Janet was not there. As he raised his head off the pillow, Billy blinked rapidly for a few seconds to re-orientate himself. He needed to shield his eyes with his hand as a bright light hit him in the eyes. *A torch?* He pressed the heels of his hands into his eyes and then shook his head to bring himself round. As his sight adjusted, his eyes widened, and his lower jaw dropped slightly. There was a racing of the pulse; he was confused and frightened and a cold dread seeped into his body as sleep transformed itself to abrupt, panicky wakefulness. At the foot of the bed sat Janet in a high-backed chair, which she was strapped to with green and yellow striped electrical tape; a short length of the same tape was across her mouth and behind the tape, she seemed to be screaming in silent agony. Her eyes expressed confusion, terror, and shock. Although her matted hair had fallen forward, slightly covering her face, Billy could see that the right side of her head was swollen and discoloured. Her face and parts of her body were covered in wounds – Janet was barely recognisable. Her head hung to the one side and there were bloodstains on her knees and shoulders. Standing behind her left shoulder was Nelly. Next to him, immediately behind Janet was Deano, his glare was enough to put ice in your veins and terror in your heart; he had a kitchen knife pressed against Janet's neck. Droplets of blood were forming at her throat. Billy pushed back a surge of bile as he swung his legs out of bed but as he stood, his legs felt leaden; his breathing, till now perceptible only in a slight flaring of the nostrils, became harsh and ragged. He tried to put one foot forward but he was unable to move his legs, they would not react as if he were being held back by hidden restraints. Billy couldn't snap out of it, it felt as though he was moving with the slow, underwater motions of a dream. He held out his hands in front of him and called Janet's name repeatedly. Finally he stumbled forward, but as he approached they seemed to be getting further away, he pumped his arms to try to accelerate, but he was held back by some unseen force. Now they seemed to be moving even further away as if they were on castors. The tape came loose from one corner of Janet's mouth and it dangled from her cheek. She was mouthing the words 'Billy help me, Billy help me,' but her voice seemed deep, slow, and far away. He was getting no nearer and he couldn't understand why. The more he tried the further away they seemed to get. Nelly and Deano wore manic grins; they fidgeted and seemed exited and overactive, their pupils were large and black as if they were on some illegal high. In a long drawn out booming voice, Deano said, 'This is what happens when fuckers like you get in our way, Crabby...' he grabbed Janet's hair and yanked back her head. He slid the blade slowly sideways across Janet's throat like a violin bow and the incision widened like a toothless grin, a wave of blood arcing through the air. Deano smiled wickedly and as Janet's blood spattered across his face...

Billy screamed the sound of it yanking him out of his nightmare. He jerked up in bed, dropping his head into his hands. Janet flicked on the bedside lamp; she held her splayed fingers across her chest and was panting heavily.

"Billy, Billy what on earth is the matter?" she gasped, rubbing her eyes with the palms of her hands.

Billy untangled himself from the sweat-soaked sheets; he mopped his brow with the back of his hand. "They were there," he said pointing at the foot of the bed. "Those bastards were there as plain as..."

Janet snaked an arm across his shoulder and gently coaxed his head onto her chest with her other hand. She cradled him in her arms. "It's just a bad dream, Billy, there's no one there, come on settle yourself down again, everything's OK."

Janet switched off the bedside lamp and they lay there in the dark. Billy's chest was rising and falling in short pants, Janet slowly stroking Billy's forehead, whispering reassurances. After a while, the strokes became slower and softer until finally her hand was motionless; Billy guessed that she had dropped off again.

Billy couldn't settle. He slept fitfully, his sleep disturbed by vivid recurring nightmares in which he was forced to watch the knife sliding across Janet's throat. When awake, he was thinking about the gang and the threats that they had made. He was as certain as he could be now that his nightmare would soon turn into reality – unless he reacted first.

Although his Mother was not at home, he thought that he probably wouldn't settle until he went back just to make sure that everything was OK. He was concerned about Sophie and if anything she was probably platting her legs, desperate to relieve herself.

Now, in the early hours, Billy found himself dressed and standing over Janet. He could have stayed there for hours just looking at her peaceful form. He so desperately wanted this woman. He felt more in love than he had ever dared to imagine, after so long in the wilderness. Kissing Janet lightly on the forehead, he felt himself start to stiffen. Her cheeks were pink and there appeared to be the slightest of smiles on her lips. He decided not to wake her and tell her his intentions, so he left her undisturbed in bed.

25

Billy drove home with both front windows cracked slightly open, letting the fresh air buffer his face. He wondered where all his energy had come from. No doubt, he would suffer for it later. Fatigue now swamped him, so he flicked on the radio. He continuously pressed the search button until he found a station that pleased him – Smooth FM 'Why do we sail on this ship of fools' a track from the eighties by Erasure was playing. He turned the volume up and whistled along to the tune. His left hand gripped the steering wheel; his right arm rested on the window ledge. Billy mused that if someone ever devised a machine for disqualifying someone for driving with fatigue, then his levels now would serve him a twelve-month ban.

There had been light drizzle; the tarmac glistened slickly in the splash of the car headlights. Despite the drizzle, the air now seemed surprisingly milder than earlier and there was a delicate aroma of newly mown grass. He stopped at some traffic lights and shot forward with a slight squeal of the tyres when they turned to green; he didn't care, he had always been a careful driver but now? What the hell.

Billy was suddenly distracted by the *blam-pop-blam-pop-pop* of a show-off Vauxhall Corsa exhaust, which had roared up behind him with its main beam on. It kept accelerating until it was virtually kissing his bumper; Billy tut-tutted; *it probably has the same engine as a hairdryer*. He adjusted the rear-view mirror to avoid the dazzle. The other driver sounded his horn and then overtook him at great speed; there was the low throb of over cranked in-car bass woofers. The driver bawled something at

Billy, but he couldn't tell what. He heard a couple of fucks and something about 'old bastards being on the road'. The young driver stuck two fingers up at Billy and sped off. In about fifty metres his brake lights came on, there was a loud shrieking of tyres and, without indicating, he turned left. *What the fuck was all that about?* Billy ground his teeth together. *Oh, if only I had more time, so many more morons could disappear.* He felt purged. All his negative energy and anger had now been shaped and tunnelled into what he thought was a positive force.

A little further on and Billy spotted several male youths standing at a bus shelter. The shelter was surrounded by broken glass and one of the gang was kicking out at the last pane that remained in one piece; his mates were cheering him on. In the gutter just in front of the gang was a large pool of rainwater – a grin began to spread across Billy's face. He accelerated and at the last second, he swerved towards the footpath and steered his car through the flooded gutter. The scene through Billy's rear-view mirror was an absolute joy. The soaking wet gang were bowling along the footpath screaming obscenities. *Oh! What a time to be without a camera.* Tears of laughter snaked down Billy's cheeks.

There was still a glow deep inside him; the taste of Janet lingered on his lips. *Well, that was an absolutely fantastic night.* He shook his head slowly. *Why the hell hadn't I done that years ago? Look what I've been missing; I've certainly got some catching up to do and in such a short space of time too.* He felt in a relaxed and happy mood and any nervous tension had drained out of his body. From somewhere he had found the energy and sparkle of a man who had left his wife for a much younger woman.

His thoughts turned to Thommo; he blinked away an image of the tattered flesh that had lain in the schools' service road. Billy had been focused on his goal but now he was vacillating between two competing sets of horribly raw, mixed emotions and his conscious was now rebelling against what had happened. Faint lines of doubt appeared across his forehead. He considered his madness, his folly and began to feel a steady, tight sickness at the knowledge that he had ended a life. His thoughts were so revolting. He had killed someone, had he been programmed from birth to eventually turn out to be a killer? On the other hand, did certain circumstances conspire to make a killer of him? Should he continue with his 'Crusade?' *Do and die. Don't and die. Great options.* The more he thought about it, the more ridiculous, irrational and perverse it became. Thommo was dead. Dead. Would he have eventually changed his ways? Would he have gone on to be a doctor perhaps, or a solicitor? He thought about his parents, his family, what would they be thinking? Huddling together on their settee sharing a box of paper tissues as they flipped through a photograph album. Thommo dressed as Spiderman at Christmas perhaps, holiday snaps building sandcastles. Was it a waste of that boy dying before having lived a full life? Billy felt it like a lead weight in an already pained stomach. Thommo would never feel that exhilaration, never feel the love for someone that Billy was experiencing right now, never be a father, never be a husband, never again feel the sun on his face, or…

Never again burn someone alive.

Billy shook his head trying to bring order to the turmoil in his mind; he was still too angry, the wounds inside still raw. He reached down to his left where he kept endless supplies of *Rennies* in the coin holder. The stress was making acid, which didn't at all help his situation.

Thinking about it would do no good. His determination for revenge countered his present thoughts and so he pressed on. *No, I'm right. He killed someone, he had it coming, I've performed a service by ridding the world of him. He's dead and can't harm any more people. His friends are still breathing, and they CAN harm people, it's black and white, and anyway, it was pointless thinking about it; I can't go back and change anything, so why worry about it now?* No, this distracting thought was not going to be enough to interfere with his mission; he could not allow what had happened to clog his mind and cloud his resolve. He had work to do.

Any lingering doubts about his actions would be dispelled

in about two minute's time.

Billy flicked the indicator arm and entered the road on which he lived. On the corner was a 'Theme' pub; live bands on Friday and Saturday night with the occasional mass brawl and a steady supply of illegal drugs. At lunchtime, though, it was a totally different venue. Full of pensioners making the most of the 'Two meals for the price of one' offer.

The car climbed the steep hill, semi-detached properties on either side with off-road parking and neat gardens. The car bore right at the sharp bend at the top. There was a commotion; two fire engines and three police cars, which were parked haphazardly, blocked the street. Their spinning domes flung out red and blue beams of light, which splashed against walls and houses. A small crowd of residents most of them huddled under umbrellas, still wearing pyjamas, and nighties, which were hidden underneath coats. They were bustling with frenzied activity as they giraffed their necks for a better view.

The attentive audience was focused on the smoke pouring from the windows of Billy's house.

Billy froze momentarily and unintentionally mounted the curb, barely keeping the back end of the car from slamming into an electricity sub-station. After he'd managed to wrestle his car back under control, and still on the pavement, he came to an abrupt stop as the car ploughed into his next-door neighbours' privet hedge. His chest tightened, and he was able to draw breath only with effort. When he lifted his hands from the steering wheel, his fingers quivered like those of an old man. He leapt from the car leaving the door open. Uniformed officers were mingling with the crowd seeking any eyewitnesses. Billy strode purposefully toward the house. A forensic investigation van was parked half on the pavement and half on the road. The area was festooned with blue and white POLICE LINE DO NOT CROSS cordon tape, which fluttered in the breeze. It stretched from a small tree in his neighbour's garden to the handle of a police patrol car. Then more tape stretched from another patrol car to a fence post in the neighbour's garden on the other side of his house. Billy didn't realise the significance of the tape. The area in between the two police cars was being used by the Fire fighters who were dashing back and forth in a well-rehearsed manner.

Billy elbowed his way through the small throng of curious night-gown-clad residents who were huddled together in murmuring groups. They fired questions at Billy, but he obviously knew nothing and so ignored them, apart from one moron who was filming the tragedy on his phone. Billy grabbed the phone and smashed it on the floor. The phones owner was none too pleased, but Billy kept on moving forward. The crowd got back to spreading rumours amongst themselves when their enquiries went unanswered. With head bowed, Billy attempted to duck under the tape but a PCSO, posted to control comings and goings, shoved an open palm into Billy's chest.

"Whoa, hold on now, sir you can't go any further, please stay behind the tape," the copper said.

Billy placed both hands on his head. "This is my house," he blurted, "what the fucks going on…"

The PCSO relaxed his restraining hand. "I'm sorry, sir but you obviously can't go in there…I'll get my gaffer to have a word with you, just hang on there a moment if you will." He twirled and disappeared into the melee.

As Billy paced the pavement in an agitated manner, he spotted a group of about ten youths that had gathered on a grass verge about twenty metres away on the other side of the tape. They were generally messing about, laughing, and pushing each other playfully. Some were swigging cheap cider from 2 litre plastic bottles. Most had hoods pulled up over their heads, some wore baseball caps. Billy recognised one of the gang as Nelly. He had a gut feeling that they knew something about what had gone on here. He elbowed his way through the crowd almost bowling a couple over, ducked under the tape and headed directly for them, ducking under the tape again on the far side. The nearer of the gang members had his back towards Billy, Billy tapped him angrily on the shoulder and Deano turned round. The look on his face told Billy that he was the last person that he'd expected to see.

"Cr...Crabby, what the...how the hell..."

"How the hell did I escape from the house?" Billy bit into the inside of his lower lip. "Is that what you were going to say?" Deano didn't answer. Billy spat, "You've done this you bastard, you're the one who's set fire to my house!"

Deano quickly composed himself, sneering on one side of his mouth; he took a nonchalant swig of cider, through the empty bottle over his shoulder and then ran a sleeve across his mouth. "Nah, not me crabby." He gestured with a thumb towards the cackling gang of conspirators behind him. "I've got a dozen witnesses here, man who'll swear I was somewhere miles away..."

Deano's sentence was truncated because Billy had taken a step forward and had grabbed Deano's jacket in his left hand just below his chin. He balled his right hand in readiness for a punch. There was clear, focused hatred in his eyes.

Deano's face collapsed into a snarl; he prodded a finger into Billy's face. "Look here, Crabby," he said through gritted teeth, "if these fuckin' coppers weren't here I'd..."

Deano stopped mid-sentence because he had been struck dumb with astonishment. And this is why. Billy was resting the tip of his nose on the end of Deano's finger. "You should have gone home and washed your hands first, Deano, you stink of petrol."

Billy released his grasp of Deano's jacket and threw a punch. Deano's head shot back instinctively and the punch landed on his breastbone. The gang now surged forward, Billy was surrounded by them, pushing, jostling and shoving him between themselves, but the PCSO's who were present had already spotted the potential trouble brewing and rapidly placed themselves between Billy and the gang. They interlinked hands and began slowly moving forward, coaxing the argumentative gang down the road to disperse them. One of the coppers asked Billy if he needed to make a complaint. Billy thanked him and declined saying he would deal with it himself.

Deano was being pushed backwards with the aid of a PCSO's palm, which was strategically placed in the middle of his chest. Deano knocked away the obtrusive hand with an arm. "Don't fuckin' touch me, pig," Billy heard him cry, "I'll fuckin' have you for Police brutality!" Then to Billy and out of earshot of the police: "Fuck you, Crabby, you're gonna die very slowly, man, very...very slowly."

Deano threw Billy a wicked sneer and then laughed a low heartless sound that chilled the bones; he was livid. Veins standing out at his temples, his face florid with such intense rage that Billy fought against the temptation to look away. Deano then drew a finger across his Adams apple in a throat slitting gesture. Nelly thought the whole episode hilarious and as he retreated backwards, he sketched a cross in the air.

Mrs. Caine, Billy's next-door neighbour, and who was now short of half a privet hedge, approached Billy and tugged at his sleeve. She was probably somewhere in her late seventies and was the road's resident curtain-twitcher. She was the type of neighbour every street has, interested to the point of nosiness. Although, in this case a distinct asset. Mrs. Caine was adorned in pink slippers and a pink nightgown, her hair was a mass of small curlers, which were held in place with a thin scarf tied under her chin in a bow. As Billy turned, still quivering with rage, she took him gently by the elbow to one side.

"Come on, calm yerself, Billy. I'm so sorry about what's happened, Billy," Mrs. Caine said softly, "it's a terrible to-do. You're lucky my son Tom got up to go to the loo, smelled smoke he did, came outside and saw the smoke billowing from an open window and then phoned 999. It was Tom who broke down your door, threw a carpet on the flames he did and then chucked water on the fire with a saucepan until the fire engine arrived. He suffered a couple of burns to his hands and he was coughing his lungs up he was, they took him away in an ambulance, just after your Mum. Well, like I say, lucky really."

Billy ran both palms down his face. "Yeah thanks, Vera,

could have been a lot worse I s'pose." He sat on the low wall, which surrounded his neighbours house and Vera joined him. He perched his elbows on his knees and stared at the pavement for a while. His brain was finding it difficult to process what was happening. This had all come unexpectedly, the events happening so quickly, his mind was awhirl. Ruffling his hair with his fingers, he inflated his cheeks…and then it sunk in what Vera had just said.

Billy leapt to his feet. "Wh…what do you mean, Just after Mum?"

Vera's face crumpled. "Ooohh, you don't know?" she placed a friendly hand on his arm. "Haven't the police told you, Billy? I'm sorry, love but your Mum *was* in the house. I saw her arrive home in a taxi about half ten, she's been taken away in an ambulance."

Billy dropped back onto the wall. This unexpected tragic news had pierced his heart like a poison-tipped arrow. After taking a moment or two to digest what he had just heard, his first thought was that he had underestimated the enemy in a major way and that he would need to up his game.

Billy emitted an agonised howl, "Bastards!"

All of the gathered neighbours and emergency service personnel turned and stared in silent unison.

26

Billy could barely keep his eyes open. He was over-tired, he hadn't slept eight hours in the past forty-eight, but the excitement of the evening seemed to be keeping him sharp. The pain! Oh, the flooding tide of pain, shooting through him like he'd been tasered. He'd popped into the loo about a quarter of an hour ago and took a small handful of painkillers and he was desperately waiting for them to kick in. He sat huddled with his elbows resting on his knees and his chin perched in cupped hands. After a while, he noticed the severity had reduced to a mild ache, so he stood tentatively and raked his wispy hair with his fingers.

To pass the time and keep his mind active he began to read the bumph that was haphazardly displayed on a nearby notice board: Clearer hearing – all the answers, we listen, you hear! Vaginal discomfort? Use *Sylk* a natural lubricant. Get your flu jab now! Affected by cancer? We can help! *Like bollocks you can.*

He sat down on a hard metal bench. He loathed hospitals. The periodic ding of the lift doors opening and closing, the hustle and bustle of the A and E department, the smell.

His throbbing head was full of 'whys and what ifs?' He jumped to his feet again and for the fourth time he began pacing agitatedly up and down the waiting room. It was a huge and elaborate Victorian room with high-cornices, cast iron stairways, and large stone archways. It was decrepit and falling to pieces. The walls and tiled floor scuffed and scarred by decades of varying types of trolley. He had a vague memory of his father telling him the building started life as a workhouse. A new, multi-million-pound replacement hospital was being built on adjacent land.

Billy was surprised at just how many people were about at this time of the morning. He heard four, possibly five languages other than his own. Everyone looked washed out, frazzled and tired. Some people sat with heads bowed or angled at the ceiling, occasionally blowing out their cheeks and constantly gazing at their watches. Others sat there in various degrees of distress: angry, tearful, and nervous. An obnoxious young man dressed in a smart suit was braying into his mobile phone. An old couple sat opposite, their anxious faces reflecting the same deep-set worry that Billy knew was on his own. There was a kid with her wrist bandaged in a tea towel screaming her head off, her parents having no luck in consoling her. There was a tattooed, drunken yob arguing with the receptionist and a security guard. He was bawling obscenities at them and they in turn wanted to know why he felt he should be seen before anyone else. *I'd soon shut him up.* A very old man sitting close by coughed and sneezed without covering his mouth; Billy slid along the bench away from him. The man then moaned something unintelligible and spat on the floor. People who were sitting in the vicinity turned their noses up in disgust, and then indulged in the typically British action of ignoring it. Mainly, though, there were furious sighs of exasperation as to the length of time that they had been kept waiting. There was something in the atmosphere that sucked all of the enthusiasm out of you.

An elderly woman of Asian appearance wearing a green overall ambled toward Billy pushing a small trolley stacked with cleaning materials. She stopped and sprayed some type of liquid cleaner onto a bolted down metallic table nearby. He watched as she wiped it off with a cloth. She looked up and flicked a thin smile at him; he did likewise, and she moved off down the corridor stepping in the phlegm that the old man had deposited on the floor. She stopped abruptly and, lifting her foot up, tutted loudly on seeing what she had trodden in. Billy's eyes widened as she took a mop, cleaned the bottom of her shoe, and then slapped grey water over the area. She placed a plastic triangular warning sign over the wet patch - 'Danger Slippery Floor', and then moved off at a slow, relaxed pace. Billy almost puked.

Staff, whom to Billy looked impossibly young, clattered past in white coats, some with clipboards some hauling trolleys or pieces of equipment. One particular white blur came crashing through swing doors to his left. She held notes in one hand and was scribbling down something with a pen, not particularly looking in which direction she was heading. Billy jumped to his feet and grabbed her by the arm.

"Excuse me!" It burst out of Billy with a little more volume than was necessary. People turned and seemed to temporarily freeze. "I'm sorry, love but they bought my Mum in over two hours ago, Mrs. Crabtree? Only I'm worried, can you find out…?"

"*I'm* sorry also," she scowled, snatching her arm away from Billy's restraining grasp. Beneath a fall of blond hair flecked with auburn, her greenish-brown eyes studied him. "There are a lot of sick people in here you know…have you reported to reception?"

"Yes, but that was ages ago, please…"

There was turmoil etched into Billy's face and on seeing water well in his eyes, she formed her lips into a tight slit and sighed heavily. She continued, "Ok, wait here I'll go and check, Mrs. Crabtree you say?"

"Mmm. Thank you, I really do appreciate your help."

Billy plonked himself back down on a steel bench. *Fucking hell, how many highs and lows can you have in such a short space of time?* He dropped forward, elbows resting on spread knees, clenched fists supporting his chin. A dog-eared *Daily Mirror* lay on the seat next him. It was soiled and well thumbed, he took it and riffled through it idly and found a small section about Thommo's death on page seven. It was a very basic account and didn't even mention Billy's name, referring to him as 'The janitor'. *Janitor indeed!* He didn't react to the story in any way; he had other things on his mind. He dropped it back onto the seat not knowing what he had just seen or read. He drummed impatient fingers on his knee, whistled something or other quietly to himself, and flicked his eyes around the room. Billy began to feel numb and bleak, but his thoughts turned back to his Mother, so he shot out of his seat and began pacing again, angry at himself for being selfish and so full of self-pity. The thought of his Mum being at home by herself and defenceless against Deano and the other gang members was almost too much to bear. Tears of guilt formed for not being there for her. If he had only been there he could have at least done something – *or I could be in a bed somewhere in this hospital covered in a white sheet?*

The nurse returned shortly, and informed Billy that his Mother had been admitted to ward D4. He took a disinfectant-smelling lift to the fourth floor as the nurse had instructed. The heavy aluminium doors parted with a 'Ping' and Billy stepped out into a wide, deserted corridor. He made his way through a labyrinth of corridors and, although his way was well sign-posted, still managed to lose direction on a couple of occasions. He finally arrived at his destination after being re-directed by a cheerful receptionist in Radiology. He stood with his arms resting on a tall, semi-circular worktop. There were four workstations but only one nurse on duty. Billy listened intently as the Nurse – a large middle-aged lady, hair close cropped at the sides of her head, three gold studs piecing her right eyebrow and a name tag pinned to her uniform reading Natalie Wigg - explained that his Mother had not sustained any burn injuries but she was presently unconscious due to smoke inhalation. They would not be able to assess if there was any lung damage until the specialist in that field arrived that morning. However, she was in no immediate danger, she was comfortable, and the nurse *thought* that the prognosis was pretty good. It was obviously not visiting time but, due to the exceptional circumstances, he could have 'Two minutes' with her.

Billy entered the ward; its rows of beds stretching both

sides of the room each surrounded by stark white curtains. On approaching his Mothers' bed, he stopped abruptly and a breath caught in his throat. He suddenly felt very hot and giddy.

Her head lolled to one side, one skinny arm lay outside of the bedclothes, a plastic bracelet was strapped around her wrist. The gnarled, bony, withered hand was shaking very slightly. He observed her chest rising and falling very slowly. Her breathing was shallow but regular with a rumble of catarrh; each intake of air made a soft wheezing sound. There were wires attached to her skull, measuring brain activity. Spaghetti like tubing snaked across the floor and disappeared under the bed sheets. Fluids were being drip-fed into her via a clear plastic bag suspended from a drip stand and running into a cannula taped to her crinkly arm. Its tubes and wires plugged into a machine with a flickering screen. The steady, changing waveforms of her heartbeat and the reading of her blood pressure. It bleeped annoyingly every few seconds. A clear plastic mask hissed oxygen; it had slipped and was covering her chin; it was obviously not doing the job for which it was designed. Black soot ringed both nostrils.

Billy took another step forward struggling to keep his composure. His heart ached as he digested how serious the situation was, tears pricked his eyes as he approached the bed. Before replacing the mask over her nose and mouth, Billy stared at the machinery, its bleeping punctuating the silence; he wondered if it might register awareness of his proximity; there was no change in the readout. *What an idiot.* He gently adjusted the pillows beneath his Mums' wispy, white hair. He took his handkerchief and wiped her eyes and then her mouth where a single track of saliva had dried; he slipped the mask back into its correct position. He took up the chart at the foot of the bed, but the numbers and graphs told him nothing. Billy kissed his Mothers' forehead; she smelt of smoke and urine. He sat at her side and wrapped his hand around her curled, inert fist; he shook her shoulder gently.

"Mum, Mum, it's me, Billy," he whispered.

The eyelids fluttered but remained closed. *She can't hear me, can she? But maybe she could...*

Billy carefully lifted her hand and dropped his forehead onto it.

"Oh Mum, Mum," he said softly, "What have they done to you? Why the hell didn't you stop at Ivy's? When I rang you, you said you were happy to stop..." his face was a mask of anger, the veins at his temples stood proud and he ground his teeth together. "I'm gonna get 'em, Mum, don't you worry, them bastards are gonna pay for this...I'm sorry. I'm so sorry for the way I've been acting lately, there's a reason...I haven't been feeling well, Mum..." he sat upright and wiped his tears from the back of his Mothers' hand with the sheet. He apologised to her for all the jobs he'd failed to do and for all the times he hadn't been there.

Billy sat with his fingers overlapping her frail liver-spotted hand. Wires protruding from her leathery skin, bruises pooling where tubes fed vital fluids. Once he thought she tried to squeeze his hand, he spoke her name aloud, but almost certainly it had been a reflex gesture.

He'd been asleep, for how long he didn't have a clue, but Janet occupied every sleeping thought he'd had.

Natalie shook him gently, "Mister Crabtree," she whispered, "you're snoring."

"Sorry." Billy sat up, immediately awake but uncertain as to where he was. He stretched, yawned, and knuckled his eyes.

The nurse placed a friendly hand on his shoulder and smiled, "I could hear you in the reception, I thought we had a Moose loose in here." She smiled, Billy didn't. "Why don't you go home and pick up a few things for her, eh? Slippers, a nightdress perhaps? Any medication she

may be taking? You can't do any more here. We'll ring you if there are any changes."

Billy threw her a pleasant smile and nodded.

When the nurse had disappeared, he took his handkerchief and, gently lifting the oxygen mask to one side, mopped saliva that had dripped from her slack mouth. He stood and poured a little water into a plastic cup and held it to her mouth, but it snaked down her chin and onto her gown. Billy replaced the mask and crouched over the bed, kissing his Mothers' forehead once more. "I'm going now, Mum, I have some tidying up to do. The people who did this? Their day will come. The maniacs who set our house on fire will pay dearly." Billy said it quietly to himself and without parting his teeth. "I'll see you later. Don't worry you'll be fine, Mum everything's been arranged, you'll be well looked after. Love you."

As if she had been listening at some level, her chest heaved, and her eyelids fluttered without opening. The monitor beside her began to bleep with increased urgency.

Billy leaned over his Mum and stared intently into her face. There was no movement; her eyelids had stopped flickering. He straightened and took a couple of steps back, staring unblinkingly at her pale, drawn face.

The monitor gradually returned to a steady pace.

27

Billy stood statuesque outside of the A&E department. Several grey paved steps led from the entrance doorway down to the footpath in front of him. A rush of absolute and eternal loneliness engulfed him, tightening his chest. He was feeling the exhaustion of a long day seeping into him. There was damp in the air and it was quite chilly; summer was going to be late this year. When he had entered the hospital, the wind had been barely a breeze, but now strong gusts carried a penetrating nip that motivated Billy to wrap his arms around himself. To clear his thoughts, he inhaled deeply through his nose several times pulling in lungs full of the frigid chill, which were expelled in little white puffs.

During the last twenty-four hours, his emotions had ping-ponged between intense excitement and intense fear. His pulse sounded in his ears and so again, he sucked in deep lungs full of the earthy, damp morning air. The rain had stopped, though there were still puddles reflecting the amber streetlights. They were showing a milder yellow, as their influence waned. The breeze fluttered his jacket as he stretched both arms out wide and yawned for long seconds. To his left, a stocky round-shouldered man wrapped in a navy blue frayed night coat with white piping. He was stamping his feet rhythmically to keep warm. In his right ear, a gold crucifix earring. His hair was receding and cropped close to his skull. His cheeks were rosy, probably from the wind-chill. The colour contrasted sharply with the dark shadows beneath his eyes; he was obviously recovering from some major surgery. He was gripping a tall steel stand fitted with castors similar to the one next to his Mums bed. Hanging from the top of the frame was a clear plastic bag, which held a clear liquid. A small diameter tube led from this and disappeared up one of his sleeves. In his other hand, the faint red glow from his cigarette cupped at his side, obviously a hardy smoker intent on shortening his life.

"Mornin'," Billy said.

The man nodded. "How'do," he said brightly. He flicked his butt into the service road and wheeled his life support unit back into the hospital. *Not in the mood for a chat, then? Same here to be honest.*

Grey streaks of dawn were smeared across the sky and birds were croaking and arguing; *there's fuck-all to sing about.* Slipping up the cuff of his shirt, he glanced at his watch and sighed heavily in the knowledge that he should be starting his shift in twenty-five minutes time.

Darkness hung over him; it had nothing to do with the weather. He ground his teeth together; he still had people to deal with, the people who had put his Mum in hospital.

Then, both palms shot up to his temples, and he cried out loud, *"JESUS CHRIST, SOPHIE!"*

28

The front lawn was littered with smouldering debris. What was once his Mothers' home of sixty years now reduced to a charred skeleton. The air smelled of bonfire night. There were still a few onlookers dotted around the scene, one filming the devastation with his phone. Only one police constable in a high-viz sleeveless jacket was left to patrol the perimeter. Billy stood transfixed for a good few minutes, staring unblinkingly at what resembled a bombsite. He noticed the copper had stopped to have a chat with one of the onlookers and so he swiftly ducked under the scene of crime tape. Fire fighters were still damping down as he made for the front door – well, the front doorway; what was left of the door was probably on the lawn somewhere. A large man wearing a white protective over-suit knelt in the doorway. He was dropping tiny bits of debris into a clear plastic bag with tweezers. *Waste of time, mate, I already know who and what caused the fire.* He didn't ask if he could pass he just slipped through the small gap between the CSI and what was left of the doorjamb. As he entered tentatively, a voice called out to him. One of the fire fighters was balling at Billy, something about the health and safety dangers, but he ignored it and continued inside. Entering the kitchen was like entering the darkest bowels of a cave. Sophie was nowhere to be seen, normally when she heard his approach she had met him with a wagging tail and wet nose. *God, I hope she managed to get out and was wondering the streets somewhere.* Sadness overwhelmed him. Sophie's basket had melted and formed what looked like a giant green cowpat across the blackened floor; she had obviously not been in it. He called out – nothing. Water dripped onto him from the floor above. He called again hoping that she would come bursting from somewhere with her tail wagging furiously as it did every time he came in from work, always so pleased to see him as if he had been away for months. Then he remembered her hidey-hole. The kitchen unit was barely a couple of hundred millimetres off the floor, but she sometimes crept under there with her tail between her legs if ever Billy had admonished her for some reason. The fire had charred it badly, but it still stood there defiantly on scorched legs. He knelt and peered underneath. Sophie had curled up into a ball obviously trying to escape from the fire. Mercifully, she seemed to have escaped the flames and had been overcome by smoke. A thick covering of soot had hidden the white patches of her fur. Billy reached out a shaky hand and stroked her head. He couldn't speak. He lifted her head. He sobbed uncontrollably; tears snaked down his face. Sophie had been his companion. He had had conversations with her - out of earshot of his Mother, obviously. It sounded stupid, probably was, but this dog had been the friend he'd never had, the wife he'd never had or the child he'd never had. "See ya, old girl," he eventually managed to stammer. He dropped his head into his hands and tears dripped through his fingers.

Originally, he'd bought Sophie as company for his Mother while he was out at work, but apart from being a great companion; Sophie had proven to be a useful guard dog, barking at anyone approaching the house. Although, when the front door was opened, she attempted to lick to death whoever the caller was.

Eventually he rose to his feet and as he did so, a hand touched his shoulder. As he spun, the fire fighter asked if he was OK. Billy threw his arms around him and hugged him, breaking down into fits of uncontrollable grief.

Billy stood as if he had been sculptured in stone, his head bowed. For a very long moment he couldn't move, paralysed with grief. The muscles in his back and shoulders screamed; he didn't know exactly how long he had stood there rocking the lifeless Sophie in his arms and crying softly. Eventually he went out into the back garden. From the shed, he took a shovel and a hessian sack. What the sack was used for he hadn't a clue, it was something his father had left behind. In the corner of the garden, Billy dug a shallow grave. He felt discomfort as the rain pummelled his head; the weather suited the scene perfectly. Cold droplets that stung when they hit his skin and ran down the back of his neck; he felt as if he had driven a cabriolet through a car wash. He hurt so bad he felt like throwing up. The pain was in his chest. His head spun.

It was a struggle to get Sophie into the sack, but he managed it eventually and placed her in the pit of the grave. Billy stood at the edge of the hole, expressionless, his face ashen white, staring into what seemed like a black abyss. A pain was growing more intense in the pit of his gut, like a large blade being thrust into him up to the hilt; he was in desperate need of painkillers.

Billy didn't know how long he had stood there, minutes? Hours? Feeling light headed and unstable as he scraped earth over her and with the back of his shovel he gently patted down the mound of soil he had placed on top of Sophie's last resting-place. The thuds were as hollow as his heart. He rammed two pea-sticks into the earth that he had tied together to form a crude cross. The driving rain mingled with the tears running down his cheeks. Dry, harsh sobs choked him. *She was such a beautiful dog, a classic Border collie. Black with white patches and sparkling deep blue eyes. Her needs were simple. She loved her walkies. She loved to be loved. She ate her food as if she hadn't been fed for a week, and then she came out here for a crap, that's all she wanted out of life.* Billy mopped away tears with the back of his hand. "Bye, girl," he said in a cracked whisper.

Billy's body then unfolded like a butterfly emerging from a chrysalis; he stood tall and his eyes widened. Adrenaline began to spike through his body. He didn't realise that he had been biting the inside of his lip so hard that a rivulet of blood was trickling down his chin. Vengeance clawed at him. He would watch and wait and soon enough the time for retribution would come. Deano's number was as good as up, and the name Billy Crabtree would be up there with the rest.

"Don't you worry, girl, it's payback time," he said through gritted teeth, "Someone is *seriously* going to fucking suffer for this."

Again, tears flowed. Billy's shoulders hunched forward, lifting and falling with each sob as he trudged wearily and solemnly across the front lawn. He hadn't a clue what time or even what day it was, so tired and lost was he on the day he buried his best friend.

Billy was startled when Mrs. Caine called out to him, "How's your Mom, Billy?"

"Mmm?"

"Your Mom, how's she bearing up? I'll probably pop along later, see if she needs anything."

Billy sighed heavily and ran a sleeve across his eyes. "She's not come round yet but I'm sure it'll help if she can hear a friendly voice…I…I've just buried Sophie in the back garden."

Mrs. Caine slapped a hand to her mouth, "Oh Billy, I'm so sorry…is there anything I can do, love anything at all?"

"No thank you. I'm sorry, Mrs. Caine I must hurry along… things to do, you know?"

"Of course, Billy you take care now."

Billy sat in his battered and dented car awhile his mind awhirl. Once again, he lost all track of time and didn't have a clue how long he'd been sitting there. Eventually, he buckled up and turned the engine over. As he slipped the car into first gear there was a loud rattle on the side window, which made him jump back in his seat; he dramatically slapped a hand to his chest.

He lowered the window. "Mrs. Caine, you nearly gave me a heart attack!"

She pushed a package through the open window, "Sorry, Billy I forgot to tell you this parcel arrived this morning and I took it in for you."

"Thank you, Mrs Caine much appreciated."

"No problem must dash, Billy I'm getting soaked, byeee!"

Billy wound up the window and placed the parcel on the passenger seat. He patted and stroked it lightly as if it were Sophie; his eyes widened. "You've come just at the right time my friend," he said through clenched teeth, "someone is in for a *very* nasty surprise in the *very* near future."

29

Co-co had been right in his assumption. Although Billy's story had been pepped up with carefully chosen words to make it as glamorous as possible, it was soon relegated to just a couple of lines as, during the night, a Dutch airliner had come down in the Middle East killing all 235 passengers on board. The nations' news editors were hungry to add their bit of gossip. Did a terrorist missile bring it down, perhaps? Also vying for the front page, particularly the tabloids, was an 'exclusive' shock revelation, one of the BBC's top male newscasters being caught on camera in a gay night-club – no doubt a worrying read this morning for his wife and two kids.

Billy had driven straight from the hospital and was happy to see the school gates clear of any media. He opened the school, let in the cleaners, who were very irate because he was late, but he totally ignored them. Then he made straight for the Leisure centre. He made his way to the disabled changing room, locking the door behind him. He was no longer tired, he had gone past being tired, he was on a mission and nothing was now going to get in his way. However, he needed to be awake and alert and so he thought that a shower would revitalise him. The room was chilly. He stepped into the shower cubicle and let hot water cascade over him. He stood for several minutes feeling the healing heat relax muscles tight with tension, warming life back into his body. He watched the rain spatter on the skylight above him. He closed his eyes and tilted his head back letting the invigorating water run over him, trying to lose himself in the pulsating spray, but he couldn't clear his mind. There were too many things invading his thoughts.

Billy decided no one needed to know about the house fire. He went straight from the leisure centre and into work. On his arrival back in school (where no one had noticed he'd been missing for an hour) he changed into his working gear and skipped his usual morning cuppa. He had no appetite and had given breakfast a miss. He glanced at his watch and knew that the administration staff should have arrived at school by now, so he made for the reception; Billy stuck his head through the hatch.

Esther was sitting where Janet normally sat. She wore her hair in a bun, which made her ears look even larger than normal. *Like a couple of Ping-Pong bats stuck to her head.*

"Well, good morning stud, how are you?" Esther said raising two immaculately plucked eyebrows.

Billy rolled his eyes. "OK, thanks, Esther," he said, his face colouring.

Her brow wrinkled slightly, "Your eyes, Billy they're very red, have you been cry..."

"Esther! Really." Janet was at the rear of the office flicking through some documents in a filing cabinet. Esther moved as Janet approached the window and slid into her swivel chair. "You'll have to excuse her...I haven't told her anything, Billy, she's just assuming that..."

"I don't know what you've done to her, Billy but she came in here this morning singing at the top of her voice, cheeks the colour of tomatoes..."

"Esther, please." Janet had raised her voice, albeit with a grin. She turned her attention to Billy and lowered her voice. "What happened to you? I was looking forward to cooking you a full English this morning."

Billy took her hand. "Sorry, Jan I had to get back for Mum, you know how she is."

Janet's brow furrowed slightly. "But you rung her from the restaurant, Billy she was staying with a friend, wasn't she?"

"Erm…yeah…but I was concerned, I picked her up from her friends and took her home."

"Mmm, that's a nice thought. Well I missed you this morning."

"I'll make it up to you. I hope you don't think I'm pushing things along too quickly, but do you think I could pop round this evening and maybe stay the night?" He reached out and tucked an escaped tendril of hair behind her ear.

She liked that.

Billy genuinely wanted to be with Janet that evening. She was nearly all he could think about now. He knew he had to force himself to focus on other things, his goal, but he just wanted to touch her, smell her, and kiss her. The fact that he had nowhere else to go was immaterial and he desperately needed not to be alone.

Esther had been eavesdropping their conversation, which wasn't too difficult with ears that could probably pick up a spider having an asthma attack at a hundred metres distance. She began quietly singing to herself, *'Sex bomb, sex bomb, you're my sex bomb…'*

Janet glanced over her shoulder. "Esther!" Then too Billy: "Ooohhh, that woman."

Billy smirked, "She's only winding you up. So, I'll see you tonight then?"

Janet raised her eyebrows and smiled. "OK, I look forward to it. Seven thirty?"

"Great, see you later." Billy winked and smiled back.

As he turned his back on Janet and strolled away, his smile evaporated and his face took on a more serious, almost evil look.

Billy Crabtree was on the hunt.

30

Deano was now back in school after serving his suspension and so Billy needed to concentrate his efforts and forge ahead with his plan. He consulted his notebook to remind himself as to what the first step would be. He nodded thoughtfully and then put it back into the top pocket of his overall. Time to get cracking, but first he needed to see if there was any news about his Mother. He dialled the hospitals number adding the extension number that he had been given. It rang four times and was answered by a certain 'Betty'. Billy asked about his Moms' progress, only to be told that there wasn't any, though things were not getting any worse. Best to phone in a couple of hours when the specialist had checked her again.

Billy left the workroom and made his way to the skip area. Two skips were permanently sited here backed up against the swimming pool wall. Along the wall, numerous bunches of flowers and cards had been placed next to candles, which were now expired. Billy guessed by the wind but more probably by the health and safety officer. Billy stooped down. What he read from the cards was sickening. Surely not about Thommo? Friendly? Kind? Best friend anyone could have? Billy nearly threw up.

Next to the two skips, a large steel container had been sited. It had been purchased by the school to house general building materials. It was a huge struggle, but Billy managed to lift three, six-hundred-millimetre square paving slabs from the container and into a wheelbarrow. He backhanded sweat from his forehead, leant against the container, and caught his breath for a few minutes. Next stop was the boiler house. Here, in the one corner, he kept an array of garden tools. He took a rake, a shovel, and his wellies and laid them on the top of the slabs. Then began the long arduous journey to the environmental area. It was broad daylight, but no one would ask him what he was up to, why would they? Staff would see him going about his duties all day and every day, if Billy had something with him, a screwdriver, a hammer, a toilet roll, it always looked like he was about his business.

It was hard work pushing the wheelbarrow through long grass, so to take his mind off his aching limbs he whistled a couple of Motown tunes that he remembered from when he was a teenager. He needed to sit down and rest for a good ten minutes when he finally arrived at his destination. Making use of a nearby wooden bench that had been donated to the school in memory of one of its pupils who had been killed in a road traffic accident. Two small holes were all that remained of a brass plaque that had been screwed to the bench in memory of the lad. Obviously, some mindless moron had prised it off and done God knows what with it. He was puffing and panting, and he needed to remove his overalls as they were soaked through with sweat.

When sufficiently recovered, Billy unloaded the slabs from the wheelbarrow and leant them against a mature silver birch, which overhung the environmental pool. Then he hid the garden tools amongst nearby shrubbery. He recovered his overall, threw it into his wheelbarrow and off he went whistling a non-descript tune.

All he needed to do now was to lure his next victim to his final resting place.

31

Billy's next victim came sooner than he had expected.

That same afternoon Billy had grabbed a mop and bucket from one of the cleaners' cupboards after receiving a phone call from reception. Some pupil had decided to throw up in the Humanities corridor. There were sixteen boys and girls toilets dotted around the school, but it was always too much effort for a pupil to go and stick their head down the pan. It was a strange phenomenon that always puzzled Billy. As far as he could remember, he had never attended a vomit situation that had happened outside of the school building, or for that matter, had occurred on a ceramic tiled floor. Kids always had to empty their stomach contents onto carpet for some reason. Lately, Billy had got into the habit of just ripping up the old carpet tiles, replacing them with new; it made the job a lot easier and after all, he wasn't paying for it.

Billy made his way through the Library quad, into the humanities social area, and from there along the humanities corridor. Here he spotted his target - although he could smell it long before he was able to see it. The kid had obviously eaten something that had been flavoured with garlic. Someone had placed a chair over the patch of sick so that the kids wouldn't paddle through it. Surprise surprise, it was on carpet. He got down on one knee and, as he got to work pulling the contaminated carpet tiles up, he began retching; one job that he had never got used to.

From the other end of the corridor, Billy heard raised voices. Then a door was flung open and a teacher appeared screaming at a pupil who had followed him out, hands deeply entrenched in his pockets. Billy stood and leant on his mop to watch the drama unfold. The teacher was red faced and wagging a finger in the pupils' face; the face belonged to Nelly. The teacher was informing Nelly how useless he was, how he always ruined his lesson, how he would never make anything of himself, and then the classic, 'You've let yourself down, you've let me down, you've let the whole class down...' Nelly had probably heard these statements a dozen times a day since he had started school and his face reflected the fact.

If pupils were disruptive in class they were usually made to drag a table and chair into the corridor and do their work out there so that they could no longer subject the class to their bad influence. During lunch break Nelly and Deano had had a bet to see who could be expelled from the classroom first. (Obviously Thommo's demise wasn't going to stop them having a 'laugh') In the early days of their school life, the three of them attended the same class but were soon split up into separate classes to lessen the disruption.

When the classroom door had been slammed shut, Billy made his way down the corridor. As he approached, Nelly had both hands clasped behind his head and both feet perched on the desk. Wires from two earpieces disappeared under his jacket. Nelly was rocking precariously back and forth on the back legs of his chair and was oblivious to Billy's presence. Nelly was wallowing in glory, under the impression that, after only five minutes, he had won his bet with Deano. Deano in fact had been expelled even before he had reached the classroom, managing to disrupt the class as they lined up for their lesson. Although a desk and chair had been placed in a different corridor for Deano's solo lesson, he was in fact in the staffroom and in the process of removing a mobile phone and purse from a handbag.

Billy grabbed the wires that hung around Nelly's neck and gave them a sharp tug; the earpieces shot out with a pop.

"Alright, young man?" Billy had raised his voice sufficiently enough to make sure that Nelly would be startled.

Nelly's arms and legs flailed around like a demented windmill as he tried in vain to keep his balance, but the chair toppled back and there was a muffled thud as his head hit carpet tiles. He sat vigorously rubbing the back of his skull for a few seconds trying to re-orientate himself. When he glanced up, his jaw drooped.

"Crabby, you dozy twat I'll…I'll fuckin' sue you for this, you bastard," Nelly spat as he retrieved his baseball cap and jumped to his feet. "What yer tryin' to do, kill me you fuckin' idiot?"

Well, yes as a matter of fact I am. Billy smiled. "Sorry about that, son I didn't know you were so jumpy." He reached out as if to look at the back of Nelly's head. "Let's have a look at that shall we, don't worry, son I'm trained for this kind of…"

Nelly knocked Billy's hand away with his forearm. "Don't touch me you fuckin' peado perve."

"OK, OK, calm down a bit, I have apologised." Billy took a furtive glance up and down the corridor then beckoned Nelly nearer with a hooked finger. He lowered his voice. "Listen, you remember the other day when you and your mates dumped me in the pond…"

Nelly snarled, "That weren't us, man and you can't fuckin' prove it, so fuck off."

"Rrriiiggghhhttt, OK, it's just that when…*someone* decided to deposit me in the environmental pool, I lost my watch. It's very upsetting, a present from my mother for Christmas…."

"So, nuffink to do with me…"

"Yes, yes, as you say. Shame really, I'd been dropping hints for years about the fact that one day I would love to buy me a Rolex…" Billy could see Nelly suddenly show a great deal of interest, his eyes were normally shadowed and calculating but now he peered at him with bright-eyed eagerness. "Anyway, it was very expensive so if you hear anything? There'll be a small reward for anyone who finds it."

"Yeah, yeah, man…I'll, erm, put the feelers out and let you know."

"Good lad." Billy patted Nelly on the shoulder. He hooked his mop over his shoulder and as he turned it *accidentally* clouted Nelly across the face.

Nelly retched and spat out bits of fibre and in quick succession drew a left and then right sleeve across his mouth. "Fuckin' wanker! I'll have you for this, crabby, so help me…"

Billy ambled down the corridor listening to a tirade of verbal abuse. He half-turned to face Nelly as a twisted, cynical smile leaked across his face. *If only he knew what fate had in store for him.* He carried on strolling along whilst Nelly pantomimed shooting Billy in the back with a dirty finger, jerking his hand back to mimic the recoil.

Billy knew that Nelly could make the environmental area long before he could so, as part of his plan, he took a short cut via a large storeroom with a fire escape at the rear. He made a beeline towards the environmental area, but this time he concealed himself behind the shrubs where he had left his garden equipment. From this vantage point, he could see way across the sports fields and playground and the school in the distance. The faint ring of the bell, which heralded the change of lessons wafted across on a light breeze.

Billy's eyes were drooping with fatigue. He was having second thoughts. *Shall I do this another time? When I've rested and regained some strength? No that's the sort of stupid thing the old Billy would have done. I'll conquer my tiredness, I can only expect to get away with this if I master my weaknesses. I was pathetic a few days ago – not now. Will he even turn up? I wouldn't be surprised if all the gang members already own a Rolex…*

A smile spread across Billy's face. Strolling purposefully with an arrogant swagger across the football pitch came Nelly, occasionally taking a furtive look behind him.

Easy, so bloody easy, I can read this prat like a book.

As Nelly came striding through the thicket of small shrubs he began kicking at the long grass which surrounded the pool in the hunt for his prize. He was smirking. *A small reward? Does Crabby think I'm fuckin' stupid? Must be worth a fortune, this watch*. He was oblivious to the crackle of vegetation behind him or the sudden flurry of activity where a bird or small animal had picked up Billy's approach and made its escape. *Wait till Deano sees my new watch, he'll be dead jealous.* However, Deano would never see it; in fact, he would never see Nelly again because Billy was standing right behind him now wearing a maniacal grin; he was holding a shovel above his head. He lowered his eyebrows; he was keen for confrontation, confrontation with someone who had subjected Sophie to a slow lingering death, someone who had tried to murder him and his Mother, someone who had burnt the family home to the ground.

As the shovel whistled through the air Nelly turned slightly catching the shovel in his peripheral vision, he tried to evade it and to a small degree he did, and it did miss its intended target – Nelly's head, but instead struck him on the shoulder. Nelly wailed and staggered back tumbling and whimpering down the length of the bench his hands groping at thin air. Billy moved in closer and swung hard striking him with the full force of the swing on his right cheekbone shattering it. Nelly felt a surge of wetness as blood spurted from his face; he roared with pain and fell backward across the bench as the world exploded into tiny stars.

"That's for my Mum and Sophie, bastard!" Billy bawled without parting his teeth. The pain and loss were still deeply entrenched within his soul.

To Nelly, Billy's voice seemed to be far off in the distance. With the aid of the bench, Nelly managed to pull himself up onto unsteady feet all at once choking and spitting blood and gasping for
breath. Billy stepped around the bench; he was grim now and silent, dedicated to what he had started. He was wild, wilder than any animal. A maelstrom of anger, rage, grief and frustration reduced to a single function, his body an extension of the shovel in his hands.

Although Nelly was barely able to see through the blood he could just make out the blurred silhouette of the shovel coming towards him, it sang as it hurtled through the air so he raised an arm in a feeble attempt to block the blow, but Billy had swung the shovel with such force it broke Nelly's arm clean in two. Nelly's legs buckled and he fell to his knees and then slumped onto his back his chest juddered and he tried to call out again but with less strength this time; he no longer knew where he was or what was happening.

Billy's actions where controlled, deliberate, robotic.

The shovel lifted again and came down square on Nelly's face and again on his shoulder and again on his forehead splintering his skull Billy moving with the zeal of the possessed his face wrenched into a knot of murderous intent the scene was being played with deadly cold ruthlessness Nelly tried to scream but his windpipe was clogged with blood and all he could manage was to gurgle blood from between broken teeth thick crimson liquid oozed from his right ear his heart was hammering in his chest Billy's face was red and hideously distorted his every instinct screaming at him to stop but he was driven on by the force inside the shovel went up and down like a piston the more he pummelled Nelly the more his movements took on a frenzied and insane ferocity he chopped slashed and sliced at Nelly's body until pain racked his shoulders arms and back muscles and although Nelly had long since stopped shuddering Billy hit him again and with more force than he knew he possessed and the only reason that he stopped hitting him was because he was too exhausted to lift the shovel above his head anymore.

For Nelly, everything had long ago faded to black.

Billy collapsed onto the bench; his overall was glued to his back with sweat, his pulse thumped in his neck. He rested his forearms on his knees, his head bowed low; he was gasping for breath.

There was the slightest sound of a gargle. Billy slowly raised his head and watched with owl-like eyes as Nelly's back suddenly and violently arched. Billy's heart pounded – *he surely couldn't still be alive, could he?* Then Nelly was still. The body jerked slightly which made Billy almost jump off the bench, and then it writhed as if in a macabre puppet-like dance. Billy stared unblinkingly as a thin stream of bloody vomit cascaded from his mouth. Nelly breathed a small number of shallow breaths and then a sharp exhalation of air, and then he was eerily still. His body was sliced open oozing the life out of him. He had slipped into darkness, his glassy eyes open and gazing out in terror. Billy stood and crouched over the recumbent figure dwelling for a short, uncomfortable moment on the horror of the scene. Nelly was very still.

It was so very quiet. Birdsong in the near distance, calmness amid the monstrosity of the scene. The stillness more curdling even than Nelly's screams. Billy's stomach was empty, but he began straining with dry heaves, he sat back down and leant over the arm of the bench; his chest rose up and down in quick, jerky breaths. Warm stomach fluids dripped from his mouth; tears flowed. *Is this a nightmare or reality? What the hell am I doing? This was madness, absolute madness.*

Billy felt like he was being torn apart by emotions. He feared what he had turned into, the insane level of hatred, the incomprehensible degree of violence, the fact that he could harbour such hate for so long, his potential for savagery and the ease with which he had embraced vengeance. This was sheer brutal murder, with Thommo he had been calm, it had been impulsive, a gut instinct.

But Billy wasn't just ending the life of Nelly; he was remembering those past hurts; he had just killed every kid that had ever swore at him, spat at him, called out to him with vial, hateful taunts, and yes, on occasions, attacked him physically. He had ignored all of that, but it had been stored away somewhere in the depths of his brain and now something had 'popped' and it had leaked to the surface.

Billy's stomach churned. He was in desperate need of a couple of Rennies. He clenched his teeth to repress his nausea and sat stiff and stupefied for what seemed like long minutes. He took in and let out deep lungs full of air to calm himself;

he realised that he needed to rapidly rein in his rampant anger, for Billy was acutely and nervously aware of precious minutes passing. His thoughts vanished like shifting smoke because now there was some tidying up to do. He knuckled the tears from his eyes and rescued his wellies from the shrubbery. After donning them, he stooped at the foot of the body, resting his hands on his knees while he caught his breath; he had found this little escapade to be more trying than he had imagined, the adrenaline rush from the confrontation had left him drained and listless.

The cadaver had already formed a milky, gossamer fluid over both eyes. The lips and skin had begun turning blue. Nelly was only recognisable by the clothing he wore. Billy sensed that, although dead, Nelly still had surprises waiting for him. For a moment, he almost expected Nelly to blink, to grin, to spring upright and grab him. Just to make doubly sure, Billy pressed two fingers against Nelly's carotid artery – nothing. Billy shifted from behind Nelly's head to his feet; the dead eyes seemed to follow him. Billy took both ankles and dragged him to the edge of the pond, as he did so the corpse wheezed and gurgled bubbles of blood in its throat. He stepped into the pond, grabbed the ankles again, and pulled Nelly into the water. Nelly's arm extended skyward as if reaching out for help. Billy grabbed at the cold, clawed stiff hand and forced it underwater. He got out. He fetched one of the slabs and placed it at the ponds edge. He glanced down at the corpse – still staring at him. He fetched the other two slabs and then got back into the pond. He placed his foot on Nelly's chest forcing him to the muddy bottom. He swivelled round, grabbed a slab, and placed it on Nelly's chest. Likewise, with the other two, one placed on Nelly's feet, the other across his midriff.

As Billy tidied the surrounding area and washed the blood away from the slabs and bench with pond water, he stood awhile leaning on his rake and stared unblinkingly into the water. He turned his eyes into slits and then knelt at the ponds edge – he moved his head nearer.

It was dim and vague, but Nelly's glaring eyes still seemed to be watching him, staring at something beyond this world and into the next. Billy watched in morbid fascination and thought that the eyes of the dead
would have no expression, but Nelly's seemed full of terror and agony. The gaze fixed intently on a distant vision, as though he had glimpsed something far more terrifying than just the face of his killer. His broken jaw twisted in a hideous smile, the violence of his death etched onto his distorted face. Nelly's hair snaked out like fronds of seaweed in a swell. Billy half wondered whether he might see Nelly sit up suddenly and pry open his milky dead eyes and just stare at him or perhaps a hand would push itself out of the water and grab at his throat – *it probably would have done if this were a horror film*. However, this was reality, there was nothing. A bubble formed in his mouth, rose to the surface and popped.

Billy's insides lurched; he gagged and spat out the bitter fluid. He stood and raked Marsh Marigolds, Water Hawthorn and lilies from each corner of the pond and arranged them over Nelly's face and body to form a living shroud.

Billy stayed there a while longer transfixed as the dark water grew still around Nelly. Nelly's eyes seemed to stay with him long after he had turned his own away.

There was no sign that a human being rested here. Billy's face was calm, empty, and expressionless although he was subconsciously grinding his teeth together, wondering again where all the senseless rage had come from. *From them, that's where it had come from, if only they had just left us alone.* He took a violent sniff through his nose. *Well, that's another bastard who's off the streets and not making someone's life a misery.*

32

Mrs. Crabtree still hadn't come round from wherever she was. The consultant had suggested to Billy that the best thing for his Mother now would be for her to hear recognisable sounds, her favourite music for example or his voice. It was, he said, all part of the recovery process.
So, instead of Billy being exhausted like he should have been and expected to be, he had gained a second wind from somewhere and had sat with her for the best part of an hour or so reciting every little tit-bit, every boring episode of his day – well, not *everything*. There had been no response whatsoever from her.

After leaving the hospital Billy drove round aimlessly for a while and then he parked up. He was thinking about the house and what might have happened if the gang had struck on a night when he and his Mum were in bed. He shuddered involuntarily. He took two caffeine tablets and a small handful of painkillers without water; they tasted awful. Resting his head against the headrest, he closed his eyes. He must have nodded off for a few moments, but was jolted back from his daydreams when he heard loud booming sounds coming from the roof of his car. Surrounding his car, a gang of sullen youths (named trainers, baseball caps or hoods, and tracksuits) had thought it hilarious to kick and thump the car with clenched fists as they passed. A couple of the youths threw Billy obscene hand gestures as one satisfied himself by urinating on the
front wheel. Billy didn't flinch or show fear as they staggered off, laughing. He exhaled loudly and ran both palms down his face.
If only I had more time, I could have added those bastards to my list.

He turned over the engine and pulled away.

A short time later and Billy found himself with his thumb planted on Janet's doorbell. The moment that Janet opened her front door Billy stepped into the hallway, pressed her up against the wall, and kissed her. She put her arms around him and held him tightly, pressing her face to the warm curve of his neck. He rubbed her back, her shoulders. He inhaled her delicate perfume, fresh and crisp, mixed with her natural scent. He kissed her neck and he was sure he heard a slight whimper. Then he eased her away and lifted her hair, slowly letting it fall through his fingers. He hooked loose straggly wisps behind her ears. Cupping her cheeks in both hands, he smiled and stared into her eyes. Billy stroked her face gently, tracing her features like a blind man would, as if unable to believe what his eyes saw. Although she was no longer young, there seemed to be a lot of little girl in her. She was relaxed, she wore a white blouse, she wore torn jeans and she wore a teenage grin.

"What an amazingly beautiful woman you are, Jan," Billy whispered.

Janet averted her eyes and pressed the back of a hand to one her cheeks. She was flushed and sparkling. "Oh, you're making me blush...do you like lamb?"

He smiled. "That was a bit random...I love lamb."

"I think you're going to like my home-made apple and rhubarb crumble too, Billy, it's to die for, even if I do say so myself." She took his hand. "Come on in I'll get us some drinks."

Billy loved the way that Janet spoilt him. Just like his Mum. He suddenly felt a pang of guilt because he knew that he didn't appreciate all that his Mum did for him, Billy wanted to apologise to her for his behaviour, hoping that his Mum regained consciousness before he... Janet asked him to lay the table for her and then disappeared into the kitchen. He pulled out a red and white check tablecloth from a cabinet drawer and shook it open with a flourish like a bullfighter showing off his cape. After smoothing it across the table, he took an empty wine bottle from the cabinet. A candle had been jammed into its neck, white folds of solid wax cascading down. He sat down at the table and set about taking an inventory of the room.

Billy hadn't had the time to survey his surroundings on his last visit, because he had been much too pre-occupied. Therefore, he took this opportunity to have a nosy. There was no mess or clutter everything looked pristine. As they chatted through the open kitchen doorway, Billy strolled round picking up certain items and photographs and examined them closely.

The sparse furniture was quite modern in design; it reminded him of the one and only occasion when he had spent a mind-numbing couple of hours ambling round Ikea with his mum. *Mmm, very now.* The fireplace was painted an eggshell-white and a black marble shelf topped it, in front of which, a three-piece suite upholstered in black leather formed a semi-circle around a black ash coffee table. A huge black and white stripped Japanese fan served to screen the fireplace. A tall glass cabinet with rows of shelved *Willow tree* figures and a huge black ash bookcase filled with volume upon volume of either romantic novels or books on fishing. *No guessing which books belonged to whom.* Walls eggshell-white, carpet black flecked with small white diamonds. A chromed television stand on top of which stood a large flat-screen Sony. Black curtains. Candles of all shapes and sizes surrounded the room, all either black or white. The room could have failed miserably if not for a huge red-orange sunset painted in oils, which adorned the fire breast. It looked very similar to one that Billy had spotted in the Indian restaurant. Overall, the room could have come straight from a scene in DIY SOS. Everything was of beautiful, elegant simplicity. Minimalist design is what Billy thought it was called. The room was orderly, just like her life, Billy imagined.

Billy glanced across the living room towards the open patio doors and made his way over, resting a shoulder against the jamb. The light was fading to a blue tinge. It was a long narrow garden, made private and impenetrable by a profusion of competing ornamental shrubs on the one side, in front of which a variety of early flowering hardy annuals, their colours muted by the failing light. Opposite was a knee-high box hedge so neatly groomed that it appeared to have been trimmed with a pair of nasal hair scissors. Weeds had found their way through gaps where the paving slabs butted. The path wound its way through grass that shone dark green, lush and as neatly manicured as the hedge. He thought about his own neglected garden, in which he had spent very little time during the last couple of summers. *I ought to have made a little more effort for Moms' sake; she would have loved to have sat out there.* He flopped into a nearby chair under the realisation that the years of loneliness had slowly eaten him up and he had turned into quite an unpleasant old man. Billy was startled back from his thoughts as the wind picked up suddenly and a flurry of pine needles cascaded onto the lawn. In the far distance, he could just make out a gate, presumably leading into a back lane.

"It was full of fruit and veg when Mike was alive." Janet had been watching Billy intently from the kitchen doorway. "I couldn't be bothered; dug the lot up…gave me something to do I'spose." She handed him a glass of Sainsbury's red house wine.

"Mmm," Billy went, "You've got it looking nice." He rose from his chair; it emitted a soft farting noise.

Billy coloured. "Ah, sorry, that wasn't me…"

Janet chuckled. "I know, Mike wouldn't get rid of that chair, thought it was hilarious."

Billy placed small kisses on her forehead and hooked hair behind her ears, so he could take in more of her beautiful face.

When Billy had finished his meal, his plate looked like it had been licked clean by a dog. Billy suggested that it would be well worth marrying her just for her apple and rhubarb crumble alone, the fact that she was smart and beautiful also, was the cherry on the cake – or crumble, he quipped. Although they chatted about this and that over dinner, they both yearned for a repeat performance of what had gone on the previous night.

And then to bed.

A trail of clothes littered the stairs and across the landing. There was no foreplay this time, they were both much too eager. Billy lay on top of her and sunk into her, filling her. The passion that Billy had never found an outlet for exploded within a very short space of time. Janet wrapped her legs tightly around him and buried her tongue in his mouth. As she began writhing he was soon hard again, and this time his movements were less urgent. This is how it should be, she thought. Gentle and slow and loving, the desire almost painful, wanting each other so badly that nothing else mattered.

Billy slept long and deep, with Janet wrapped in his arms purring gently – AND he was pain free, which surprised him after his emotionally and physically exhausting day.

During the weekend, Billy and Janet hardly spent a moment apart. They ate together, showered together. She took him to the cinema and they had a pub lunch. Billy monitored his Mothers' condition with occasional short visits and telephone calls.

Saturday morning turned out to be a chilly, but a vibrantly gorgeous sunny day. Only a few small bloated clouds scudded across a deep blue sky as they strolled carefree and smiling around the local park. Towering pines, birch and oak trees dappled the pathway as they walked leisurely hand in hand. You could forget where you were, and it certainly gave Billy a break from all his troubles. He would have loved nothing more than to have done this with Jan perhaps thirty years ago and maybe pushing a pram with *his* son or daughter in it. It was all he could do to stifle a few tears.

Janet had taken a couple of slices of bread to feed the ducks. As they stood near the water's edge Billy noticed a man crouching down with his arm around his young son. The lad was sweeping a fishing net back and forth through the water; on the bank beside them was a jam jar full of dirty water. Another pastime that Billy would have loved to partake in with his *son.*

As the two of them tossed bits of bread at the rapidly gathering army of Canadian geese, Billy slipped down the bank soaking his one trouser leg up to the knee. Janet fell to bits with laughter and Billy too saw the funny side. They had found time for a long slow snog against an oak tree, which brought a certain amount of derision from a passing gang of young teenagers. 'Eeeerrrr, that's gross, man,' was one comment that they had overheard. They had laughed it off and carried on hand in hand. They walked a long way that morning.

They returned to Janet's home for a spot of lunch.

And then to bed.

The afternoon had been spent shopping, another alien activity to Billy. Janet had suggested that Billy's attire was more suitable for a Hovis advert, which Billy couldn't argue with; his Mother had purchased all his clothes from her friend Ivy's catalogue. After donning certain items of his new wardrobe, he looked a little more 'Dapper', Janet had suggested. He didn't have the heart to tell her that he would be getting very little wear out of them.

And then to bed.

Sleep, food, sex. Sleep, food, sex. Sometimes they went to bed not to make love, but just to lie in one another's arms, just for the comfort of it, to put an end to loneliness. No one was complaining. Billy certainly found that it gave him a lift, and, with her encouragement and positive outlook, he quickly began to regain the fragments of his shattered self-esteem. Expecting to feel totally knackered at the end of the weekend, he felt as though he'd recharged his batteries, and Janet had rediscovered all the excitement of adolescent love.

"You know," Janet had said earlier, "you ain't bad in bed for an old'n."

Billy had laughed, "You know why, don't you?"

"No, tell me."

"Because you never know when it might be the last."

Janet had thought that to be a strange comment but didn't press him for a further explanation. She hit him over the head several times with a pillow and chased him naked into the bathroom where they had made love under the shower.

They sat naked on a rug in front of the glowing coal-effect gas fire sipping red wine and chatting. Before they had realised it, a few intruding flares of sunlight stabbed through chinks in the curtains. They illuminated little but were just numerous enough to highlight what Billy thought to be Janet's perfect form.

And then...

When they had finally crawled up the stairs, and after making love again, Janet had ruffled Billy's hair and kissed him goodnight and then corrected herself wishing him good morning. She dozed, and Billy lay on top of the bed with his hands clasped behind his head. He stretched out naked on the duvet, his body almost floating with a sense of relaxation although his heart still raced from his exertions. *And I can't feel any pain whatsoever, perhaps they should prescribe it on the NHS!*

The bedroom was dimly lit, courtesy of a bedside lamp, which Janet had forgotten to turn off. The room didn't appear to belong to a woman of Janet's age. It held more of a childlike quality, it was girly. Cushions, stuffed animals, and candles littered the place. Billy thought that, surely you only need one candle in case of a power cut? There was a hint of pink satin emulsion on all four walls, and a darker shade of floor-length pink drapes edged with white ruffles adorned the window, which matched the canopy over the bed. The matching furniture was finished in a white satin effect; pink satin sheets were draped over his midriff. A small portable TV stood on a white tallboy directly opposite the bed. The top was covered with an array of makeup and perfume bottles and a set of rollers and several prescription tablet containers with childproof caps. He felt exhausted, but his eyes stayed open. He ruffled and smacked his pillow several times but still he tossed and turned trying to get comfortable, but the bed wasn't the problem. What was keeping him awake were the returning thoughts spinning around his head.

Billy took a glance at the bedside clock; it read 5:17a.m.

Too early to get up. Too late to sleep. He took a glance the other way. In sleep, Janet looked so beautiful and peaceful. She was snoring softly; he smiled; he liked that. A noise that irritated millions of couples the world over and *he* loved it. *My torture has always been waking up alone and this, this is fantastic! Shit, shit, shit, shit, shit, why couldn't I have had just a few more years of this?* His life was now almost over and could never be re-lived. The self-despising element at the centre of his psyche did not believe he was meant for this and now it had happened against all the odds...*Thank you so fucking much, God.* He sighed heavily through his nose. He turned to face her, propping his head on the pillow and just stared, and stared, and stared, drinking in her beauty. Billy's ridiculous grin would not subside. When he did finally drop off, it was an extremely uneasy sleep, anxious even in the land of nod about the day that loomed ahead of him.

He woke with a start. Glancing at the clock - which is all that Billy seemed to be doing of late - a quick calculation, told him he had in fact been asleep for just twenty-three minutes. Janet was snoring loudly; he smiled then thought about his recent purchase, which he'd placed in the boot of his car. *I may not get a chance to use it if I'm not quick, some plans work better with very little planning.*

On an impulse, he slipped very carefully out of bed, took his clothes from where he'd draped them over a nearby chair, and got dressed on the landing. He made his way down to the kitchen and rifled through Janet's drawers until he found a Tesco carrier bag. Holding his breath, he pocketed Janet's set of keys and clicked the front door shut behind him. He opened the boot of his car, and placed his new purchase into the carrier bag. There was no way he could muffle the engine as he fired her up but guessed that Janet was too far gone to be disturbed.

Billy cruised the streets. He had almost given up looking for what he hoped would be his next target, and his next target was only added to his list as a recent afterthought. He had been driving aimlessly round the side roads of his estate when a little luck dropped on him. The black Saburu with the darkened windows roared up behind him, sounded its horn, and then overtook him with a squeal of tyres; the passenger gave Billy a two-fingered salute through the open window. After about two hundred metres, it pulled into the kerb with yet another squeal of tyres. Billy also pulled over about fifty metres behind it. He killed the engine, grabbed his carrier bag from the boot, and began walking slowly along the footpath constantly looking behind him, although it was unlikely there would be anyone around at this time of day. The driver was continually revving the engine and Billy thought of the poor locals lying in their beds listening to it and too scared to come out to ask for quiet. Billy ruffled what little hair he had and altered his gait to a stagger; he looked for all the world like a homeless drunk. As he neared the vehicle, he noticed that the passenger window was open. On drawing level, Billy placed one hand in his carrier bag and bent down.

"Morning, boys," Billy said jovially and louder than was necessary.

The mixed-race youth took a slight jump sideways. "Fuck me, it's granddad again," and then to the driver: "this twat ain't learning no lesson, man, where's my fuckin' baseball bat?" He rummaged around in the footwell of the rear seats and found what he was looking for. He turned sharply and put a hand on the door handle ready to teach Billy a lesson, but instead he turned to stone. His mouth opened to say something, but nothing came out. He was frozen in his seat; deep furrows appeared across his brow. His brow had furrowed because he had never looked down the shaft of a crossbow bolt before. And before his brain had time to evaluate the situation Billy squeezed the trigger, and the powerful weapon kicked in his hand. The bolt entered the youths left eye and there was a pop! followed by a red blur as it exited through his right temple. Billy quickly fumbled in his bag for a second bolt but as he glanced up, he relaxed because not only had the bolt gone straight through the youths head, it had lodged in the side of the drivers' skull. It was only due to the feathered flight bringing it to a halt that it did not pass all the way through. The impact on the driver had forced his head against the door window showering the road with splintered glass. The passenger slumped sideways, and his head landed in the drivers' lap.

"Mmm," went Billy, "well that's saved me a bolt… granddad, indeed."

Billy held the crossbow above his head admiring his fantastic new toy. He mumbled quietly to himself, "Should have bought me one of these years ago." He began chortling in a spooky manner as he quickly scanned the street for any witnesses – the street was deserted.

"Where have you been?" Janet slurred.

"Just popped to the loo, pet, you go back to sleep," Billy whispered.

"Mmmm, let's make a seat."

Billy pressed his back into Janet's belly and she slipped an arm round him. Billy closed his eyes and smiled to himself. He didn't see himself as a brutal killer; his only thought was of the probable lives he had saved because two evil suppliers were off the streets forever. It was a little naïve of Billy to think that, because they would be replaced in a matter of days, but his hope was that other despondent citizens across the country would follow his example and carry on with his 'crusade'.

This is fantastic, who would have guessed after all these years looking after my ailing Mother that me, Billy Crabtree would find love – albeit short lived. Janet had soon dropped off again and Billy nestled his erection into her bum cheeks. Within seconds, he too was in a deep sleep.

The minute Janet opened her eyes on Monday morning she lit up from within. She wasn't one of the slow risers who shuffle about yawning and moaning about Monday mornings, she literally beamed.

As they ate breakfast Janet, a towel twisted around her hair, damp still from the shower, placed a hand on top of Billy's across the table. "How long can this last, Billy? I don't know why but I feel that something's going to happen, I think the bubbles going to burst." A slight crease appeared across her brow.

Billy smiled and shrugged casually to put her at ease. "I've told you, Jan, until the day I die."

He had told her the truth but at the same time felt guilty. *Will she think I've used her? I hope not. I never intended that, I truly love the woman.* He had visions of the aftermath of his actions, the newspapers, and TV hounding her for her side of the story. He swallowed hard.

"I said you'd better make a move, have you seen the time?" Janet said.

"Sorry miles away then." Billy replied, stifling a yawn into the back of his hand. He massaged his wrist; the kickback from the crossbow had given him a slight sprain.

Janet had prepared sandwiches for Billy, which he stuffed into a carrier bag; he grabbed his coat. He leant over the table and, gently placing a finger under her chin, lifted her head. He kissed Janet on the forehead. "Love you," he said.

Janet snaked an arm around his neck and pulled him nearer, kissing him on the lips. There was something deeply tender and vulnerable about him. "Where have you been, Billy Crabtree?" She asked.

Billy smiled and thought, *Mmm, I could tell you where I've been, but you would NOT believe where I'm going. Have we just been killing our pain with each other? No that's cruel it's just me.* He mentally shook his head and bollocked himself inwardly. *Always the negative, Billy, always the negative. I really love her, and I hope she loves me.*

Billy needed to leave the house a good deal earlier than Janet, so he could let in the cleaning staff, check the boilers, check the swimming pool etc., etc., so he went out to his car, a twelve-year-old Renault scenic he'd owned for seven years, and drove off.

The next part of Billy's plan depended on a little luck and he was hoping that today would be the day that both he and Deano would cease to exist.

33

Luck was not on his side.

On numerous occasions during Monday, Billy had made his way to Deano's locker and had surreptitiously taken a quick glance inside courtesy of his master key. The one item that he required, the item that Deano would jump through hoops for, what he would probably die for hadn't been there. Ditto Tuesday, but it did give Billy time to hone and perfect his plan and act out several trial runs.

When Billy turned up for work on Wednesday morning, the school was already open. It happened on occasions. The Headteacher and the deputy head were both key holders and would arrive particularly early on occasions if they needed to get work done before the start of school. Indeed, as Billy had arrived he had spotted the Headteachers car on the car park and another vehicle parked next to it, which he didn't recognise.

Billy went straight to his workshop where he leant over the sink and splashed cold water onto his face. He stood up and let droplets trickle off his face and onto his shirt; grey strands clung to his forehead. Dabbing his face with the towel he gazed into the mirror. The face looking back at him was a really bad copy of the one that he remembered from just six months ago: slack and pallid, almost black under the eyes, the eyes themselves half-closed and vacant. *What the hell does Janet see in that?*

The telephone didn't ring all day. Billy continually paced around his workroom, trying to keep busy but every few seconds he would be gazing at his watch, gazing at the clock, making himself coffee. He went around straightening things that didn't need straightening. He began to nibble at his lunch, but his stomach wasn't having it - no appetite. Considering what he had planned, he was pretty calm and relaxed. What he wanted more than anything now was a quick dignified exit, and not to go out like his father. He was quite certain though, that Deano would not appreciate the time and effort that Billy had put into *his* exit.

During the day, Billy went about his duties as normal, stopping off at Deano's locker a couple of times during the morning. As the day wore on, anticipation again soured into disappointment. The most significant excitement was a year eight student who had 'accidentally' lost a shoe on the roof of the school. This usually meant that someone had thrown it up there and if she 'squealed' there would be consequences.

Billy's calmness was evaporating and he was getting increasingly concerned that his plan was taking a lot longer than he had hoped, but during the afternoon his luck changed. On opening Deano's locker, there on the top shelf was the one thing that Deano, and indeed most of the kids today would be unable to function without, his mobile phone. Billy took a furtive glance left and right and then dropped the phone into his pocket. Slipping back the sleeve of his overall he glanced at his watch, it read 2:58p.m. *Shit, that doesn't give me long, I must get cracking.*

Billy hurried back to his workroom. He took from his bag a sealed envelope, on it, written in biro, simply 'Janet,' and underlined twice.

34

He strolled around kicking at this and kicking at that; he knew that he would find something here after watching many minutes of CCTV. Was it instinct, experience? He didn't know, he just *knew*.

He ran his hand along the backrest of the bench and stopped at a small rusty coloured patch. He went, "Mmm."

From a trouser pocket he pulled out a used tissue, sixty pence in loose change, and a Cadburys éclair. He un-wrapped the sweet and popped it into his mouth, throwing the wrapper into the pond. He rifled through other pockets and from the last one, the inside pocket of his jacket, he pulled out a small plastic evidence bag. Once again he went through each pocket in turn and eventually found his Swiss army knife in the other back trouser pocket along with two crumpled parking tickets and a tatty folded picture of Carol Vorderman. With the knife he scraped some of the rusty debris into the bag. He didn't give a toss about protecting the integrity of a potential crime scene. The 'evidence' would be for scare purposes only. He slid the bag into an inside pocket of his jacket.

There *was* something here he could smell it. He kicked out at a stone and it skittered into the pond. The ripple moved a Lilly pad and he caught sight of something small, white and shiny. His eyes slowly turned into slits and again he went, "Mmm."

Finding the small saw blade in his multi-tooled knife, he cut a metre length of branch from a nearby silver birch. He lowered the branch into the water to gauge its depth and then crouching down, moved the Lily pad to one side. An opaque glazed eye glared at him from the depths. He stood slowly and removed his herringbone trilby, then ran a sleeve across his forehead. He went, "Mmm…Jesus fucking Christ!"

35

"Hi-ya," Billy chirruped, shoving his head through the open sliding glass doors of the reception office. "Can I have a quick word?"

Janet smiled, "Sure, Esther can you take over the window for me for a couple of minutes please?"

"Yeah, no probs," Esther called back.

Janet rose from her swivel chair. She looked good. When he had last seen her that morning she was sitting at the breakfast table in her night coat and with a towel wrapped around her head. *She looks even gooder now.* Billy thought knowing the word didn't exist, but it summed up his feelings. Her hair was neatly brushed back from her face. Her makeup was careful and quiet. She wore black trousers and a white blouse open at the throat. On a thin, silver chain around her neck hung a pair of rectangular shaped, black rimmed bifocals.

Billy took Janet by the hand and led her down the corridor. He stopped outside of the ladies toilet, glanced quickly left and right and, on seeing no one about he pulled her inside, locking the door behind him. He wrapped his arms around her and pulled her close. She returned the embrace with similar enthusiasm, their lips met, then her mouth opened, and her tongue slipped inside his. She pressed her body into his, moaning quietly and then suddenly realising where they were, she quickly extricated herself from him.

Janet admonished him with a wagging finger, but in a light-hearted manner. "Billy Crabtree, have you gone insane, what the hell…"

Billy placed a hand gently over her mouth. He said, "You smell great, Jan." he slid his hand away from her mouth and they melted uncontrollably into each other's arms. Billy kissed her hard, pushing a hand up beneath her hair, fingers slowly massaging her neck. Janet closed her eyes and her mouth drooped open. She froze for a second or two and then went limp, returning his passion. They stood there for a long moment, taking in the closeness. Finally, she pushed herself away from the comfort of his embrace.

"Don't you think we're a little too old for this, Billy Crabtree?" she whispered, albeit with a smile. She fingered her hair back into place.

"You're probably right." Billy said.

So, they did it again, this time for long minutes.

"You're gonna get us both sacked if we're not careful," Janet said as they broke apart. She straightened her clothing; her smile was radiant.

"I love you, Janet Westwood."

Janet wrinkled her nose and smiled. She placed an open palm gently against his cheek. "What's all this about, Billy? You're acting strange."

"Nothing, I was missing you that's all…Jan, can you make me a promise?"

Janet's brow creased slightly, "Yes…yes of course." She cupped his cheek in the palm of her hand.

Billy sighed heavily. "No matter what happens, no matter what you hear about me, I want you to promise that you won't think badly of me. There is something I must do and there is a very good reason why I have to do it, I hope that you will find it in your heart to forgive me. I love you, you know that don't you?"

When Janet looked into his eyes she swore that they looked a little wet. *Is she reading my mind?* She wiped at his eyes with a thumb, confirming his suspicion. She had immediately seen in his face that something was wrong and felt that the bubble that she had mentioned over breakfast was about to burst and the skeletons in his wardrobe were about to be exposed. A conflict of emotions tumbled through her mind. A tear escaped and snaked slowly down her cheek, but as Billy was holding both of her hands now, she couldn't wipe it away. *My God, she even cry's beautifully.*

"You're worrying me, Billy, what's the matter? What's going on? Tell me please." Janet's look of genuine, brimming concern mirrored that of Billy's; but hers was so much more attractive.

"There's nothing that you need to know now. Nothing. Just promise me, please?"

"Yes, yes I promise but..."

He kissed her hard again and then said, "I have loved every second that I have spent with you, Janet Westwood. We must go now before we're caught."

She gazed into his eyes unblinkingly and Billy wondered how much of what he was thinking she could read from his expression.

She took a deep, shuddering breath, "But, Billy that sounds like a goodbye..."

Billy felt an urge to weep but contained it for fear of alarming her even more. She looked so forlorn, he hated keeping things from her, but there was no way he could reveal the shocking episodes of the last few days and the shocking episode that he had planned for Deano.

A shockingly loud school bell shrieked, which made them both jump a little.

Billy placed a finger over her lips, "Ssshhh, we must go."

Janet popped her head through the door; the coast was clear. As they made their way back to the reception, Billy informed Janet that he had found a mobile phone and if anyone came looking for it he could be found in the boiler house.

There was a wolf whistle as they entered the office. "Put him down for a bit," Esther called out.

Janet shook her head slowly and sighed, then brushed a single tear away from her eyes. "Ohhh, that woman..."

She's just having a laugh," Billy said.

"Mmm," Janet went, then in a lower tone of voice, "I wouldn't be surprised if we found her under our bed one of these days...what are you smirking at?"

"You said *our* bed."

"Yeah, well, it is isn't it? Although the mattress may need replacing soon with the amount of action it's seeing." She giggled but at the same time wondered if it *would* see any more action.

It took all of Billy's resolve to stifle a tear; he cleared his throat. "By the way, Jan, I need to borrow your car keys, there's a drain I need to get at and you're parked right over it."

"Yeah, OK." She fumbled in her handbag and handed Billy her keys.

"Back in a tick."

There was no drain. It was just a ruse so that Billy could place the envelope on the passenger seat of Janet's car. He sat there for a while in the drivers' seat. He could smell her. He longed to see her again and again and again...to be with her for the rest of his...tears flowed again. *Pull yourself together, Billy, miracles do not happen.* His face hardened perceptibly; there was work to be done.

On placing the car keys back into Janet's hand, he took her balled fist and held it tightly. She stared up at him pleading with her sorry blue eyes for him to tell her what was going on. She placed her head on his chest; her arms clung on to him tightly, wishing she could heal whatever was bothering him.

Billy's pain was palpable; a single tear snaked down his cheek and hung on his chin. He gently disengaged himself and straightened up. "Something in my eye," he said in a tone thick with suppressed emotion. He ran a sleeve across his face.

Carefully he lifted her face with the tips of his fingers; she was giving him a quizzical look. Billy mouthed the words I love you; he leant forward and planted a brief kiss on her lips. Janet placed her hands on either side of his face and just gazed into his eyes, eyes that were as vulnerable and uncertain as a child's. She smiled, which warmed his entire body, but it was a smile of worry.

"Don't leave me Billy, swear you won't." She didn't know why she felt a sinking and unnerving feeling, but something was up, Woman's instinct maybe? They drew close again and Billy held her against his body, squeezing her tightly and rocking her like a child. He buried his nose in her hair.

"Don't ask me for something I can't give you, Jan." With that, Billy turned. She watched him as he slowly trudged down the corridor.

"Billy," Janet called.

He stopped, and half-turned. She looked simply sensational. He had found her smart, bubbly, funny, charming, and sexy. *This is the first time, as well as the last time I have loved and it was perfect. It's all ended too soon, but if I had spent the whole of my life with her, it would have ended too soon. I think all I ever understood was Janet.*

A couple of slight wrinkles appeared between Janet's eyebrows. "Please, Billy..." her voice shook as she truncated her sentence, her voice clogged with emotion. She breathed in and when she spoke again her voice was steady. "Tell me what's bothering you, I love you, Billy, and I want to be with you."

Billy's face crumpled into lines of distress and sombre weariness. *I feel the same way.* He couldn't say the words thinking it would be unfair. It was hurting him to hear Janet sounding so worried. The blood pumped around his body and his heart ached with competing emotions of guilt and joy. He tried not to allow himself to feel too much, not while faced with the task ahead. He placed a finger to his lips and tears filled his eyes. They didn't fall, just gathered at the rims. An urge came over him to sprint down the corridor and fling his arms around her again.

"Billy, I love you," she told him again.

Unbelievable. "*You* love *me*?" he whispered incredulously to himself. It sounded so, so good. "And I will love you always." But he knew he would never see her again.

She held out her hands palms up. Billy walked towards her and laid his palms on top of hers. They stared at each other for a moment; it was strange to have been so intimate with a woman, *this* woman, this beautiful woman.

He smiled, turned his back, and continued his amble down the corridor, but he had only gone a few paces when he suddenly stopped. He always thought that good things would never happen for him and, in the end, it had – and in a way hadn't. He wondered about the life that he could have had if this horrible illness hadn't got to him. Janet had visions of him turning and then both of them running towards each other in slow motion like in a film. Billy's head dropped and then quiet sobs, he didn't want to break down, but the enormity of it hit him, he was just glad that he had his back towards her. Right at that moment a little chunk of his soul had fallen away like an iceberg breaking up. He coughed, managing to turn it into a choking fit. Could he really leave her like this? Right now, he felt as if his boots were super-glued to the floor. "Goodbye," he said to himself because he couldn't say it to her. The word sounded as final as a cyanide capsule. Finally, he was in motion and he trudged on until he was out of sight. He wondered how it was possible to feel so free, so good, and yet so bad at the same time. His heart pounded sharply in his chest, it was an odd kind of tearing sensation unlike anything he had felt before. Already, deep down, Billy felt a sense of loss and he had only left her seconds ago.

Janet stood forlornly in the corridor as Billy disappeared through the door. Her lips formed an inverted crescent of sadness; she sensed that things wouldn't be the same again. She closed her eyes and a tear escaped from one.

36

Billy made straight for his workroom, trying his best to fight off the surge of regret building up inside him. He felt guilty about pouring out the insane things that he had done in the last few days in the form of a letter to Janet. He should have explained to her why he could never again be with her, why making any long-term commitment would be impossible. He felt it was the cowards' way out, but it still didn't quash the thought of being apart from her now. It had been physically painful, because each minute that passed was one that he didn't have with her.

Drawing in a long, calming breath Billy donned a clean overall. He had found traces of Nelly's blood on his other overall, so he had cremated it by putting it inside the boiler. Once again, he flipped through the pages of his notebook. *Well, this is it; I won't need this anymore.* He tossed the notebook onto the workbench. As he made his way to the door, he half turned and his eyes roved. *I've enjoyed being here. One or two bad ones, but overall I've had some good times.* He shook his head and focused on what he had to do next. He felt weary to the core now, weary but strangely renewed and alive.

As Billy opened the door to leave, Detective Inspector Collins stood there with a clenched fist frozen in the air as if he were about to knock the door, which indeed he was.

"Ah! Good timing, sir," the detective said with a broad smile. He held out a hand for a shake. Billy took the hand. The detective had a strong grip and he looked into Billy's eyes with a measured gaze. Tucked under his armpit, an A4 sized manila envelope.

"DI Collins, sir, you remember? We met last week? I was investigating that poor boys' tragic accident involving the school mini-bus."

Perched on his head a herringbone trilby. The DI flashed his warrant card in front of Billy's face although he had done the same thing the previous week. Force of habit.

"This is constable Mc.Given," he continued, pointing blithely to someone out of view.

Billy poked his head through the door and said, "Afternoon," and then to the inspector: "why didn't you phone to warn me that you were coming?"

'Warn'? 'Tell' would have sufficed. He spotted these things he was a copper.

"Can we just have a quick word, sir, mmm?" The detective said politely; it was phrased as a request, but Billy felt it wasn't one, the tone indicating it was an offer not to be declined.

"If you're not too busy?" He took a step forward, taking advantage of Billy's confusion; he was going to have a quick word whether Billy wanted to or not.

Billy slipped back the sleeve of his overall and checked his watch as obviously as he could. There was a nagging sense of urgency now, a quickly looming deadline. "Well, I am in a bit of a..."

The inspector placed a hand gently under Billy's armpit and led him into the workroom. "Won't take up too much of your time, sir."

As the inspector brushed past Billy, there was that funny smell again, the one that Billy had noticed when the inspector had seen him on the day of Thommo's 'accident'. Billy couldn't quite place it, but it was similar to the aroma that attacked your sinuses when you opened the door to the P.E. departments' lost property cupboard.

The constable removed his helmet, tucked it under his

arm, and shadowed them. He was of slight stature, barely five feet seven; he looked about thirteen. His shirt was white linen, its collar fastened with a small, ornate gold pin. There was not a hint of lint or fluff anywhere on his immaculately pressed uniform. He obviously had no fear in lining up on parade each morning to be checked out by the station sergeant.

"Tea, coffee?" Billy enquired.

"Yea…" began the constable.

"No thank you, sir," interjected the Inspector, "we're rather busy. Now if I can just ask you a few questions?"

"Sure," Billy said, "please, sit down." He glanced at his watch again.

There were four chairs in Billy's workroom, none of them matched; all had been salvaged from the skips.

The constable made to sit, but on seeing the condition of the chairs, he wrinkled his nose and said, "I'd rather stand, if you don't mind?" He then took a notebook and biro from his tunic pocket and flipped it open with a dramatically flamboyant flick of the wrist.

"Put that thing away, son," The inspector said, pinching the bridge of his nose between forefinger and thumb.

"Sir!" bawled the constable.

The inspector inflated his cheeks and then placed the manila envelope on one of the chairs. He took time fumbling in several pockets before taking a notebook from the inside pocket of his jacket; the jacket had seen better days. It was green tweed with leather patches at the elbows and would have been out of fashion forty years ago. He made a few strange noises from his throat as he rippled through the pages of his notebook, stopped, coughed, and then scratching his head flipped the pages back and forth; it was purely for effect.

Bloody hell, is this the best they have? A podgy Colombo was an afterthought.

"Be with you shortly, sir can't read my own writing." The

DI said, tapping a biro against his notebook, which he referred too much longer than was necessary.

"No problem," Billy lied, the muscles at his temples twitching. He glanced at his watch, regretting having let the police in. The timing of his final plan needed to be set in motion a.s.a.p.

"Ah, here we are, Mister Crabtree, can you tell me if you are familiar with these two young men? Mister Neil Dunn and a Mister Craig Dean?" The inspector glared at Billy to read his reaction.

Billy placed a balled fist on one hip and scratched his head with the other hand. He braced himself not to let his voice waver. "Erm…yes, yes I do they're both pupils here at the school."

The inspector made a little sound like 'mmm' in the back of his throat. He stood where he was for a while thrumming his chin with his fingers. He then strolled over to Billy's workbench, took a hacksaw off the tool rack and ran a finger along the blade. He snatched his hand away and inspected his finger for any signs of blood; he replaced it into its holder. He turned and leant against the workbench. Consulting his notebook again running a finger down one of the pages. "You had some bother the other evening, Billy did you not? A number of youths apparently throwing missiles at your house and daubing graffiti across your garage door?"

Billy stared at him open mouthed. His lips formed an uneven grin, the slightest of tremors around the mouth; he released an inward sigh, hoping the relief on his face wasn't too evident. *So that's what this is all about.* "Yeah, little shits," he said brightly, "why can't they leave people alone, huh? And you think this pair are involved do you?"

"Maybe, Billy, maybe. Although if that is the case then one of the youths in question is already dead. A mister, mister…"

"They call him Thommo I believe," Billy jumped in.

"Mmm, Thommo is dead courtesy of your schools mini-bus. Now then, information given to us by one of your neighbours, a certain Mrs..." consult notebook again flicking the pages back and forth staring at the notes as if he'd lost his place..."Griffiths, she has volunteered some CCTV which shows three youths walking away from the area at about the same time as your Mother rang us. I take it it was your Mother who rang, sir?"

"Yes, yes that's right." *He obviously doesn't yet know about the fire at the house.*

"Mmm. I've played the tape to your Headteacher this morning and he has had no trouble in recognising one of the youths involved, he couldn't make out the other two, they were wearing hooded tops, but, as he has stated to me, these three... sorry it's two now isn't it? Anyway, these *two* always stick together so we could have a very good guess as to who the other one might be."

"Well *I* know for a fact who they are," Billy stated firmly, "the one stuck out like a sore thumb, even though he had his nose and mouth covered. Ginger hair, scar through the eyebrow..."

Billy stopped talking because the detective didn't seem to be listening to him. Instead, he was again flipping through his notebook, turning pages forward then back. Billy wanted to snatch the notebook from the inspector's hand and shove it up his...he nodded pleasantly at the constable who smiled back and was still standing to attention as if rigor mortis had set in. there was a long awkward silence.

"Ah, here we are," the inspector said, thrumming his chin with his fingers again. "Now then, Billy, can I tell you something that I am concerned about?"

"What's that, inspector?"

"Well, this line of enquiry is normally delegated to a much lower rank but when I found out that one of these young men is dead and one of them has gone missing, well this starts twitching..." he was tapping the side of his nose with a finger... "What are your thoughts on that then, Billy?"

Billy shrugged. *Shit, I can't believe he's been reported missing so soon, his Mother must have reported his absence.* "Erm, well, what can I say? The accident involving Thommo was erm, just that, an accident. And Nelly, well he's always going AWOL."

Billy's narration had lost its complacent, reasonable rhythm, uncertainties and hesitation was very apparent.

The inspector began to pace, to prowl but not taking his eyes off Billy. Glaring at him with mixed feelings as though a lie was written all over his face which in fact he knew for a fact there was, but he thought he'd continue with the chase, slowly wear him down after all, it's all good practice. He knew he should be more involved in the administrative side of policing, spend more time at his desk but *God* he'd miss this side of the job. He narrowed his eyes into slits of suspicion, which normally gets the nerves jangling in the opposition. His internal antennae had picked up on something and he was determined to find out what. How many times had he spoken to people who seemed genuine, but how many times had he seen perfect acting from the worst type of criminal? The corners of his mouth drooped; he fluttered his eyelashes, nodded gently and went, "Mmm." If it was possible to make 'Mmm' sound condescending, then the DI had managed it.

After long seconds in deep thought, the inspector again went, "Mmm." He turned to the constable who had been playing the game: shoulders thrust back, hands clasped behind his back, legs slightly apart, and eyes glaring straight ahead. "Constable stop standing there as if you've crapped yourself, man, leave us for a few minutes would you please?" He flicked his fingers in the constables' general direction as if to shoo him away.

The constables' brow puckered and the corners of his mouth turned down slightly. "Do you think that would be wise, sir? Surely that would be a professional breach of ethics?"

Deep ridges creased the inspectors' forehead. "Don't talk

bollocks, just go...*now*," is all he said.

"Certainly, sir." The constable didn't need telling twice. He gave a crisp salute, turned with drill precision and left.

The inspector sighed heavily through his nose and shook his head slowly from side to side. "I don't know what's happening to the force nowadays, Mister Crabtree he's come straight from the Cubs and into uniform." He clasped his hands behind his back and stared at the closed door for what seemed like long minutes. Billy felt that there was a sudden change in the atmosphere. Then the inspector averted his gaze on to him, studying him intently; Billy changed his position on his chair almost imperceptibly.

The inspector sank heavily into a seat and put his feet up on the one next to it. "And how do you know it's Nelly that's gone missing, Billy?"

First name basis, the inspector thought, reduce him to an inferior status. How superbly patronising, an old copper tactic.

"You just said that…"

"No no no, I didn't mention any names, Billy now did I?" The inspector asked reasonably and spread his hands out in front of him. He lifted his eyebrows and shoulders questioningly. He was enjoying himself now but tried to keep the pleasure out of his voice. He stared at Billy for a quarter of a minute, allowing him to marinate in the atmosphere.

The silence wasn't overtly threatening, and Billy regarded the inspector seriously, but he showed no signs of outward distress – or so he thought. He cleared his throat and swallowed hard but there was no spit there. Billy feigned interest in his nails.

The inspector had the ability to see what was invisible. Observing what was odd in what seemed to be natural; he read the signs as if they had been tattooed across Billy's face. The fidgety panic of someone with something to hide. Having no formal training in such things, over many years he had picked up the art of body language from word of mouth, experience and from what he had read. From the moment Billy had opened his mouth the inspector had known there was something not quite right, Billy's posture and demeanour were all wrong. As a long-established expert in putting up fronts, the inspector had a sharp ear and eye for minute uncertainties of tone, manner, non-verbal behaviour like a minute change in the nostrils and the pupils of the eye. 'The human lie detector' congratulated himself inwardly on the subtlety of his questioning; he had spotted stress so now he needed to probe the topic a little more, raise the stress factor.

Billy scratched an eyelid.

A blocking gesture.

"Well…erm, I just *assumed* that it was Nelly, he's always disappearing. Kids, ay?" Billy laughed nervously as he tried desperately to keep his breathing regular, attempting to suppress any tell-tale signs of nervousness. It wasn't working. Billy looked away and begun fiddling subconsciously with his hands.

There, again, the inspector noticed, a faintly different timbre, a sudden increase in agitation. He was already feeling the thrill of the hunt; he lived for it. If you had played this game long enough like he had, then you learn to trust whatever it was that raises the hairs on the back of your neck. Nothing compared with the elation of winning the game, of seeing the target led away in handcuffs, but of course he already knew what the outcome was going to be, after all, the boy's body had already been found but he was going to hold back this nugget of information. This was all jolly good practice, wasn't it?

The inspector stood and smiled towards Billy, but he seemed to be thinking about something else. He wasn't thinking about anything in particular; he was letting Billy stew in the silence. He began pacing; he didn't speak for a long time. Billy could feel the perspiration starting at his hairline.

Eventually the inspector said, "You seem to know a lot about him, Billy, huh? Considering there are well over a thousand pupils who attend this school."

Billy just shrugged feebly. "Yes…well, every year we get

kids passing through the school that *everyone* gets to know from day one. *He* and his two mates have been a thorn in the schools' side since the day they started."

The inspector resumed, "Mmm, anyway, his Mother contacted us on Saturday morning apparently he'd nicked seventy-five quid from her purse. Seventy-five quid? Where the hell do these dole scroungers get that kind of money from, eh Billy? She'd been phoning him for hours apparently, according to her he would always answer. A typical kid, phone permanently stuck in his hand. Anyway, it was the last straw, she said. She's had enough of the little scrote nicking stuff off her and she called us in, it was also his birthday at the weekend; she thought it strange him not turning up what with all the expensive presents waiting for him."

Damn and fucking blast! What are the chances of it being his birthday? Just my bloody luck. This wasn't in the script.

The inspector said, "I don't know how they do it. Single Mother never worked a day in her sodding life and I goes round there on Saturday and there's this great fucking flat screen tele stuck on the wall, leather suite, knee deep in shag pile carpet... makes the blood boil it does. Do you know how many times we've had that little shit and his mates down at the nick?"

Billy held out his hands, palms up, his shoulders rose and fell.

"I've lost count to tell you the truth. We pick him and his two mates up..." he consulted his notebook.

"Thommo and Deano?" Billy prompted.

"Yeah, we pick these bastards up and they're back on the streets doing the same damn thing before I've finished my fucking paperwork, *and* I've had to be civil to 'em too, but I must keep going because if I don't, Billy then the other side has won. Justice, sir! It's why I do what I do. I love locking up villains simply because it makes the world a better place. If you ask me, running that bastard over was the best thing for everybody."

Billy's eyes widened, and his jaw dropped open. He couldn't believe what he was hearing. Here was a man who thought the same way as he did, and *he* was a member of his majesty's police force!

The inspector strolled over to Billy's desk, his ears now flushed. There he found a chaos of neglected paperwork. He moved some of the papers round with a finger having no idea what he may be looking for. It was simply an exercise in serendipity. "It's obviously my job to bring criminals to justice, Billy," he said without turning, "now, there's people out there that view things differently. Their priority is to save the Crown Prosecution Service unwarranted expense in pursuing cases where they might not secure a conviction – it's all bollocks!"

The inspector took a handkerchief from his trouser pocket and, tilting his hat back on his head, ran it across his forehead. "This job has given me two fucking heart attacks, Billy. Anybody in plain clothes tells you he doesn't drink he's a fucking liar. This job affects you like that. I ain't supposed to drink, I can't eat what I want to eat, and I ain't supposed to smoke. It's the shitheads out on the streets that's done this to me, Billy not what I put into my body." He blew his nose into his hankie and stared at the discharge for a few seconds before replacing it in his trouser pocket. "*I* know how to rid the streets of crime, Billy and I think you are on the same wavelength, eh? We must make sure the scum I arrested five years ago are still inside after five years. We must make time inside impossible to do. Make it mind numbing time, back breaking time. Make 'em carry a sack of rocks from A to B and then from B to A all day, every day. And when you're not doing that, teach 'em that it doesn't pay to do what they did, and whatever they did wasn't playing by the rules and so they're gonna be treated like the shit that they are. I want these arseholes to know we mean business, bad people should go to bad prisons…you agree with me, don't you, Billy?"

Billy nodded enthusiastically because he *did* agree with everything the inspector was saying, and as he opened his mouth to reply…

"…You want to go out and do it again? I fuckin' hope so, because next time you'll do even *harder* time. And then when you get out you'll be telling everybody to keep away from the nick 'cause it's no picnic, it's hell, because the food is shit, there's no tele or radio or gym or heating or mobile bastard phones, bedclothes and toilet seats are made from barbed wire. When I pull somebody in I just want to mention the word prison, Billy and they shit their pants. For all our endeavours this country is growing into a more dangerous place, I find it difficult to swallow, Billy this rising tide of violent crime. The community is crying out for things to return to normality and I can't reassure them, Billy, and that pisses me right off. Tell me, Billy," he paused momentarily to loosen his shirt collar with a hooked finger, "did you ever watch Colombo?"

Billy's eyebrows slowly moved towards the ceiling and he chuckled.

"Something amused you, sir?" The inspector enquired.

"No, no it's just that…earlier I thought…never mind." Billy tried to smile, but it seemed uncomfortable under the force of the inspector's stare. Then: "Yes is the answer to your question, I do remember Colombo."

The inspector took off his hat and perched it on the armrest of the nearest chair. He ran a sleeve across his brow. Then he removed his jacket and threw it onto the seat, covering the manila envelope; dark wet stains adorned his shirt around the armpits. He strolled over to the workbench and took Billy's notebook. Billy's visage turned chalky white and his eyes turned into saucers; the inspector began fanning his face with it. As the inspector paced up and down the workroom, Billy's eyes never left his notebook; his teeth ground together. *Please don't open it, pleeeaaassse do NOT open it!*

"That's what they call me back at the station you know, Colombo. I don't mind, in fact I go about my work in a very similar way to him, seems to work for me, anyway. If you remember, sir he would always know who the killer was in the first ten minutes of the program and he would even go on to tell them how they did it, reverse detecting I think they call it. Do you remember, sir?" He continued fanning his face with Billy's notebook.

Billy shook his head to regain his train of thought. He was so very tired and very frustrated; his very thin patience was wearing very thin. It took great effort to keep his tone light. He wrinkled his brow in a parody of remembrance. "Yeesss…I think so, but where's this getting us, Detective inspector Collins? Why are you interrogating me like this? Shouldn't all of this be following a set procedure? Down at the police station with audio and videotaping, a solicitor perhaps?"

The inspector held both hands up in a pacifying gesture. "This isn't an interrogation, sir we're just having a little chat, a few background questions, there's no harm in that is there? Mmm? Believe me it's standard procedure."

Billy glanced at his watch, "Look, inspector I am rather…"

Billy's words were cut short as the inspector threw Billy's notebook back onto the workbench and approached him. Billy sucked in an inward sigh of relief on seeing his notebook back where it belonged. The inspector leant, flat-palmed on the armrests of Billy's chair with his weight forward on them. Their noses were no more than the length of a biro apart. Billy caught the stale smell of alcohol and tobacco. Billy looked up and met the inspectors' eyes. They were hard and predatory.

There were times to be subtle and times when you simply needed to listen. Sometimes though you needed to push, to goad, to provoke a response. The inspectors' face leaked a slow, humourless smile. He looked to left and right as if there were others in the room that might be listening in; he leaned in further and lowered his voice conspiratorially.

"Well now, sir," he said, fixing his fiery, bloodshot eyes on Billy's in order to intimidate him with the seriousness of the situation. "Have you ever noticed when you read detective novels or watched films how there's something that always bothers the detectives' subconscious? Some little oddity of behaviour, which, when he recalls it, proves the key to the whole problem? Well, that's you Billy; my obstinacy and hunches are inexhaustible. It's not so much an occupational disease, rather an essential requirement. Billy, let's skip the foreplay, eh? I have a strong suspicion that you deliberately ran down Mister Thomson, and I have an even stronger notion that our Mister Dunn is no longer walking Gods

earth. *I*, Billy, am in no doubt that *you* in fact murdered those two boys. I can feel it, taste it."

Billy's eyes widened and glistened. He jerked his head up and found that he was staring down the throat of a man who picked the likes of Billy out of his teeth at the end of the day. His mouth slowly dropped open; his upper lip was beaded with perspiration now and he didn't have a clue as to what to say or do, he was falling apart and didn't know how to cope with it. He couldn't hold the inspectors gaze; his eyes moved quickly to the floor.

"Lost our tongue have we, Billy?" the inspector smirked. "You don't want to say anything? Fine by me, we can carry on with this little chat back at the…"

"You *are* joking I take it, inspector?" Billy interjected; his bottom lip trembled but he sat up straight and determined, folding his arms in a show of defiance. A little gasp, half laughter, half exasperation burst from his lips. "I mean you *are* joking, yeah?"

The inspector smirked humourlessly. "I have been known to take a stab at humour on occasions, Billy, unfortunately this isn't one of those occasions. This, as far as I am concerned, is a murder enquiry and I have a knack of ferreting out murderers. I apologise if I've disturbed your sensibilities at all, but awkward questions must be asked. Normally I would have sent out someone junior to have this little chat with you, but I like getting out in the field it's my style especially when I can break someone down into confessing. None of this would be allowed back at base camp, that's why so many guilty toe-rags are walking our streets."

"What the hell is this? I'm the caretaker," Billy stammered in a voice cracking with emotion. He pushed himself out of his chair, almost knocking the inspector off his feet. Billy began pacing the room agitatedly. "You can't come in here and accuse me of murdering kids!"

The outraged citizen now. They all fell into certain groups – fake depression, anger, denial, or negotiation, but guilty or innocent, they all became outraged at some point in the questioning...or *expressed* outrage. One thing he knew for sure, he had never come across anyone who was immune to his type of questioning. Asking the right questions was just as important as spotting certain body language or analysing answers.

"It's, it's ridiculous, I-I-I've been vetted, DBS checked..."

"Yes, Billy, and so had Ian Huntley. My philosophy is Billy that we are *all* capable of murder given the right incentive. During my career, I have been in the presence of real killers and genuine evil. I can smell and taste it. I've met clever ones, stupid ones, those who have lost it and killed, and those who have enjoyed every second of it. The social predators, people with a glint of cruelty in their eye, parents who have killed their own kids, those who have claimed the voice of God telling them to do it or a message from the devil in a Black Sabbath song. Senseless deaths but they have all tried to justify what they had done. It was everybody else that got it wrong, not them...sit down, Billy."

Billy slumped down into his chair, head in hands.

The inspector parked on the arm of the chair opposite Billy.

He continued, "I remember many years ago there was one particular creep who had kidnapped, tortured, and raped an eight-year-old girl. He went into minute detail when he was in the dock, smiling as he related
the story his eyes never leaving the parents. Scum like that makes me so angry, Billy that I could stick a knife in them myself. He was given life but surprise surprise he's walking the streets nine years later, completely..." he drew quotation marks in the air with two fingers... "*Rehabilitated* he was. Mind you, that one turned out well. The girls' father tracked him down and run the piece of shit down in his Range Rover. Like you, Billy, in your own way you probably think yourself as noble ridding

the world of a disease. Some have had motives that I could understand and I've felt nothing but pity for them. *But,* it always comes as a surprise to them that society doesn't agree with them."

The inspector stood and locked his hands behind his back. "I'm trying to be nice here, Billy but that can all change. I've been a copper for twenty-seven years, I'm serious about it, if I wasn't I'd have done something else for twenty-seven years. So, after the amount of years that I've put in you get to know when people are lying, you know it in your bones when someone is guilty. You, Billy? You're so transparent I was never in any doubt about your guilt. If you were to tell me it was Wednesday I would feel the need to look at the calendar just to confirm it." He strolled over to a racking system that held various types of screws, nails, wall plugs etc. He took a box of wall plugs off the shelf and for some reason sniffed it and then replaced it. "I've got a copper's nose for these things you know, Billy, if you haven't got the nose then you're not a proper copper," he confided, without turning. "There are kids coming out of university straight into this job and call themselves detectives. Detectives, ha! Haven't got a fucking clue, couldn't detect piss in a bog. Always got an eye on promotion without the necessary commitment of hard graft. It's a new era, Billy, which demands a different kind of copper. Cases today are just as likely to be solved using a laptop, it's just a fancy bit of hardware and it's only as good as the intelligence going into it. OK, there's a place for 'em, but I can crack a case by finding that one tiny little piece of the puzzle that you can't find on any computer. You need to have the ability to interpret what you see and hear. In my world it's guilty until proven innocent that's my philosophy, Billy. They hate my archaic approach and my 'hunches' and the fact I may deviate or finesse a procedure or two from time to time. Laws are written so that coppers like me can figure out a way around them...call it intuitive insight. A copper has to feel crime before he can detect it. It was much easier years ago. Smack someone's head up a wall, frame them, plant evidence, alter paperwork, but there are still ways, Billy, silent ways to intimidate the scrotes."

He paused for a while, waiting for Billy's response to his last piece of verbal brilliance.

"I see," Billy said, unseeing.

"Mmm, I've never been a conventional copper, Billy. I've always sailed close to the wind and I know I provoke disapproval and exasperation from the top brass. *But* because of my constant, dogged results, Billy they don't question my methods they turn a blind eye. Guess who has the best clear up rate?" He didn't give Billy time to answer. "It's all PR, community liaison, social integration, and all that bollocks nowadays. I have spent days attending seminars with white boards, overhead projectors and motivational roll-play. At the end there's always a question and answer session and I always put my hand up and say, I could be out there right now arresting scrotes instead of listening to this crap. And there are huge sighs and shaking of heads. The force is changing, but I'm the type of copper who doesn't fit in with the modern ethos. I can't even fart nowadays without referring it to the CPS. I'll be retiring soon so I'll be buggered if I'm going to change or adapt now at my age. They think I'm a joke and there are only a handful like me left. *I* am the stuff of legend in the eye of the younger recruit. Oh yes, they decry our lack of sophistication but deep down I think I am viewed with great affection. I still play by the rules as far as possible, but the rules only get you so far sometimes you must bend things a bit. On occasion I have spoken of things in court that I hadn't strictly seen, but if they're guilty they're guilty and sometimes, especially with the shit system we have in this country, you have to persuade people and steer 'em in the right direction. The nature of society has shifted, Billy, I sometimes feel left behind, part of the past. No, I'm from the old school, mate and like all good coppers of my age I make my own luck and I ain't afraid of pursuing it no matter what unlikely direction it takes me in. Give me an hour with some thieving sociopath scrote down a dark alley, a quick knee in the bollocks and I have my fucking confession no probs. It's getting harder though, Billy. A few years ago, I'd arrest some tosser and he'd be banged up for five years. Now, I arrest him, and I find myself sat behind a fuckin' desk churning out paperwork for days on end. Put a dot or comma in the wrong place and the twats back on the streets." He then opened and closed two drawers, taking advantage of the chance to snoop, commit to memory, part of his nature.

"I've been with your Headteacher for most of today," the inspector continued. He belched generously and placed the back of his hand against his mouth. "'Scuse me. We've spent a nice day trawling through hours of video footage…you appeared in it quite a lot, sir."

Billy sat back in his chair and perched his chin on steepled fingers; his eyes everywhere except on the inspector. The walls seemed to be closing in; he tried to keep his face blank, unreadable. *This is going to end unsatisfactorily, and not like most of the works of fiction that I've read where all the loose ends are tied up. I haven't finished what I set out to do; all I need is just a little more time, shit! How the hell did I think I was going to get away with this? This is cold reality I may as well have left a paper trail or have erected a sign 'Murderer this way.'* Things were sliding from bad to worse; he squeezed his eyes shut; it was suddenly hard to breathe.

The inspector began fumbling in his trouser pockets for something.

Not a-fuckin-gain. Billy massaged his temples with his fingers.

The inspector then began rifling the pockets of his jacket, eventually retrieving a packet of Embassy No1. Tapping one out, he ignored the formality of asking Billy if he didn't mind lighting up. He placed it between his lips and then offered one to Billy hoping he wouldn't reach out because the pack was empty.

"No thanks, I gave up five years ago," Billy said, and then: "I'm sorry but smoking on school grounds is strictly forbidden."

"So is murder, Billy I would imagine." The inspector smiled, and then lit the cigarette with a lighter, which was adorned with the figure of Betty Boop. A woman he had been questioning a few months earlier had offered him a light and he'd 'inadvertently' slipped it into his pocket. He inhaled deeply. He held it there for a long time and then exhaled in deep satisfaction. Although Billy hadn't smoked for years, watching the inspector light up bought on an instant craving, Chinese torture.

The inspector resumed the narrative, his voice stern, unemotional, working his way under Billy's skin. "Now there was one interesting little sequence that we came across which happened on Friday afternoon," he said flicking ash onto the floor. "We see you heading towards what I think you call your environmental area…?"

The inspector raised both eyebrows at Billy. Billy went, "Mmm."

The inspector gave an expressive pout of his cracked lips. "Mmm…indeed, Billy. And then low and behold a minute or two later our Mr…Mr…can't believe it, it's gone already." He flicked open his notebook and made a show of consulting the page in front of him. Eventually he raised his eyes. He might have done this a good deal earlier if he had wanted because the page was completely blank.

How fucking irritating is this man, just like the real Colombo.

Ash fell from his cigarette; he held Billy's stare, waiting for him to say something, to crack, but Billy broke away to study his feet.

Whilst consulting his notebook, the inspector absentmindedly excavated the contents of an ear with a little finger and then closely inspected the brown goo that he had extracted. He wiped it on the back of a chair. "…Ah, here we are Mister Neil Dunn, yes he follows close behind. A

while later you return but our Mister Dunn does not, and he hasn't been seen or heard of since. Strange, don't you think?"

"There are many ways to get to and from the environmental area, inspector without going anywhere near our CCTV system…it's just a coincidence."

The inspector inhaled and exhaled smoke every three or

four sentences. Billy had refused a cigarette, but the smoke was getting to him, he was getting a nicotine fix just sitting in the same room.

"Quite right, sir, I realise that if you happen to believe in coincidence...which I do not. It's unusual that no camera picked him up anywhere in the school for the rest of that day. It's as if he followed you to the environmental area...and never came back."

Billy tried to hide a nervous swallow.

"So, you didn't catch sight of him at all?"

"N...no, I would have said."

"Mmm."

The inspector retrieved his jacket yet again and annoyingly felt in every pocket until he found what he was looking for in the last pocket he tried; he dropped the jacket back down again.

Billy ground his teeth together. *He's doing this on purpose.*

The inspector frowned slightly as he wriggled his tongue in the corner of his mouth attempting to dislodge a piece of bacon trapped since breakfast.

"You wouldn't have such a thing as a tooth pick by any chance would you, Billy?"

Billy sighed loudly. "No, 'fraid not."

"Mmm, never mind." He waved a small plastic bag in front of Billy's face. "Anyhow, you see these specks of debris in here, sir? Well, I scraped these off the bench in the environmental area; they look amazingly like dried blood to me. I would bet a year's wages that this sample would match perfectly with our Mister Dunn's DNA in our database. What do you think, sir?" He knew full well that the DNA of such a young man of Nelly's age wouldn't be held in the police computer system. But he also knew full well that it *was* Nelly's blood and that he was at present marinating in a black, watery grave just a few hundred metres away.

Billy sat grim and silent with his head bowed, elbows resting on the chairs armrests like a boxer who had just gone eleven rounds and didn't want to come out for the twelfth. *Oh my god!* Billy spotted an unsettling smear of blood on his right shoe. *Is that mine or Nellys? I'm sure I put my wellies on...mind you there was a lot of blood, it could have easily transferred...or it could be Thommo's?* He slowly slid both feet under his chair. An expression of panicked concentration was now etched deep into his face. He thought he had been punctilious to a fault in his preparation.

Billy needn't have bothered; the inspector had spotted the blood as soon as he had entered the room but he didn't mention it; didn't want to spoil the game.

Now, with Billy slumped forward and the air sour with the smell of anxious sweat, the inspector recognised that he was almost at the acceptance stage and that Billy's burden was lifting.

Billy tried one last pathetic attempt at wriggling out of his predicament; he slowly sat upright; his forehead creased with a painful frown. "Could be anybody's," he croaked feebly, "or...or a bird or a rat, and anyway, there's dozens of kids get injured here every week. I mean, can you seriously suggest that *I* or in fact anybody would set out to kill three students? OK, if it turns out that it was these three that attacked my house...yeah, OK, I'm gonna be mad, but kill them? There are proper, legal procedures..."

Billy's sentence was cut short due to the inspector spinning round sharply. "What do you mean, Billy, kill *three* students? We're only talking two here...or are we?"

"I, I, I meant two...slip of the tongue," Billy said to the floor, now unable to meet the inspectors gaze. His brain was now moving in too many directions.

"Mmm. I suppose it does seem ridiculously absurd and far-fetched, Billy...but not impossible. I never ignore anything as being too unlikely, Billy because in my line of work you get to meet the weirdest of people who do the weirdest things. Now, let's say for example if something were to arise that *enabled* you to get away with it? You're the Caretaker, Billy. If you were away on sick leave no one would notice, am I right? Staff here don't know you, they don't listen to you, and they look through you as if you are not there. They only want you when some little shit has thrown up over their desk or little Timothy has written his name across the bog wall in crap and now you're pissed off with tapping people on the shoulder aren't you, Billy? You're sick of being a doormat. I encounter many people like you, Billy. People who live their lives passively with anger and resentment slowly building up inside of them year in year out and then suddenly..." he clicked his fingers in the air; Billy jumped. "And now you're gonna hit 'em with a sledgehammer..."

"No, no, you're wrong, you're wrong..." Billy's forehead lowered, a portrait of dejection. He slumped forward, cradling his head in his hands. "I have nothing more to say, why don't you just leave me alone?"

"I think not, Billy no one gets left alone when I am looking for a murderer, and if you aren't the one I'm looking for, sir then pigs can fly and I am Robbie Williams." The inspector placed a balled fist on one hip and fingered his chin with his other hand. The smoke from his cigarette irritated his eyes; he wiped them on the back of his hand. "Let's say...for arguments sake... you were dying, Billy, it would be a whole new ball game then wouldn't it, ay? It would change the rules somewhat, wouldn't it? Make thing's a whole lot easier for you?" The inspector took a long draw of his half-finished cigarette then dropped the butt to the floor and ground it out under his heel; he instantly regretted the act; it was his last one.

Billy clamped his teeth together and raised his head; their eyes met. He felt sick. He couldn't rid himself of a sense of foreboding. After several seconds, Billy's eyes filled with salt water.

"How...how on earth..."

"I told you, Billy I'm good, very good even if I do say so myself. All it took is this," he said, tapping the side of his nose with a digit, "and a couple of phone calls. When I visited your Mother, there was a picture of the two of you on the sideboard. I asked when it was taken, last summer in Weston-Super-Mare she said. Looking at you then and now, Billy and it's obvious there is something drastically wrong. Then, a quick call to your doctor – phone number courtesy of your Mother – and he confirms your predicament."

"So much for patient confidentiality," Billy moaned.

"Mmm, indeed, it didn't take much. You're doctor works for us on occasion and I knew he'd appreciate me ripping up a recent speeding ticket he'd received in return for certain information. I'm very sorry about the situation you find yourself in, Billy…how long…"

"I don't know…weeks…months maybe…"

"Mmm."

This is why he had become a copper; the thrill and excitement of knowing you were about to pull in a criminal, especially a murderer. He had had discussions on occasions with his superior about the possibility of promotion, but that would mean being tied to a desk. He'd miss the buzz of doing exactly what he was doing right now. "I have a sixth sense, Billy I can see what others cannot, and anticipate what others cannot. You see, Billy I need to look into the killers' face when I finally nail 'em."

Billy's brow creased slightly; he hadn't understood that last sentence, and unbeknown to him, the inspector hadn't understood it either, it was something he had memorised from a detective novel.

"It's all supposition and guessing," Billy said, still clutching.

"That's called detection where I come from, Billy. Anyway, I don't do this job for the money, although I'm very well paid for what I do. Oh no, I do it for the thrill of the chase, the excitement of pitting my wits and skills against the low life. It's something no drug can recreate. There's always the adrenaline rush when you've cracked a case, Billy…like now, for instance. And anyway, as I said earlier, I can understand why some people take matters into their own hands, I can understand why you've taken the course that you have everybody's felt like that at some point."

"Everybody? Do you think so?"

"Yes, every person has the capacity, in fact some of the shit I meet, Billy I could quite easily kill two or three of them a week and not bat an eyelid."

The inspector took his coat and again went through all the pockets.

Billy's face crumpled. "What the hell are you looking for now?" He said without parting his teeth. The inner anger sent bile up into his mouth.

"Temper temper," the inspector said. "You know, Billy I could have sworn I bought an envelope in here..."

"It's there," Billy said jabbing a finger, "there on the chair right in front of your nose."

"Ah yes. Now then, there something in here that I'd like you to look at, Billy."

The inspector slid out several enlarged photographs and flipped through them. The scene of crime guys had done their job thoroughly, but only he had spotted something that no one else had. He pulled one out and handed it to Billy. "What are your thoughts on that, Billy?"

Billy glanced at it and then looked up puzzled. "It's just a picture of the school mini-bus," he said handing it back.

"Mmm," went the inspector as he flipped through the pile again. He pulled out another one and handed that to Billy. "And this?" He said.

"Well, it's the same photograph but it's been enlarged, again...I don't understand, inspector, what am I supposed to be looking for?"

The inspector took a pen from Billy's desk and, leaning over his shoulder, he ringed a part of the photograph. "And now?"

Billy's forehead ridged, "No," is all he said.

"Mmm, well maybe I was expecting too much. It's ok, I've shown these to some of my colleagues' back at the station and they missed it too. Like I said earlier, kids out of college. Too many coppers, even good coppers, overlook certain facts that are staring them in the face. You see Billy some things are so obvious we sometimes can't see them. Look again. You told me that on the day that you hit Mister Thomson, you were barely travelling at ten miles per hour?"

"That's correct, I can't be exactly sure of the speed, but I remember that I was moving very slowly."

"And I believe you, Billy. But although you were driving slowly you hit the brakes so hard that it still produced small skids marks."

"And?"

"Look again, closely. What puzzles me, Billy is that there appears to be approximately a hundred millimetres of tyre marks in *front* of the mini-bus...as if someone had come to a halt, reversed and then drove forwards again. Any thoughts on that, Billy?"

Billy didn't answer; his mind wandered off into a void of hopelessness; his narrow shoulders rolled forward, and his head dipped into his hands. He began sobbing. He then rested his head on the back of the chair, covering his face with open palms. *All I needed was one more day, Shit! Why didn't I go for Deano first? I must have been an idiot to think I could see off all three of them without being caught.*

Billy slid his palms down his face and opened his eyes. "Why now? Why leave the photographs until now?"

The inspector grinned and chuckled quietly; he held out his hands, palm side up. "For the sport, Billy, for the sport. You should have stopped yourself a long time ago; if you find yourself in a hole, Billy then stop digging." He chuckled some more. String him out, he thought, he's close to snapping. Once again, he began fumbling in his coat pockets until, from the last one he tried, he found a set of handcuffs. "Now then, let's wrap things up, shall we? Mister Billy Crabtree?"

Billy jerked upright in his chair, trying to maintain composure and control.

A broad smile appeared on the inspectors' face as he jangled the handcuffs teasingly in front of Billy's face.

Billy's jaw clenched, and he ground his teeth together. He slowly raised his eyes and looked determinably and unblinkingly into the inspectors' eyes. "They had no morals, inspector, and no respect for their fellow human beings whatsoever. People have a right to be protected from monsters like them. *They* set the ground rules, and I just played by them. If, and it's a big if, they ever went to prison, they'd be out in no time doing exactly the same thing. You've just said so yourself. I don't want that…*I* wanted to kill them! *I* wanted to watch them die!" He slumped back in his chair and slid both palms down his face.

37

Billy felt as though he was free falling, plunging helplessly into a dark void. *To be so close and not finish?* The thought was unbearable. It was looking very unlikely now that he would be bringing Deano to justice. Billy's own special kind of justice.

The inspector continued, "Mister Billy Crabtree, I am arresting you on suspicion of the murders of Mister Thomas Thomson and Mister Neil Dunn. You do not have to say anything, but it may harm your defence if you do not mention when questioned something which you later rely on in court. Anything you do say may be given in evidence…is precisely what I will be saying to you when I come back later in the week and slap these on you for the murder of these two gentlemen." He smiled and raised his eyebrows rapidly several times.

Billy's face collapsed. "Wh…what on earth…you're *not* going to arrest me *now?*"

The inspector crouched down until his nose was almost touching Billy's nose. He whispered, "I can arrest you if you like, Billy because I am as sure as the fact that I've got a hole up my arse that if I wasn't so shit-hot at my job, then a certain third member of the gang would have eventually and mysteriously disappeared. Am I right, Billy? Huh?"

"I don't understand, I…"

"I think you do, Billy. I can't arrest you just yet. You haven't said that you've actually killed anyone, just that you wanted to and that's a totally different thing." He slowly stood upright and clasped his hands behind his back. He stood in front of a calendar just to his right, admiring a panoramic shot of a Dutch bulb field. "Do you know how many murders I've investigated over the years, Billy?" He continued before Billy could answer, "To tell you the truth I don't know myself, probably runs into three figures. What I do know is that I've solved all of 'em... except one, one case that I have failed to close, and it's haunted me. The young man who burned alive in his flat on the Shorevale council estate about a year ago, do you remember that case Billy?"

"Yes, yes I do," Billy whispered.

"Failing to close that case has tormented me, Billy; every copper has got that one case that pisses him off. There ain't a week goes by where I haven't studied that file. Police work can affect you like that; people you *knew* were the culprits but couldn't nail. Some coppers can let them go, but me, no it's an obsession."

The inspector took in a deep, slow breath through his nose. "That poor guy is never far from my thoughts, Billy because I attended the scene of crime and the autopsy. Terrible sight. The mans' skin had crackled and bubbled as he boiled, the ligaments shrivelled, his hands turned into bird-like claws, huge blisters had formed and then quickly burst spitting hot droplets of blood across the walls and door of his hallway," he fingered his chin thoughtfully. "Mmm, terrible sight, you never get used to seeing things like that, Billy and I've seen everything believe me. Every inch of every murder scene is imprinted on my brain and they haunt me sometimes especially that one."

Billy swallowed hard. The inspectors graphic description had made him feel nauseous. If Deano were standing in front of him right now he would have gladly gouged out both of his eyes.

"What's this scribbled on the calendar – B.H.?"

"What?"

"B.H, on the calendar."

Billy shook his head. "Erm...it's a bank holiday."

"Oh, right. Anyway, I know who killed him. Everybody on his estate knows who killed him, the three perpetrators names came up dozens of times on social networking sights and in anonymous phone calls and letters but they somehow managed to squirm through our fingers. I'm sure that you know who killed him too, eh, Billy?"

Billy raised and then lowered his shoulders.

"Oh yes you do Billy. Anyway, lines of enquiry slowly fizzled out and other cases took precedence. It will never officially be filed. Using my methods..." he drew quotation marks in the air with two fingers..."they'd have been put away for ever, no doubt in my mind. However, things must be seen to be done right. You know I had those three bastards and other members of the gang in for days questioning them for hour after hour. I put them in separate interview rooms and kept returning to ask the same questions to see if they wavered from their previous answers. Sat there smug as you like they did nothing I said or did to them touched them emotionally. Sneering, smirking, looking bored, the cynical smiles, not a bit of remorse between 'em. No comment to this and no comment to that. Even at their age, they've already developed a sense that they cannot be caught. You know if I were a judge the first time I heard a 'No comment', I would be a hundred percent certain that the fucker was guilty. Their solicitors were constantly butting in, you can't do this, and you can't say that. Nowadays justice is all about who has the best legal team. Murders' don't even make the local news now because it just ain't news anymore, Billy. It's become common, we tolerate things we never used to, society has become immune to it and it's all down to the 1998 human rights act, what a load of bollocks that is! I have a list as long as your arm of unsolved muggings, robberies and so forth, I could clear most of 'em tomorrow if my arm wasn't being bent up my back. Then you've got the welfare authorities pussy-footing and fannying about, which encourages these young thugs to continue with their activities. Maniacs are being put back onto the streets by institutions from a different planet. There're people out there I know for a fact are guilty, but I can't touch 'em. If you can't get enough evidence to interest the Crown Prosecution Service, then you can forget it. When I first started this job, it was *them and us.* The only weapon I had was the law, Billy, now the law's their weapon too so now I must use whatever I can lay my hands on. I have to be out there, on the streets, I'm too wrapped up in the system, so I have certain…let's say, acquaintances that I can turn to who stand outside of it. Wrong and right have all been turned upside down, and we don't even know half the difference anymore. The whole political correctness shit pisses me off no end. I have spent all my working life hunting down scum like them, they think nothing of destroying lives and livelihoods, and they see the law as something to be tested, sneered at, and broken. I once believed that being a copper meant that you were involved in protecting the property and safety of the people, but I've seen law and order being eroded away, Billy. The government are telling people that the crime rate is dropping. Bollocks! The scum today are almost encouraged to carry on with their activities. No one gets involved anymore. No one intervenes it just gets worse and worse."

The inspector glared into space and thrummed his chin for several seconds. "I've lost track of what I was saying…oh yeah, that case ate me up inside, Billy. I spent a lot of time and effort on it without getting a result. It represents the only blot on my record. I've tried not to think about it, but it's a case close to my heart and I can't let it drop. There's a family out there, Billy unable to lay their past to rest, they want closure, I want closure, and I think you do too, sir, huh?"

Billy glanced up, nodded imperceptibly, and then dropped his head back down.

"The thrill of the chase is still there, and I would have loved to have wrapped that case up, it would be a fine way to cap my long service and justify early retirement. Well, that's what I've told the wife. I should be retiring this year y'know, but I'm the type who'll never stop chasing the bad guys. As long as there are the Deano's of this world, Billy I'll never stop being a copper. That case has kept my brain active. I didn't want some four-eyed young twat coming straight into the job from Uni and finishing the job, although I doubt whether they'd know where to begin. Now, I think justice is about to prevail, I think that case is about to come to its conclusion. If I can't get enough evidence to convict the shits who burned that poor man alive, then perhaps the culprits should have a taste of their own medicine. If murder is ever considered justifiable, Billy then the murder of those three scumbags is justifiable. They have been a thorn in my side, Billy and I think you are the man to pluck it out. An eye for an eye and all that bollocks, ay, Billy? That's what you believe in isn't it? The law of the jungle, Billy?"

Billy had been absentmindedly thrumming the table with his fingers.

"Are you nervous, sir or just bored?"

Billy shrugged feebly; his mind was somewhere else. The minutes seemed to be moving very slowly.

"Billy Crabtree, I see you as the British Charles Bronson, you are fucking special! You're special because people are going to remember you. People love the idea that the bad guys don't always get away. There are millions of Billy Crabtree's in this country who are cowering behind their curtains, they think things but can't carry them out. It's action that makes heroes, Billy, like *you*..." he flung a pointing finger at Billy "...you are prepared to get up off your arse and do your country a service, Billy, you will be followed. With those three cunts off the scene, the crime rate on their estate will drop by a huge amount! This is just the tip of the iceberg!"

A cold and instant realisation spread across Billy's face; his brow furrowed, his eyes opened wide. "You *want* me to kill Deano don't you? That's what this is all about. That's why I'm not being arrested. You want him dead, but...but you're the police, surely these kind of tactics are little, if any better, than the criminals and you're telling me to..."

"Oh no no no, sir. I ain't telling you anything." He approached a potted plant that was sitting on the windowsill and stuck a finger into the soil; it was bone dry. "I, Billy have to be *seen* to play by the rules; it doesn't mean I actually *have* to play by them..."

"You're stepping over the mark..."

"There's NO fucking mark, Billy! There's getting things sorted, and not getting things sorted." The inspector mopped his brow. "Morality? I'll sort out the morality questions when I retire, Billy there'll probably be quite a few, but I'll get over it. I don't normally waste my time on bullshit like red tape all I'm saying is I need more time, Billy. More time to get this sample analysed. There is evidence to be carefully checked and prepared and time-consuming liaison with the CPS. And anyway, I'm a very busy man; I've got other cases on my books, dozens of crimes going through the post-arrest stage." He tapped the side of his nose with a digit and winked. The inspector then took his coat from the chair over which it had been casually thrown and shrugged into it. He held out a hand for a shake. Billy took it, albeit limply.

"Like I have stated, there is this one big case that I have failed to close – it haunts me, it torments me, it's got me by the short and curlies and there is not a single hour of the day that it's far from my thoughts. Billy, as I've said I'm from the old school and if needs be I'm quite prepared to lie and cheat to get my man, so there's no sense in me apologising for something that's gonna get me the result that I'm looking for...*we're* looking for. It's results that matter rather than how you get them, as long as I can close the file, I'm happy. I couldn't get to 'um, Billy, the scum around them made too good a job of covering their tracks like most of the crimes that they have committed. So, if it doesn't come now, then when they do eventually release me into the wild and put me out to graze, then I will be applying to join the Cold Case Unit. They're a bunch of old farts but they're still itching for answers like myself."

The inspectors' brow had collapsed; he had lost his train of thought again.

Billy raised his eyebrows, "The guy who burned to death?" He prompted.

"Oh yeah, that's right. Me, you, the guy who burnt to

death? He was someone's son, Billy. For Christ's sake he was a divorced man with two kids, what if they had set fire to his flat at the weekend when the kids would have normally been staying there? I don't give a shit if the guilty people spend time in nick or are buried under someone's patio; the end result is the same, except the latter one is a lot easier on the taxpayers' purse. I feel responsible in some way for all of them, and the pain of his family weighed so heavily that even my broad shoulders were close to bending." He clenched a fist in front of Billy's face; "I *promised* them on more than one occasion that I'd bring the guilty people to justice. This case has left its mark, which can only be erased by justice in whatever form that takes." He unballed his fist and placed a friendly hand on Billy's shoulder; he smiled, "Look, Billy, there is the opportunity here to remove this cancerous Deano animal from God's earth. Him and his two mates? They're not *people*, Billy; they're something less than human. They say that children are born innocent. I no longer believe that, Billy not in the Britain we've built today. It doesn't matter what counselling they have, essentially there are still evil people about." Forgetting to mention that this was probably his only chance for some kind of professional redemption. "So, then Billy, I'll pop round on…" he waved a hand vaguely in the air, "… Friday? Shall we say Friday? Is Friday OK for you, Billy?"

"Erm, well I think we both know that everything you've said in the last minute or two is a load of old crap?"

The inspector feigned a hearty laugh.

Billy threw his shoulders back and stood tall. He sniffed violently through his nose and said very quietly, "*But*, Inspector, I want you to know that no matter how hard I've tried to be good in this world and do the right thing, I've always ended up on the losing side. But now I'm dying I don't give a shit. I am *not* some nut-case vigilante, all I've done is take on a personal war against crimes that have involved me and my family, I just wanted to save innocent people from…" he sighed heavily, "*look*, inspector, I don't want to leave this unfinished. I do not regret for one second giving those bastards what they deserved, in fact it satisfied me greatly. Our society will have five less pieces of shit to worry about. I think what I have done is morally correct although I am under no illusion that in your eyes I am a murderer. I hope I am setting an example, I hope others will study it and think about it. Everything that's been tried with these...*boys* has failed and so I have concluded that the system failed and that's where I come in, you have to fight evil with evil."

"Fight evil with evil, erm, I'll have to remember that one, I like that, Billy." His face collapsed. "*Five!* You said...*five?*"

Billy smirked. "Oh, come now, inspector, do try and keep up. I have left a letter explaining all."

The inspector ran an open hand down his face and let out a rush of air from his mouth. "Indeed, Billy, indeed. I've been around a long time, Billy and I thought I couldn't be shocked by anything, but you..." he shook his head slowly trying to grasp what Billy had just told him. "And who..."

"It's all in the letter. I've only targeted people who deserved what they got, if we had a system that handled these things better, well...?"

The inspector arched a single eyebrow. "Mmm, ok, yeah, mmm that's the spirit, Billy."

"So then, I'll ring you when I've got some news...leave it with me."

It was very rare for the inspector to be flummoxed; he quickly regained his composure and scratched at the back of his head. "My God, Billy you have been a busy bunny. Anyway, until Friday then, sir?" He held out a hand for another shake, which Billy took. To the inspector, Billy seemed to have grown in physical stature, becoming broader, taller. He rifled in his pockets and pulled out a card, which he wafted in front of Billy's face. "If you think of anything else, no matter how trivial, or need anything, Billy, my mobile numbers on there, don't hesitate to call OK?" he thrummed his chin with his fingers. "You know, Billy I've a feeling we're gonna make a good team me and you, I like you, you get the job done." He placed the card on the table. "I'll see myself out." As he turned he let rip a corpulent fart. He flapped a hand in front of his nose. "Last nights' mushy peas," he stated by way of an apology.

As the inspector shut the door behind him, Billy slumped back into his seat not quite believing what had just happened. The last half-hour or so had been so surreal; he rested his head on the back of the chair and stared wide-eyed at the ceiling. *'Just the tip of the iceberg' the inspector had said. Was he planning to use me to bump certain people off before I die? Other members of the Subway rats perhaps until the whole gang had disappeared?* That thought gave Billy a bit of a thrill. He gave a little jump when there was a knock at the door. Billy sighed heavily and got up to answer it.

"My hat, sir?" The inspector said.

"What?" Billy said, exasperated.

"My hat, sir, I've forgotten my hat."

"Oh right...right." Billy fetched the inspectors' hat and handed it over.

The inspectors' thin smile didn't translate to his voice. "Thank you, sir." He placed the hat on his head at a jaunty angle. As Billy went to shut the door the inspector turned and put his foot against it. "By the way, sir, just one more thing?"

Billy had a powerful urge to tell the inspector, *'Just fuck off!'* "Yes, inspector?"

"That plant of yours needs a drop of water. Good day to you."

My god what an irritating twat he is. Billy closed the door after him. He stood where he was for a while, half expecting a knock on the door again. Shortly, he sat himself down again and rolled his head around on his neck to untie the knot that was tightening between his shoulder blades. He now realised how naïve he had been and that in normal circumstances he had been playing a game he couldn't possibly have won. *However,* these were not normal circumstances, and Billy knew that with the little breathing space he had been handed, he *was* now after all going to win the game.

The inspector was dead right; he's certainly shit hot at his job. He was also dead right about the third member of the gang disappearing but it's gonna have a slightly different ending to the one that he envisaged.

Billy Crabtree would definitely *not* be wearing handcuffs on Friday. He stood and ambled over to the table where he picked up the card the inspector had left. He shook his head slowly from side to side and a smile spread across his face. *Well, I can't do much with the inspectors' library card now can I? If you were to write a crime thriller with DI Collins in it, no one would ever believe in his character.*

Billy's roller-coaster ride was now almost at its apex. He rubbed both palms together and began chortling gleefully, slowly expanding into a raucous rush of laughter.

38

Billy gulped back the dregs of a stone-cold cup of tea. He leaned back in his chair and studied his little workroom. A small workbench fitted with a vice. A phone, three shelves stacked with files containing contractors contact details, asbestos rules and regulations, the safe handling of chemicals and a health and safety manual that had never been opened. A rack carrying various tools. *Not much to look at, but it's amazing what has gone on in here over the years.* He'd picked up many skills from various courses he had attended. He had even been invited to teachers' homes to carry out the odd little job on occasion: erect shelves, replace taps, fix toilets, etc., etc. *A welcome bit of pocket money and all tax-free. Nice people most of 'em, but useless with their hands and no common sense whatsoever.* He shook his head to dismiss his reverie. He was very fatigued but knew there was no time for rest. He had to remind himself that his work was far from over. He must keep calm and collected, keep his mind sharp, and rally every ounce of discipline available in his weakened physical and mental state. Glancing up at the clock on the wall and then checking its accuracy against his watch, Billy jumped to his feet. The inspector had disrupted his schedule. *Should I go through with my plan now or leave it until another day? Now! It has to be now; I've left a letter in Jan's car.* Everything was in place and ready to go; he was resolutely determined to see this through to the end. What with the copper hot on his tail and the fact that he would have to explain why Deano's phone was in his possession,

Billy was going to go for it. *However, I'm gonna have to be quick about it.*

Moving with purpose now, Billy retrieved another two sealed envelopes from his bag; he placed them upright against the telephone. On one was written simply 'Police.' Not wanting the police to waste time and effort trying to unravel what Billy had been up to, he had written down everything about his recent escapades, although from what he and the inspector had just discussed, he was already aware of most of it. He had logged how he had done what he had done and why he had done it. The second envelope was addressed to the 'Social Services', informing them where his Mother was at present and outlining what he expected them to do for her in his sudden and unexpected absence.

Just to refresh his memory he flipped open his notebook, quickly read from it and tossed it back onto the workbench; he had no need of it anymore. He took a roll of gaffer tape from the shelf and items that he had placed there earlier: a short length of string, which he had cut from a roll, a small glass jar with a screw lid and a plastic vending machine cup. He rammed all the items into his overall pockets.

His first port of call was the swimming pool plant room. As he made his way there, the floral tributes, bunches of flowers, teddy bears and cards placed there for Thommo had almost doubled in size. He had a quick glance at a few of the messages. They were bleating the loss of - 'A great friend'. 'You'll be missed'. 'Waste of a great soul'. *Are they talking about the same Thommo?* If he wasn't in such a rush, he may have added a card of his own. 'Gone and already forgotten', perhaps? Or 'Good riddance to bad shit'?

Staff rarely made their way down here; in fact, most of them didn't know this place existed. Chemicals were dosed into the swimming pool automatically and the only tasks that Billy was expected to perform were to change the barrels and drums of chemicals when they were low or empty and log daily chlorine and pH readings that were displayed via a digital readout.

From the left pocket of his overall, he took the small, screw top jar. He unscrewed the top from a barrel of sulphuric acid and very carefully poured a small amount into the jar screwing the lid back on tightly. Next, from his right pocket, he took the now misshapen plastic vending machine cup. He slipped a respirator facemask over his head, lifted the lid off a tub of chlorine and half-filled the cup with granules.

His next destination was the boiler house where he deposited both containers on a shelf just inside the doorway together with a cup of tap water. Finally, the shipping container. Stored here were various building supplies, old desks, cupboards, scenery from different plays and musicals, etc., etc. Right at the back, there were television stands of various heights and widths, which had been gathering dust over the years since the introduction of flat screen TV's. These were fitted with castors and allowed the easy transportation of the heavy, old type television sets around the school. Billy took the one that he had run a tape measure over earlier and wheeled it into the boiler house.

Job done. Now all he had to do was wait for his last victim.

39

Billy sat on the edge of a raised concrete slab, which supported one of the boilers. He hummed a nondescript tune in a soft tone as he chewed his thumb and worked on finding focus for the last push. Exhaustion was etched deep into his face; he rested his back against the boiler and mentally shook his head to clear it of all thoughts. He pressed the heels of his hands against his eyes to enable him to concentrate. A clear head was needed, closing down any distractions. If he wasn't careful, he'd soon be thinking about Janet again, which he really couldn't afford to do right now.

Raising his eyes, the flameproof, tiled ceiling had been discoloured by veins of rusty coloured water. *The roofing company is coming out to look at that tomorrow, should have left 'em a note. Hey-ho, never mind.*

He closed his eyes and his mind tossed up an image of Nelly's face. Was this reality or was this a nightmare that he would soon wake up from? He knew the answer to that, but perhaps after all these years of suppressing his anger he had now lost the ability to think rationally. He'd managed up until now to push the whole nightmare from his thoughts. Billy just couldn't believe the instability of his actions over the last few days. He had a short fuse, he knew that, but he had lived his life with order and control and then suddenly out of nowhere…his eyes shot open, his breathing quickened.

He waited.

The boiler turned off automatically one hour before the end of school and so it was still quite warm. He sighed, dropped his head against the warm side panel of the boiler, and pressed his fingertips into his temples; it felt good. Raising his arm, he watched the second hand of his watch intently; it seemed not to be moving. It took all of thirty seconds of willpower, but his thoughts did return to Janet and the fragile, despondent, and abandoned look on her face when he had left her in the corridor. He contemplated going to see her for one last time but talked himself out of it, how many times could he see her 'for one last time?' He would have cherished one more night of warmth and companionship. *Mmm, that would be fantastic.* No, he didn't want to see her looking at him like that again. Like she loved him, cared deeply for him. He hadn't realised just how badly this would hurt. *What did she see in me? I'm not exciting and not especially good looking. The sex had been great, though. Beautiful and intense. She loved the fact that I spoke to her tenderly throughout and was more interested in giving than receiving. At least I'm not going to my grave a virgin.* He shook his head internally then cursed himself inwardly for not ending on a better note. Soon it would all be history. If only he were able to turn back the clock. Now it seemed so very far away. Would she forgive him? *I doubt it, why would anyone?* He had said that he would love her until the day he died, which of course he had meant absolutely. He hadn't actually told her that that might be sooner rather than later, so he hadn't *really* told her anything that wasn't true. He would give anything for the time, the opportunity to do it again. He had loved her with all of his being and hadn't realised just how badly this would hurt. Billy felt fulfilled on one hand yet strangely empty at the same time.

He waited a bit longer.

I wonder what I'd be doing now if Thommo hadn't stepped off the curb at the precise time I was passing in the mini-bus? I may have had a couple more weeks with...

Feeling sorry for himself wasn't going to get much accomplished.

Patience was never one of Billy's more obvious virtues; he slipped back the sleeve of his overall and glanced at his watch again. Tutting loudly, he was even impatient whilst waiting to die. There were only four minutes left until the end of school bell would be sounding. He bit the inside of his lower lip, and then took a sip of coffee that he had bought with him. Billy barely needed the caffeine hit; he was still running on the adrenaline that had been fuelling him for the last few days. His eyes were red-rimmed and began drooping with fatigue. Perhaps the adrenaline was running out – whatever adrenaline was. He downed what was left in his mug in one go.

Janet had been unhappy with her husband for years, she had told him so. *Perhaps if I had approached her years ago...there I go again, what if, what if, but I have experienced love. OK, only for a few days, but what a few days...fantastic. If I were given the choice I would gladly re-live my short time with Janet rather than live a lifetime with anyone else.* He now desperately craved what he couldn't have, but at least temporarily he'd had everything he had ever wanted - a woman who loved him, and who he had loved more than life itself. They had spent only a few days together in a sea of happiness; he wept. Not openly, he wept inside, and that's where it hurts the most. The shrieking of the school bell startled him into action.

Billy leapt to his feet, adrenaline coursed through him again manufacturing a sudden wide-eyed alertness. He experienced an unrivalled and unprecedented high. He made his way to the boiler house door and unlocked it, leaving it slightly ajar. Already he could hear the screaming voices of kids as they discharged themselves from the front of the building, gushing out in their hundreds.

Billy made his way to the only window in the room. It was constructed of louvered glass panels, which allowed the heat from the boilers to escape. It was so filthy and opaque he could barely see out of it; he rubbed the corner with his fingers to create a small spy hole. From here, he could survey the main entrance door to the school. Within seconds his intended victim appeared. Deano vaulted a low fence and was heading determinedly across the front lawn straight towards Billy; on his face was etched irrepressible rage; he lit a cigarette as he stormed toward the boiler house. *Keep off the grass you sadistic, murdering, bullying, moron, and welcome to the rest of your life, which will be a very short time indeed.* He smirked; Deano had obviously been given the message about his mobile phone. Billy took an envelope from his inside pocket and tipped into his palm the remaining sleeping capsules that he had taken from his Mothers' bedroom. He swallowed the lot with the aid of the cup of water. He had calculated that it would be approximately thirty minutes before they entered into his system and began to take effect. Turning off all the lights bar one, Billy then stood in the shadows next to the door. The door was booted open; the aluminium door handle hit the wall behind it and shattered into several pieces.

"Crabby! Are you in here, Crabby, I want my fuckin' phone..."

"Right behind you, son," Billy didn't raise his voice, but it was enough to make Deano give a little shudder. Billy's face was half lit and half in shadow and looked eerie.

Deano spun round. He had a look on his face that said he wouldn't mind eating Billy's heart. His pupils were fully dilated, almost covering the iris; he had obviously popped something on his exit from the school building.

With one hand, Deano grabbed Billy's shirt at his throat and shoved a finger into his face. "You've got my mobile, Crabby," he demanded, his voice low and threatening. "You nicked it outa my fuckin' locker, I'll get you the fuckin' sack for this, you thieving..."

"I found the phone in the humanities social area..."

"That's bollocks, Crabby..."

"OK, OK, calm down it's here on the shelf, just hang on a bit." He pushed himself away from Deano's restraining grasp and offered him his back.

Deano leant against the door jamb; he took a long drag on his cigarette then flicked the butt in Billy's direction. It bounced of his leg. Billy half turned, the corners of his mouth turned upward slightly, he then heeled the butt into the concrete floor.

Billy's reaction was not what Deano had expected. A slight crease formed on his brow; he sunk his hands into his pockets.

With his trademark sneer Deano said, "I ain't got all fuckin' day, Crabby, I want my phone, twat," his voice a furious hiss.

A short while ago Billy would have found Deano's reaction annoying and anger would have bubbled up inside him, but now, he found his goading quite amusing, and he laughed louder than the situation warranted.

The creases on Deano's brow deepened significantly. His morose response was, "You're a mental twat, man, gimme my fuckin' mobile *now!*"

Billy turned around and was holding the phone between finger and thumb; he smiled and 'accidentally' let the phone drop to the floor. As Deano glanced down and instinctively went to grab at it, Billy balled his right hand and thrust it forward catching Deano in the 'V' under his ribs where the sternum ends. Deano gasped and hinged over at the waist, hands propped on his knees struggling for breath. Billy immediately took advantage of his opponent's shock and surprise and brought his fist up, chopping at the bridge of Deano's nose; blood spouted as Deano crumpled to his hands and knees. It was the perfect stun factor; the last thing Deano would have expected would be a physical assault by a member of staff. The blows that Billy had delivered were a lot more significant in real life than they are in films where two men batter each other around the head for ten or fifteen minutes and are still standing. Deano was just where Billy wanted him, conscious but groggy.

Billy flapped the fingers of his right hand in the air; he smirked. "I've a good mind to sue you for nutting my fist, Mister Dean," he said.

Deano tried to say something, but nothing came out. He had curled into a foetal position with both palms covering his face.

Just to make sure he had Deano fully incapacitated; Billy sucked in a huge breath and held it. He took the lid off the jar of sulphuric acid and poured in the cup of chlorine granules. Dropping to one knee, he pulled one of Deano's hands away from his face and wafted the jar under his nose. One inhalation was all that was needed. Deano flipped onto his back, his hands around his throat gasping for air. Every hoarse and ragged breath he took caused an explosion of throbbing agony between his ears. Deano grimaced and wailed as pain continually cut into his head like a lance, his face quickly reddening to that of a tomato, his lips turning blue. Blood roared through his veins and his heart knocked against his ribs. Then his brain shut down and his world went dark. He lay quite still, quietly moaning, semiconscious at best, eyes closed.

Billy smiled satisfactorily. He stood and took a couple of steps backward. "Not very nice is it? I know exactly what you're going through, son," he chortled.

And he did.

Billy knew from his COSHH (Control of Substances Hazardous to Health) training that calcium hypochlorite, or chlorine, as well as sulphuric acid were pretty much stable when sealed in their respective containers, but when mixed deadly chlorine gas was emitted.

A couple of years previously there had been an accidental spillage in the plant room and Billy had barely managed to get out, collapsing onto the pavement outside. He had spent a full day recovering in hospital on a ventilator breathing in pure oxygen. It had caused permanent damage to his lungs and he had needed to use bronchial inhalers on a daily basis ever since.

Taking both containers, Billy went outside and threw them into the skip. He took the opportunity to blow out and suck in lungs full of fresh air. Predictably, it was a fine sunny day, the air tinged with the crispness of late spring. It was the kind of day that made him believe that this was the perfect end. There was just enough breeze to send little puffs of clouds drifting across a deep blue backdrop. Billy smiled and dug his hands into his pockets. The adrenaline now coursing through his bloodstream gave him an alertness that he had never experienced before. A pleasant euphoric sensation overcame him, which he allowed to surface in the form of a light almost soundless whistle through gently pursed lips. *My last look at the sky, my last look at the birds.* In the distance, at the edge of the playing fields, a lone kestrel rode the thermals, sharp eyes alert for prey no doubt. Above him, about a dozen seagulls were circling slowly. Soaring with their huge wings outspread, they looked massive. They seemed to sense when the kids had left the site. They invaded the school grounds for their hearty feast of discarded sandwiches, biscuits, and cakes with which the kids had decorated the school grounds. Until recently, seabirds had never been spotted this far inland, but after they had cleared their gourmet meal at the school, they would head back to a nearby landfill site where they would find more rich pickings. Another disaster courtesy of the town planners.

Many years ago, a consortium had made offers for a disused quarry and surrounding woods. Their idea was to turn it into a theme park based on Robin Hood and olde England, with the prospect of creating hundreds of local jobs and a boost to the local economy, but no, they much preferred to turn it into a giant tip.

Hey-ho, no good worrying about it now. Billy closed his eyes and took in several more lungs full of sweet air. It was glorious. What a great day to die. As the school was situated on the outskirts of the town and on a slight rise, this side of the premises overlooked woods and farmland, which stretched out as far as the eye could see. *For how long though?* The mist that enveloped the school earlier was now dissipating in the mid-afternoon sunshine. Everything seemed to be edged by glittering, shimmering light, it was so intense that it almost made Billy gasp with surprise. *Why hadn't I seen this before? Does everyone see this before they are about to die?*

Apart from the drastic drop in temperature when he had stood outside of the A&E department, an unusually warm spring had folk strolling outdoors in their short sleeves. Billy had a fluttering notion to quickly go and see Janet for one last time...no; he had started now and must see this thing through, although his heart had not yet processed the pain. He shook his head slightly. His whole body tensed, his jaw clenched and with his face pulled into a determined frown, he took one last deep breath.

Fate had cruel timing, which was life's lottery.

On re-entering the boiler house he tried to lock the door behind him, but the handle was destroyed on the inside thanks to Deano. He fetched a shovel and jammed it against the door. No one could enter. Deano was rolling around on the floor with open hands covering his face; a mound of puke lay in a small heap at his side.

Formulating any form of coherent thoughts was impossible for Deano. A thick fog seemed to shroud his brain and the spikes of pain that lanced through his temples had begun to disperse; he tried to focus on where he was and what had happened to him. He looked around through streaming, bloodshot eyes in an effort to find his bearings; it was like looking through a stained-glass window. It took quite a while before he was back in control of his senses sufficiently enough to recognise Billy standing over him. He managed to push himself to his knees but couldn't muster the strength or balance to stand. He crawled a short distance to one of the boilers oil feeder pipes and used it as a crutch to help him stand, scrambling to regain his orientation. Billy placed a foot on Deano's shoulder and pushed him back down onto the floor; he hit the ground with an "oooofff!" Billy dropped a knee sharply into the small of Deano's back directly where his kidneys sat, pinning him to the rough concrete floor. Deano clenched his teeth as another wave of pain engulfed him.

After a couple of minutes, Deano's anger started up and grew brighter and hotter as his mind cleared. He had recovered sufficiently enough to let rip with a tirade of expletives in between coughing and gagging fits. Billy took the roll of gaffer tape from his pocket and twisted Deano's arms up behind him. Deano struggled furiously to break free but with Billy now straddling him, he was helpless. Billy bound Deano's hands and then his feet, not worrying unduly about inhibiting his circulation. He then flipped Deano over. Billy ripped off a small length of tape, which was meant for Deano's mouth. As Billy stooped, he noticed deep grazes across Deano's left cheek, which was imbedded with dirt and bits of tiny gravel picked up from the floor. In addition, it was obvious that his nose was broken and bleeding, breath bubbling in the blood. Billy smoothed the tape across Deano's mouth. With his mouth taped, Deano could only breathe through his nose, which he found very difficult because it was partially blocked; he couldn't get enough oxygen into his lungs. He sniffed violently and began panicking; his breathing became hysterical making his nostrils flare.

Billy decided to leave him there awhile until the initial shock had died away.

Deano continued to twist wildly but the more he struggled the tighter the tape cut into his wrists, the more out of breath he became and the less air he was able to take in. He tried again to scream out; all he managed was a muffled whimper.

Deano's head throbbed with fire. After a few minutes, he realised that thrashing around on the floor was futile, so he calmed down and lay motionless on his side, feeling the floor under him, wondering what the hell had happened. Slowly he began to show signs of waking to full alertness. He remembered. He rolled over onto his back.

Billy was leaning against the wall, arms folded and smiling; he wanted him as scared and demoralised as all the people who had had the misfortune to cross his path over the years. When Deano tried to move, he realised that he had been bound with something – wrists tied behind his back, ankles lashed tight. Again he began thrashing about maniacally in an attempt to loosen his bonds but they held firm. The struggle had left his wrists and ankles raw, but the tape was as tight as it had been when he started. Once again, he calmed down. Beads of sweat snaked down the side of his face and into his ears. He was still snorting heavily through his nose and he turned his red, soulless, veiny eyes in Billy's direction.

Billy knelt at Deano's side and ripped the tape from his mouth.
Pain seared Deano's lips as the adhesive was pulled away and he felt as if the skin had been ripped completely off; it was stinging like hell and he did not like it one bit.

"Ow! What the fuck are you playing at, Crabby? You better let me fuckin' go, man," he bawled in a voice that was hoarse and ragged but also full of loathing, the words coated with venom. "Oh, you are *so* fuckin' dead, Crabby you are *so* going to fuckin' suffer." He forced a smile, baring his teeth, "have you ever seen flesh burn in petrol, Crabby? Eh? It gives you a buzz, man, and when I get out of…"

"So, there was more to come was there?" Billy's face was deadpan, his voice quiet, and calm. "That's all I wanted to know."

Billy ripped off another length of tape.

Deano frantically rolled his head around trying to thwart Billy's attempt to replace his gag. He screamed, "You bastard, Crabby, I'll kill you, I'll kill you, you cun…mmmmmm."

With the tape secured over Deano's mouth, Billy wheeled the television trolley from behind one of the boilers and placed it at Deano's side. Billy planted clenched fists into his hips and stared down at his immobilised captive. Deano's cold eyes returned Billy's gaze with hatred so intense that, although Billy was in the driving seat, he involuntarily shuddered.

"You, son," Billy was glaring unblinkingly, "are nothing more than a lame-brained…pox-faced…fucking…evil…moron." *Oh! I enjoyed that.* The corners of his mouth turned up slightly and he continued in a jovial tone, "funny, ain't it, how a nice day could turn out so shit in just a few seconds, um?"

Billy took Deano under the armpits and struggled to get him upright, leaning him against the wall. Next, Billy turned Deano through one hundred and eighty degrees and then, with great effort, he laid him across the trolley. Deano looked like he was about to be wheeled into an operating theatre. Billy pushed the trolley round to the back of one of the boilers where he rested for a short while, inhaling and exhaling several breaths as a calming exercise.

They were in front of a large steel hatch, hinged at one side and secured by a large iron lever. In the centre of the hatch was a small circular glass inspection window. He took from his pocket the piece of string and tied it to the top of the large lever. Opening the hatch Billy trailed the string across a small 'V' that he had earlier cut into the door insulation. This would allow the string movement even with the door shut. The remaining length of string he loosely trailed on the side of the boiler that he would soon be occupying. Next, he flipped a couple of small securing catches, which were situated just inside the boiler. He grasped a large steel handle and tugged. The whole of the burner unit slid out on steel rollers like a mortician would pull out a body from its chiller unit for viewing. Again, he took Deano under the armpits, he struggled and writhed, but Billy had the upper hand. As the television trolley was virtually the same height as the burner unit, Billy found no difficulty in sliding Deano onto the roller bed, face up. Deano's eyes were intense and, probably for the first time in his life, he looked a little scared. He fought fiercely to free himself, but that caused him pain that was even more excruciating, and so he soon calmed once more. Blood trickled from his nose and into an ear. Billy was trying to suppress a grin of satisfaction.

With Deano safely tucked away, Billy approached the main boiler control panel. He set the override boiler timer so that the boiler would re-ignite in thirty minutes. He then returned to Deano. Deano's brow crinkled and his eyes bulged as Billy lifted himself up and slid onto the roller bed, lying next to him.

Billy was now in a state of nervous excitement; even more adrenaline pumped through him, he grinned, turned his head to face Deano and said, "Enjoy the ride, kid."

Deano's eyes said he didn't want a ride; he strained against his bonds; his head and torso thrashing around in panic.

With that, Billy placed his hands on either side of the boiler doorway and slowly inched them both inside closing the hatch behind them. It was almost too narrow for both of their frames. Billy's shoulders were straining against Deano on the one side and the boiler wall on the other. Billy's arms felt constricted and his heart was pounding. It had been very hard work to get to where they were now, and he towelled the sweat from his eyes with his sleeve, the salt stinging them and making it hard to focus.

Deano went, "mmmm, mmmm," and began writhing; jerking his body back and forth trying to loosen something but there was very little room to do so. He had gone from feeling merely constricted to claustrophobic in a matter of seconds. His eyes were saucer-like now as he strained uselessly against his bonds. Billy thought how meek, insubstantial, and pathetic he looked. He took the piece of string and tugged on it. He rolled his head back and saw the lever drop down through the small round inspection glass. *Well, that worked a treat, just as I had planned and practised.* They were now hermetically sealed in and it would now be impossible to get out unless the inspection hatch was opened from the outside.

"Quite cosy in here ain't it Deano?" Billy said, his voice smooth and calm. He smiled. "Now then, young man..." Billy started brightly as he turned his whole body to face Deano who was glaring back at him with a look of intense hatred. "...I'm going to remove the tape from your mouth so that we can have a little chat, and I mean a *proper* chat. If you start mouthing off I'll put the tape back over your fat gob, understood?"

Deano's haunted eyes said bollocks, but he nodded almost imperceptibly in agreement.

Billy leant across and ripped off the tape. Deano winced at the shock of pain as the adhesive tore free of his lips; he turned his head away from Billy, spat blood against the boiler wall and then filled his lungs several times. Deano then turned to face Billy, baring his teeth in a way that most people do only for the dentist. The eyes were callous and empty. He didn't so much as look Billy in the face, he looked through him, and the words came from his mouth like a stream of vomit. "Crabby you bastard, when I get out of here I'm gonna fuckin' kill you so very very slowly, I'm gonna make you suffer, man..."

"Now now, remember what I just said, Mister Dean?" Billy said, holding up a hand as if stopping traffic. "It really is pointless lying there, young man spewing out a constant stream of empty threats when your hands and feet are tied, and you're totally enclosed in a steel sarcophagus with no hope of getting out." He then continued matter of factly, "You'd be better off making more use of your time because in exactly..." he slid back the sleeve of his overall to expose his watch. "...Twenty-two minutes time you will be dead." He flicked his eyebrows a few times and grinned a wide grin.

The boilers confined space echoed with Billy's words; he let them settle in the stillness. Deano knew what he had heard, but somehow it seemed unreal to him, a silly joke. His mouth was open, but no words came out for a good minute. Billy's remark just did not register at all. Perhaps his thoughts were still muddled by the lingering effects of the chlorine gas.

Deano still managed a smug and sinister smile. He emitted a single, husky laugh; it was a nervous laugh mixed with tension, and just to show how 'hard' he was, he belched in Billy's direction. He said, "You've had your fun, Crabby, the jokes gone far enough. Look, man get this tape shit off my hands and feet and I'll tell you what, we'll shake and pretend this never happened, we'll call it quits, OK?"

Billy raised his eyebrows. "Do you realise that you didn't say one 'fuck' in that sentence, that's got to be a first for you hasn't it, Mister Dean? What's happened to good old fashioned cold, bloody-minded malice, uh?"

Billy struggled onto his back, clasped his hands together across his stomach and intertwined his fingers. A peace and serenity had replaced the turmoil that had been haunting him for so long. "I don't think you've got the message have you, sonny-Jim. School's...Out...For...Ever!" He enunciated with exaggerated clarity. His forehead puckered slightly, "Who sang that?" He lowered his voice and repeated what he had said more slowly. The bass resonance echoed around the boiler chamber. "School's...Out...For...Ever!" He raised his eyebrows and glanced at Deano, "No? Was it Pink Floyd? No, I think it was Alice Cooper. Never mind." Billy crossed his feet and let out a diminutive sigh. "Anyway, I digress. You see, kid, I have my own simple ideas about crime and punishment. This includes doling out the kind of pain to the attacker, which he or she has inflicted on the attacked. Last year you and your so-called mates killed an innocent man by setting fire to his house. I cannot measure the pain of terror that that man felt, so, in a way, you are at this precise moment in time being tortured. Not physically...yet, but mentally. You have about twenty very short minutes to cry, shake, beg, or shit yourself. Whatever you decide, I shall be enjoying every second of it. Something is needed to rid my England of filth like you. Something better than we have at present...I've said as much in the letters that I have left behind. I could have made this far easier for myself. I could have run you down with the school mini-bus and then gone home to bed with my sleeping pills and a bottle of whisky. However, you see, son, I think it appropriate that you experience what *he* went through. I can't for the life of me imagine what that poor man went through inside his burning house during his last few moments. He knew he was going to die and he had no way of knowing why and who had ultimately condemned him to death. With premeditated malice and extreme cruelty, you also killed my dog and tried to kill my Mother and me. You are an unequivocally evil parasite who takes great pleasure out of the suffering of others. You have no concept of right and wrong. You know I've actually had a teacher crying on my shoulder, you demeaned her so much that she lost all of her pride. She left shortly afterwards. You have made so many people's lives a misery and you laugh about it, you are scum and an evil vicious bastard who takes great delight in destroying lives. You are completely pathetic, a contemptible little shit, and those are just your good points. To be honest, you make me ashamed to be part of the same species. Believe me, son when you've gone people will be putting flowers on my grave as a thank you. I consider getting rid of you as my own personal form of charity. Now then, would you like to indulge yourself in a valedictory?"

Deano screwed up his face. "Ay? What the fuck are you drivelling on about, Crabby? Say all that again, man in English."

Billy sighed through his nose. "Would you like to say a few last words?"

Deano felt his throat constrict as a sickening dread rose up from the depths of his stomach, but he still managed a sneer. "Look, stop talking shit, Crabby. Just let me go now, and I'll…I'll go to the police and own up to the fire I promise…just untie me, man you know you're gonna have to eventually. I mean, you ain't seriously telling me you're gonna lie here and set fire to your fuckin' self, now are you?" He laughed, but very nervously. His jocular tone obviously false, because Billy's face revealed that, yes, he was serious.

Billy's eyelids drooped, and he forced them open; his Mothers' medication was kicking in a little sooner than he had expected. "Why not? I'm dying anyway, so why not here? It's quick and I won't feel a thing because I'll be in a deep sleep."

Deano let out a ruthless chuckle and then broke into a wheezing cough, the chlorine still hot and burning in his lungs. "It ain't funny anymore, Crabby the jokes gone on too long…"

"No Joke, son. You see, you and your so-called friends are disgusting people, capable of doing such violent, disturbed things and you need to be stopped." Billy very slowly turned his head; the two of them were looking right at each other. Deano's eyes were wild; Billy's eyes were unblinking and placid. "Like it was no joke when I killed Nelly and Thommo."

Deano's forehead puckered and for an instant, his breath became instinctively shallower which then caught in his throat as terror swamped him. He was trying to form a sentence but had great difficulty speaking. His visage drained of colour so dramatically that even his ginger hair seemed to whiten. His face gradually folded in bewildered incomprehension. "You… you killed Thommo and Nelly?" The penny had finally dropped.

He seemed to have lost his ability to blink, his eyes suddenly owlish. There was a sense of fear in his voice edging towards terror.

A disgusting odour hit Billy's nostrils; he realised Deano's bowels were beginning to loosen, which pleased him immeasurably.

"Yep, and the two dealers of death who ponce around in the Saburu. Well, they're probably awaiting a post mortem as we speak…I think they got the, erm, *point*."

Billy threw his head back and began laughing raucously, which sounded quite eerie as it echoed around the cold empty chamber. "Is it sinking in now?" Billy surprised himself by how easy it had been to tell someone that he was as good as dead. "You see, son there are some bad people in this world and there are some very bad people and then there's morose people like you and your cowardly gang who have, over the last few years, infested society like a swarm of maggots…is it a swarm? Could be a pack or a herd…anyway, whatever. You may have grown up in a tough environment, I don't know. You may even have been abused but it doesn't mean you have the right to kill and take out your rage on others – which you won't be doing anymore. Your weakness disgusts me. You may say that what I am doing is no better, you may be right, but as far as I am concerned I am committing a wicked deed to eliminate a greater wickedness. You, sonny-Jim have been one of the devil's star pupils but now you are going to pay for your crimes." Billy raised his arm and glanced at his watch again. "Mister Dean I doubt very much that what I have just said has sunk into that infested, walnut sized brain of yours. This is it son, the end, it's over, it's finished, you are *not* going to escape custody again for a crime that you have committed, but more importantly, you will not be killing another human being ever again. And, if it still hasn't sunk in yet, you definitely will not be opening your ratty little eyes to a nurse holding your wrist and looking at her watch like hopefully my Mother is doing as we speak. So, you have only eight minutes to contemplate your short, miserable, deformed, and diseased life and its imminent and inevitable end."

Billy was really struggling to keep his eyes open now; his eyelids felt as though they had bowling balls pinned to them. Nevertheless, he was being kept alert as Deano's breathing became heavy and laboured, his heart slamming back and forth off his ribs. He broke down, whimpering, not from remorse for what he had done but because he feared for his own life. He pleaded and pleaded until he became so utterly frightened that, as his mouth opened to protest, his lips fluttered helplessly. Billy wondered how someone who had caused so much fear and misery in his short life could look so frail and pathetic now. All his bluster, all his machismo had evaporated. Deano's ashen face with its expression of panic and fear told Billy everything he needed to know - the bully had become something even more despicable – a coward. Billy hadn't thought it possible, but his hatred for this worthless piece of scum notched a little higher.

"There's an old saying, son," Billy said, "He who lives by the sword, dies by the sword although you probably ain't got a clue what I'm talking about. Anyway, how about we go out with a rousing song ay Mister Dean? Join in if you know the words to Jerusalem…which I very much doubt."

Billy only knew the lyrics to one song all the way through, and that was the Jerusalem hymn by William Blake. Every remembrance Sunday - which he remembered as always being a cold, wet November day - his parents had literally dragged him down to the small cenotaph situated in the centre of the town. It wasn't until his late teenage years that he understood the meaning and significance of this most special of occasions. Over the years, Billy had memorised all the words to this particular rousing poem, which was later set to music. After his father had died, he had willingly and enthusiastically attended every year with his Mother.

Billy's stomach lurched and there was a fresh spurt of acid into the back of his mouth, but apart from that he felt totally calm, which surprised him a little because he had been walking a knife edge of emotion for so long. Serenity had settled over him like a warm, snug duvet; he ran his tongue across his cracked lips and then began to sing in an almost strengthless whisper:

*And did those feet in ancient times
Walk upon England's mountains green
And was the holy Lamb of God
On England's pleasant pastures seen...*

Deano's mind was a swirl of panic as his tiny brain raced to process the situation he was in. He began to buck, thrashing back and forth violently in a futile attempt to free himself, even trying to head-butt Billy but his bound body would not respond to his will. Sweat sheathed him, hot and sticky on his face, cold along his spine. His pale lips skinned back over bare teeth, almost lupine. After a short while, he could only thrash weakly; he gasped in inarticulate protest, "What the fuck are you doing? You're mental, man, let me go, let me fuckin' go ain't you never heard of forgiveness and mercy aaahhhggg..."

Billy snorted a laugh, "*Forgiveness...Mercy!* Ha! Are you joking...MAN!"

Deano spewed out a string of obscenities that lasted a full twenty or so seconds before Billy lifted an extended finger to his lips, shook his head and shushed him. Billy continued...

*And did the countenance divine
Shine forth upon our clouded hills
And was Jerusalem...*

Deano let fly with another short bombardment of expletives.

Billy tutted loudly, leant across and replaced the tape across Deano's mouth. "You had your chance, son, even in the situation you find yourself in your heart is still rotten and filled with hatred."

Billy's mouth sagged, and his pupils slid up under his eyelids; he was fighting to keep unconsciousness at bay, cracking his eyelids open every few seconds. He emitted a long yawn and lay back down. "Now then, where were we?"

Bring me my bow of burning gold
Bring me my arrows of desire
Bring me my spears o'clouds unfold
Bring me my chariot of fire...

Again, Billy yawned long and hard; he felt a strange tranquillity within, no inner turmoil. The intense hatred and anger that had boiled deep inside had now subsided as the capsules that he had swallowed were making his head swim. He felt extremely weary, but very relaxed. Suddenly his eyes flipped wide open. "I've just had a thought, son I owe you something." He sniffed violently through his nose, turned to face Deano and spat into his face. Deano's eyelids fluttered rapidly; Billy's spit had formed a gossamer film across Deano's left eye. His lips were stuck firmly to the adhesive, yet still he continued with muffled, wordless pleading.

Despite the seriousness of the situation, Billy managed to chuckle weakly. "There's only one thing I regret about all of this, Mister Dean and that is the fact that I will be unable to piss on your grave."

I will not cease from mental fight
Nor shall my sword sleep in my hand...

Another long drawn out yawn, his eyes fluttering almost shut now, succumbing to the welcome fog of heavy sedation.
Then, barely audible:

'Til we have built Jerusalem
In England's green... and pleasant land
'Til we have built... Jerusalem
In England's...green... and pleasant...

Billy's eyes closed for the last time. Played on the back of his eyelids like a movie he could see swirling snapshots of time. His Mother packing a suitcase for their annual caravan holiday in Weston-Super-Mare. His father dressed in long trousers, shirt, and tie although the sun was scorching. Kicking a ball around on the beach. Other occasions, birthdays, Christmas's and some moments, which were quite boring. But then he could see Janet smiling that smile at him as plain as day. Over the last few days he had thought of so many plans, so many things he would have loved to have done with her – health permitting. The corners of his mouth turned up slightly. Then a thought came into his head, he didn't know why or where from, a book maybe or a film perhaps? As you get older never pass a toilet, never waste an erection, and never trust a fart. *Well, all three could certainly apply to me in the last week.* Although his eyes were shut tight, he chuckled to himself. Deano's brow creased significantly and if Billy could have seen him, he was glaring at Billy with eyes that were on fire.

Billy felt no remorse in the fact that Deano would never face trial, no remorse in dishing out vigilante justice. *On an average day, just how different am I from the hateful bastard lying beside me?* Fighting injustice wasn't a license to break the rules, he knew that, but still he carried no shame or guilt for what he had done. He wasn't proud of the fact; it was just the way he felt. He thought of his Mum. There was no house to sell, but the insurance company would pay out a tidy sum. There would be enough there to care for her comfortably for the rest of her life. *What will she think of me when she wakes? Well, it's all pointless now, she'll be well looked after I'm sure. What if she never wakes? Well, if there is a heaven then I'm sure we'll be going in completely opposite directions. That's a thought. If there is a heaven and hell, then Mister Dean and me will be meeting up again in the very near future!*

Billy Crabtree would never again see his Mum or Janet in this world or any other.

Very soon, all of his failings and humiliations would be gone. After fifty-eight years of mediocrity, he was about to leave a lasting reminder of himself for history. As Billy sank into a dark pool of emptiness, his eyes twitched behind their lids as if he were experiencing a nightmare. He wasn't, it was the effect of the drugs that he had taken. As his consciousness gradually faded, he finally pondered on what he could have...*should have* done with his life...memories swirled around him, all that loneliness, sadness, bitterness, all that regret and heart rending pain...and if he could just have had one more chance... How many opportunities had he missed? He wasn't one for stating his feelings but if only he had experienced more relationships, intimacy with the opposite sex, to say I love you...but he was grateful that he hadn't added Janet's name to the roll of missed chances and would have forfeited all of what he had missed just for the incredible time that he had spent with her. She had awakened feeling's in him that he thought had long since vanished.

In a very short space of time, Billy had experienced such a range of emotions, from intense fear to soul destroying sadness to such surprisingly violent anger and of course deep deep passionate love. He struggled to comprehend the events that had brought him to where he was now. Just a few weeks ago he was floating in a world of solitude and now everything was different.

Will I be a famous 'hero' or an infamous 'hero'? Perhaps there are a few people like me who think they're just correcting God's mistakes, after all, he must be a very busy man and he's bound to slip up occasionally. How else would people like Deano exist? At the beginning of the month if someone had told him he'd taken five lives and would be lying next to Deano in a boiler with just a few minutes to live, he would have suggested that they be institutionalised for something that was too far-fetched to be credible. But here he was, doing precisely that.

Although Billy was fading fast, he summoned up one last thought. It was very weak, like everything else about him, but through the haze in his head the last few days with Janet rapidly tumbled through his mind. The kiss in the park. Sitting on the bench in her garden holding hands. Her beautiful tipsy smile across the restaurant table. Her bedroom…but now it was different. Everything was white. Endless white expanding before him. White walls, white curtains, white silk bed sheets, Janet and he in white silk dressing gowns. He was holding her tightly and stroking her hair whilst she slept. He could actually smell her. Billy felt tears threatening but swallowed them back; tears were for the weak. Instead, a happy, satisfied smile spread across his lips; he somehow appeared ten years younger. His hands were clasped across his chest as if he were lying in an open coffin at the undertakers.

Nevertheless, this is exactly what he wanted; he still wanted to die.

Billy Crabtree was exultant. The only thing he was regretting was the fact that he wouldn't witness the final moments of Deano's helpless, racking terror.

Deano meanwhile had been probing his bonds to see how much give there was; they held firm. He tilted his head back as far as it would go, glaring unblinkingly at the upside-down boiler house through the inspection hatch. His pale watching face, dotted with pearls of sweat, waiting for the rescue that would never come.

Billy was somewhere he should not have been, with someone he should not have been with. He had hated his life, hated his disease, hated the pain, but to have Deano next to him, who he hated even more than all of that, was invigorating in a bizarre kind of a way.

Now he was drifting away, and off towards…*where?* He wondered. There was no pain now, just his dad quietly calling to him from somewhere. Then he saw him smiling, his arms extended looking just like he remembered him before his illness struck. Blackness now enveloped him; it was absolute and impenetrable. Slipping into a sleep undisturbed by dreams or thoughts, he had finally found the peace he had craved for many months. It was an odd, unaccustomed feeling. Dying was going to be much easier than he had ever hoped, certainly easier than living.

The last thing Billy said before he stopped breathing was "Janet." Soft as a whisper…and then he slipped into the abyss, amongst a confused jumble of images, pictures and flashing coloured lights.

Deano hadn't given up. He still thought that this was a sick stunt and that any minute now Billy's eyes would fly open and he would go, *'Ta, rah!' got you there, kid!'* and an accomplice would fling open the door and release him. He whipped his head from side to side in an attempt to loosen his gag. It flapped free and stuck to his cheek by one corner. There he lay alone, continuing with his fruitless struggling, screaming garbled and unintelligible obscenities - until he heard a loud click; it was the boilers starter ignition firing up. There would be a short delay whilst its small internal computer checked through the list of its built in safety procedures before the main burners burst into life. He became rigid, mute, and terrified; the capacity to speak had deserted him as a mind numbing, paralysing fear grabbed him. His eyes turned to saucers and he snatched in a breath and held it. If the safety check got the green light, then there would be only seconds before the burners ignited. He quivered and gave a choking little sob as a wet patch began to spread out in his trousers.

Then Deano the murderer, the self-proclaimed hard, ruthless, seemingly emotionless vicious thug, lost control of his bowels.

On the school car park, an opened letter lay on the passenger seat of Janet's car. She had been staring at it unblinkingly for a long time. She had read it more than once in trembling hands; her eyes had took in the words, but her mind couldn't comprehend them.

My Dearest Jan,
    You are by far the most amazingly beautiful lady - both inside

and out - that I have ever met. I have loved the time that I have spent with you and I hope that you feel the same, that Is why this letter will come as a terrible shock to you. But I feel I must tell you my story before anyone else and I hope you will feel it in your heart to understand what I have done and why. If my plan has succeeded then I will become notorious.

You will hear things about me, Jan, a murderer, a monster. My heart aches knowing I have left you, but I had no choice...

Billy goes on to explain why he did what he did and why he hadn't told her about his illness. He didn't want to spend the next few weeks shrivelling up and dying in front of her eyes. Above all, he asked for forgiveness. He poured out his feelings for her and how he had enjoyed and savoured every second with her, and if he apologised to her a million times it would never be enough. A paragraph was dedicated to how his father had lived out the tragic last few weeks of his life and hoped she would understand why he didn't want to go through that also.

Billy had drafted his letter so many times that he thought he would suffocate in the collection of tight paper balls that surrounded him in his bedroom.

The world around her had slipped away leaving her behind. Tears and grief ravaged her perfect make-up. She slumped forward cracking her head on the steering wheel, but she felt nothing. She gripped it with both hands until her fingers turned skimmed milk white.

Janet's forehead was rutted into lines as deep as the sadness in her heart. She was bowed down with grief. Salt water welled in her eyes and then she began crying hard, tears coursing down her face over the pale curve of her cheeks. Throwing her head back against the headrest, she ran both palms down her face marbling mascara across her cheeks. She reached into her handbag, took out a tissue, and dabbed moisture from her eyes. Once again she took up the letter not believing what she had read. There was a stain on it, ink mixed with salt water where warm tears had fallen onto it. Annoyed this time, she screamed and beat her fists against the steering wheel with the heels of both hands so hard that it made her teeth rattle. *Not again, why is this happening to me again? Am I that bad that I'm going to be left alone and miserable for eternity?* There would be mental scars. The events of the past few weeks had been fantastic and the gentleness of this man had astonished and touched her. But that would rapidly fade because alas, what she had gone through in the last few minutes would be lodged in her memory like a painful splinter for ever. She was helpless and at the depths of despair as more tears slid down her grief-stricken face.

A long breath escaped her as she sat in ashen silence for a while, her florid face creased with wistful dejection. Then again, as intense tears streamed in single torrents, she slumped forward across the steering wheel breaking down into bitter, wretched sobs. She was so utterly devastated that she could barely breathe – Billy was gone, and she was suddenly alone once more; Billy hadn't foreseen this event. Billy hadn't foreseen her ever-deepening slide into depression.

For how long she had sat there, she didn't know. Janet felt her temples throbbing and she stared blankly ahead through a haze of tears, sniffing into a soggy tissue; the school building seemed to shimmer in front of her. Once again she slumped forward and rested her head on the steering wheel.

She was oblivious to the scream, which came from the direction of the boiler house. It rose in intensity and pitch into a long, high keen of terror and shock.

Seagulls scattered in all directions, then a deafening absence of any sound.

Brief author history:

Born in Wolverhampton in 1953. After leaving school at 15 with virtually no qualifications, I tended to go where the money was as opposed to carving out any real career for myself. If I was working that was all that mattered. Later on in life it dawned on me the importance of education. So, for two years I studied electronics at Walsall College, which enabled me to find employment as a vending machine service engineer. A few years later I had a brief spell as a self-employed television engineer, which ended abruptly when the Japanese invented flat screen disposable TV's. Bless 'em. I have recently retired from my job as Site Technician at the local high school, which I thoroughly enjoyed for sixteen years.

I now have the time to take up interests, which I never seemed to find time for when I was working – golf and a Motown/soul DJ.

Betty and I have been married for 45 years and we have one daughter and one granddaughter.

I have no writing experience whatsoever, but there is a saying that everyone has a book in them and this one is mine. 'School's...Out...For...ever' is a crime/murder thriller based on my experiences and observations whilst working in a school environment.

Printed in Great Britain
by Amazon